CHARADE

Other Books by Gilbert Morris

Jacob's Way
Edge of Honor
Jordan's Star
God's Handmaiden
The Spider Catcher

GILBERT MORRIS

CHARADE

ZONDERVAN™

GRAND RAPIDS, MICHIGAN 49530 USA

We want to hear from you. Please send your comments about this book to us in care of zreview@zondervan.com. Thank you.

ZONDERVAN™

Charade
Copyright © 2005 by Gilbert Morris

Requests for information should be addressed to:
Zondervan, *Grand Rapids, Michigan 49530*

Library of Congress Cataloging-in-Publication Data

Morris, Gilbert.
  Charade / Gilbert Morris.
    p. cm.
  ISBN-10: 0-310-24702-0 (softcover)
  ISBN-13: 978-0-310-24702-9
    1. Computer programmers—Fiction. 2. Disguise—Fiction.
  3. Revenge—Fiction. I. Title.
  PS3563.O8742C475 2005
  813'.54—dc22

                           2004026273

Published in association with the literary agency of Alive Communications, Inc., 7680 Goddard Street, Suite 200, Colorado Springs, CO 80920.

Interior design by Michelle Espinoza

Printed in the United States of America

05 06 07 08 09 10 11 12 /❖ DCI/ 10 9 8 7 6 5 4 3 2 1

To Fatty Bigs
(Aka Pastor Rick Long)

CHAPTER ONE

I, Ollie William Benson, am obsessed by mirrors. It's not that I want to collect them, or that I'm fascinated by them. *Au contraire!* I wish that I lived in a world where there were *no* mirrors. The problem, you see, is that when I look into a mirror, I see myself.

That may sound strange to "normal" people. Obviously, mirrors were made for just such a purpose. But ever since I became aware that I was different from other people, I've hated mirrors and avoided them whenever possible. When I say "different from other people," you probably think I have a hideous deformity— maybe something like John Merrick, the Elephant Man—but I don't. On the other hand, maybe I really do, for at the height of exactly six feet I weigh four hundred and six pounds.

I don't think anyone of normal size understands what it means to be obese. You have to be there. When a normal person flies in an airplane, he buys one ticket. But I have to go first class or buy *two* tickets. I can't waltz into Tommy Hilfiger's and buy a shirt or a pair of slacks. I have to find a shop on a back street that makes clothing that could be worn by whales with arms and legs.

I guess you have to be obese in order to recognize the disgust and pity that flickers in the eyes of people when you meet them for the first time. I'm sure that some doctors can feel compassion for the obese, but most of them I've met seem to have a covert attitude of: *The big tub of lard, he ate himself into this.*

It's his own fault. They smile and say comforting things, but that's what they really think: *He brought it on himself.*

So that's my problem. I'm fat, shake like a bowl of jelly, and at the age of twenty-nine, when most young guys are at their best, I spend my life hiding from the world in my little cubicle at the rear of Maxie's Electronics. Then I scurry home to my apartment and pull up the drawbridge to keep people out. I cook meals that I know I shouldn't eat but eat anyway, wondering from time to time what it would be like to be a normal person. What would it be like to have a girlfriend? What would it be like to put on a pair of swimming trunks and not feel like a pale hippopotamus?

Maybe if I had a family, things would be different, but my dad died before I was born, I lost my mom when I was only seventeen, and I didn't have any other relatives living nearby. Even before Mom died, I was a fat freak.

So that's why I hate mirrors, and that's why I don't have any in my apartment—except in the bathroom. I got rid of all the rest, but that one was built in as part of the decor. It's three feet wide and goes all the way to the ceiling. It must have been designed by a bodybuilder or a beauty queen, someone who loved to look at themselves.

As soon as I moved in, I knew I couldn't face taking a shower, stepping out, and seeing a mountain of gluttonous fat, which is what I've become. My solution was simple enough. I simply bought a life-size poster of John Wayne, a still taken from *Stagecoach*, his first big hit. You've seen it—the one where he's carrying the rifle and standing beside his saddle. I fastened it over the mirror with Scotch tape so that when I got out of the tub, instead of seeing myself, I saw the Duke.

Over the next couple of years, I changed the poster several times. Steve McQueen did his duty for a few months, and he was succeeded by Randolph Scott—an actor nobody remembers except us old-movie buffs. Lee Van Cleef was one of my favorites, and he lasted nearly six months. The most recent one was Clint Eastwood wearing his Mexican serape and his flat-crowned hat, with a thin cigar clenched between his teeth. I suppose a shrink would probably have something to say about how all of these dudes were what I was not—strong, virile, lean, mean, and ready to face anybody down before or after breakfast. Well, let them say it.

When I think about all that happened, it seems to have started that Friday night with the mirror in the bathroom. Just an ordinary day, nothing special. I got home early, took off my sweaty clothes, for it's hot in Memphis in July, and threw them in the hamper. I turned the water on as hot as I could stand it, and soon the room was filled with steam. It was almost as good as being in a sauna—or so I thought, although I'd never been in one. That's another of those things I would never expose myself to—getting into a small room naked with normal men.

By the time I was about ready to vaporize, I turned the water off, flung the curtain back, and stepped out of the shower. Then I stopped dead still.

Clint Eastwood wasn't there—

I was there!

The steam had peeled the Scotch tape from the mirror and the poster lay coiled in an obscene sprawl on the floor. I stared at myself, unable to move. No way could I avoid seeing the double and triple chins, the flab that hung on me, and the stomach that looked as if it had been inflated by a huge bicycle pump. Everything about me was disgusting, and suddenly I was trembling uncontrollably. I grabbed a towel and wheeled away from the mirror, trying to forget—but I have a very good memory, *too* good in fact. Even as I toweled myself down, a scene flashed on the back of my eyes in full color and with stereophonic sound. I could even smell the odors of the weight room where I had gone to try once again to lose weight. I was on the stair-climber, which I had set at the very lowest level. The little red dots were all across the bottom of the screen, and I was huffing and puffing, trying not to fall off.

Then a girl eighteen or nineteen, wearing a tight, white spandex top and black shorts that clung to her like an extra skin, stepped onto the machine next to mine. She set it on max, with all the red dots at the top, and as soon as it was going full speed, she moved with an easy rhythm.

I remembered that when she finally stopped the machine, she turned and looked at me, fat and huge and gross and sweating like crazy. She smiled, showing a lot of teeth, and said cheerfully, "Keep at it. You'll make it."

But I saw the pity and disgust in her eyes, and when she walked over to her friend on another stair-climber, I heard her whisper, "Hippo will never make it, he's too far gone."

I shoved that memory back into a dark closet (knowing full well it wouldn't stay there). Well, we all have things to get over. I dried and put on my underwear, and then I went back to the bathroom. The rodeo guys say when you get thrown by a horse, you go get right back on.

I picked Clint up, fastened him back using twice as much tape as I'd used before, then walked over to the lavatory and studied my face in the small mirror that hung there for shaving. What did I look like under all that excess flesh? The Shadow knows, I guess, but nobody else. I had grown so used to seeing my fat face that it was just a blob to me. I took in the light brown hair and the blue eyes and the beard that was a mistake. Rather fair skin. Just a skull covered with doughy fat.

And on that night, I had a date—which didn't happen often. Just the thought of going out with a woman scared me silly. My hands were not steady when I trimmed the beard, but I combed my hair, went into my bedroom, and began to dress.

I'd bought new clothes for this date—from the Big Men's Shop, of course. They were the most expensive threads I'd ever bought, a pair of charcoal slacks and a navy-blue sport jacket, single vested, more or less a blazer. I sat down and put on the new Johnson-and-Murphy shoes, a hundred bucks a shoe, then I braced myself and walked back into the bathroom and stared at myself in the mirror. For a moment I didn't move, then I said out loud, "Ollie Benson, you look like a fat, ugly baby with a stupid beard!"

The sound of the phone ringing turned me around, and I walked out of the bathroom and picked it up. "Hello?"

"Hey, Ollie, are you about ready?"

"Jimmy ... I ... don't think I can make it."

"Can't make it? Hey, what are you talking about, man, you *gotta* make it!"

"Look, Jimmy, I just don't date. You know that. I don't know why I ever let you talk me into this."

Jimmy Douglas was my best friend. He worked the counter and dealt with customers at Maxie's while I did all the work on the computers in the back. He was as small and lean as I was gobby fat, a swift talker whereas I was pretty silent, a sharp dresser where I wore whatever I could get on. Pretty much the opposite of everything I am. Still, we'd worked together for three years, and he was the closest thing I had to a friend. He had been after me for some time to go out on a date with him, and finally, in a weak moment, I had agreed.

"Look." Jimmy had a sharp, staccato voice and a habit of repeating himself. "Look, you gotta go. I mean you *gotta* go, man! You can't stay in that stupid room all your life. Get with it—*get with it*, man! I ain't takin' no for an answer. We got these girls lined up, and you know how hard I been tryin' to get Tammy to go out with me."

"I know, Jimmy." All I had heard for the past three months was the name Tammy McNeil. She had been the second runner-up in the Miss Tennessee contest the previous year, and Jimmy had been in ecstasy when she had said she'd go out with him. "The catch is," he said, "she's got this cousin from Ohio or Nebraska or somewhere—some dumb state that ends with a vowel." Just like Jimmy to not know the difference between Ohio and Nebraska. "She won't go out with me unless I find a date for her friend."

"Jimmy—"

"Don't say it—don't say it, Ollie. Look, you gotta do it. We're friends—we're friends, ain't we?"

"Sure we are, but I'm just no good with girls."

"Ah, you'll be great with this one, you'll be great. Tammy says she's smart—like you. She's gettin' her degree in sociology—or maybe it was psychology or something else. Anyway, she's real smart, and you two will get on fine. Come on now, don't let me down."

A sense of doom settled on me. I had no happy memories of going out with girls. I had tried a blind date three times, and those three times were reminiscent of the sinking of the *Titanic*, the fall of the Alamo, and the destruction of Hiroshima. Each of those three times, I had vowed never to go out again on a blind date—but now I heard myself saying fatalistically, "All right, Jimmy, but I can tell you it won't work."

"Sure it'll work—sure it'll work! We'll make it fine. Come on now. We don't want to be late."

∽

I hung up the phone and walked slowly around my apartment. It wasn't much, to tell the truth. The living room had a couch, a chair, a huge TV, a window, and a door.

The bedroom was pretty much the same: four walls, a floor, and a ceiling, along with a bed and a chest of drawers and a small closet.

Of the two rooms where I actually lived, the computer room was my hiding place. In there, I was king of the world. I stepped inside it now, glanced around, and wished fervently that I could simply go in, sit down, and play with the computers.

My latest toy was the newest, fastest Powerbook made, and I ran it lean and mean for maximum speed. It was less than an inch thick and weighed less than five pounds. With my discount, I got it for only two thousand dollars with all the bells and whistles. Maybe I loved it because it was so small and I was so huge. And what would Freud make of that little gem?

The other room I spent my *real* life in was the kitchen. It was spotless and contained every expensive laborsaving gadget devised by the mind of man for the art of cooking. After computers, cooking took up most of the rest of my life, and once again I felt myself longing simply to create a magnificent meal and sit down and eat until I was groggy.

But Jimmy was my friend, and I had promised. So I left the apartment and waited until Jimmy pulled up in his '01 Infinity. I opened the door and got in and, as always, felt the car tilt to starboard. Jimmy grinned and reached over and punched me on the arm. "Hey, now," he yelped. "We're gonna get with it tonight. Watch our smoke!"

"Yep, we're gonna get with it," I tried to say cheerfully. And then I thought, *Maybe it'll be different this time. The girl may be homely, but maybe she likes to talk. Maybe we'll hit it off.* I nourished that little fantasy as Jimmy sped around the streets of Memphis, until finally he pulled up in front of a tan brick apartment building on Sycamore Street.

"This is it," Jimmy said. "Come on, let's go get those women!"

I got out of the car and followed Jimmy, who was practically dancing with excitement. We mounted the steps, Jimmy rang the bell, and almost at once the door opened.

"Hey, Tammy, this is my friend I told you about, Ollie Benson. Ollie, this is Tammy McNeil, the almost Miss Tennessee."

"I'm glad to know you."

"Pleased to meet you," I muttered, but I had seen the look in her eyes and the quick contraction of her mouth at the corners. How well I knew that look! Translated, it meant, *You brought this fat slob as a date for my friend? You must be crazy!*

Jimmy noticed nothing; he was too busy telling Tammy how gorgeous she was. Then another young woman stepped out and I heard Tammy say, "This is Lorraine Patterson. Lorraine, this is—what'd you say your name is?"

"Ollie Benson. I'm glad to know you, Lorraine."

"Glad to know you too, Ollie."

Lorraine was an even worse actress and less adept at covering her feelings than Miss-Almost-Tennessee. The disgust that flared in her eyes shut all my systems down. Even Jimmy must have seen it! Her jaw muscles tightened as she ground her teeth together, and I would have given the most expensive computer I had to be away from this place.

"Well, come on," Jimmy said. "Time's a-wastin'—time's a-wastin'!"

I walked woodenly toward the car, opened the door for Lorraine, then walked around and got in the other side. This time the car tilted to port, and the springs squealed under my weight. Jimmy got in, started the car up, and said, "Hold onto your hats, kids, we're gonna get loose tonight!" Jimmy has a real way with words.

Jimmy rattled on to Tammy, and soon I felt I had to make some attempt at conversation. "I understand you're in college."

"Yes, I'm a psych major."

"That must be very interesting."

"What do you do?" The woman looked at me. She was a little overweight herself—nothing like me, of course. She had brown hair, rather smallish brown eyes, and was pretty in a sort of bovine way. Her eyes were what frightened me. She looked at me as if I were a mouse in a cage being prepared for some sort of experiment. She said suddenly, "Have you ever tried to get professional help for your problem?"

I could not speak. Nobody had ever said anything like that. I'm sure they thought it, and they no doubt talked about it when I wasn't there, but Lorraine Patterson came right out with it.

"Not really," I mumbled.

"You should. There are some marvelous new treatments—psychological, of course. You realize, don't you, that obesity isn't a physical problem? You have a severe *psychological* problem. All you need to do is get that solved, and you'll be perfectly normal."

For the rest of the ride to the club, she talked about how many fat people had been helped by psychology. I couldn't think of a word to say and was relieved when we finally got to the nightclub.

Lorraine didn't wait for me to come open her door. Jimmy grabbed Tammy's arm and the two fled, then Lorraine followed and I had to hurry to catch up.

By the time we got inside I was sick. I knew I'd made a bad mistake but couldn't think of any way out of it. It was rather a small place, but it made up for its lack of size by a great deal of noise. A band of some sort was making something that sounded vaguely like music. To me it was almost torture. I followed the other three to a table where we sat down, and a waiter hovered over us, saying, "What's it gonna be?"

Jimmy ordered a cocktail, Tammy a martini, and Lorraine a margarita. The waiter looked at me, and I said, "Just a Coke, please."

The waiter stared at me. "Just a Coke? That's all?"

"That's all."

In disgust he left, and Jimmy said quickly, "Ollie here doesn't drink."

"How nice for him," Lorraine snapped.

The drinks came, and we all tasted them, and then at once Jimmy was up saying, "Let's dance, Tammy."

He hauled her onto the dance floor, and Lorraine got up. "Well, I guess we may as well dance too."

"I–I don't dance."

She stared at me in disbelief, and I could see that she'd had enough of Ollie Benson to last her the rest of her life. She sat again, picked up her drink, and began working on it.

Einstein said something about time being relative, and the next hour proved his theory true. Time crept by, each second lasting half an hour. Jimmy and Miss Tennessee danced, and I tried valiantly to carry on some sort of a conversation, but Lorraine grew more silent and as frigid as polar ice as time went on.

Finally I excused myself and went to the men's room. I stayed there as long as I decently could, but there's a limit to what you can pretend to do in a men's room. When I got back to the table I saw a tall guy standing there, smiling down at the others. When Tammy looked up and saw me, she said, "Oh, yes, this is—what's your name again?"

"Ollie Benson."

"Oh, yeah. Ollie, this is Carl Patterson. He works for a movie studio in Hollywood."

We shook hands and Jimmy said, "Yeah, they're shooting a film here right down on Beale Street. Hey, Carl, sit down and join us."

"No, I'd be the odd man out."

Patterson was a well-built man with slightly curly hair and a cleft chin. He turned to move, but I said quickly, "Hey, why don't you stay, Carl?" To the others, I said, "I'm not feelin' well. If you don't mind, I think I'll go home."

"That's too bad," Lorraine said quickly, "but you should take care of yourself."

"Yeah," Tammy said just as quickly, "good to meet you."

Jimmy looked worried. "You okay? I'll take you home."

"No, I'll catch a cab. You guys have a good time."

They all made "sorry-about-that" noises as I turned and left. When I stepped outside, I felt like the Count of Monte Cristo when he finally broke out of his prison. Quick as I could, I got a taxi and left the scene of the crime.

When I got home I shucked off all my clothes, threw them on the floor, and put on my usual costume in the summer—a pair of shorts, a Hawaiian sport shirt with enough material to make the sails for the *Mayflower*, and soft chenille flip-flops.

I went into the kitchen, got a king-size bag of Doritos, a box of Little Debbies, and a quart of chocolate milk. Then I went to the computer room and sat down in my chair. It was a massive office chair, the biggest one I could find—the only one I'd ever seen big enough to carry my weight.

I ate a half-dozen Little Debbies, washing them down with chocolate milk, then I reached out and touched the mouse.

When I begin to work with a computer, something comes over me. I'm in another world, almost like a parallel universe. It's like that movie *The Wizard of Oz*. At first everything is gray and unhappy, and then suddenly Dorothy wakes up in a Technicolor world. I'm lost in the beauty of the computer and would love to stay there for all eternity.

I don't know how long I had worked, probably two or three hours. Once again, Mr. Einstein's relativity kicked in. I looked up just in time to see my mouse, the real one with fur. She had started visiting me maybe two months earlier, but by this time she came every night. She had lost all fear of me. In the darkness of the room, illuminated only by the screen of the computer, her eyes were as silver as the screen itself. I reached down and gave her a morsel of a Little Debbie and watched as she sat up and delicately nibbled at it. Her paws were tiny and a miracle if I ever saw one. I remembered that Walt Whitman once said, "A mouse is miracle enough to stagger sextillions of infidels." How right you were, Walter!

Suddenly the memory of the evening came back, and a great wave of bitterness swept over me, a tsunami of rage and frustration. I thought of Scarlett lifting her hands to heaven and vowing, "I'll never go hungry again!"

So that night, when it all started, I closed my eyes for a time. Then I opened them and looked at the mouse, and I said, "Miss Mousie, I'll never let a woman humiliate me again!"

Miss Mousie stared at me for an instant and then calmly resumed nibbling at the Little Debbie.

CHAPTER TWO

"Hey, Ollie, you about got that X-17 put together yet?" I glanced up to see Jimmy standing to my left; as usual, he was practically hopping with nervous energy. He snapped his fingers rapidly, shifted his feet nervously, then said, "The guy's outside, and you never saw such a guy in all your life. He acts like he owns the place. You all finished with it?"

"All done." I gave the X-17 a slight shove, then tore the repair record from the pad to my left and handed it to Jimmy. I watched his eyes fly open wide, as if they were window shades. He whistled low, saying, "Holy smoke! He's gonna scream when I give him this bill."

"That's what it cost to fix it." I was glad, at that particular moment, that I didn't have to face whoever it was. At times I felt isolated and cut off back in my little cubbyhole, never doing anything but seeing the insides of machines, but I would be rotten at Jimmy's job. He could turn on the charm when he wanted to, an ability I lacked. I turned back to my work, but Jimmy tapped me on the shoulder.

"Hey, Ollie, how about what we talked about last night?"

"About what?"

"Ah, you know, the Ice Capades. I got two extra tickets. Great seats, and I can get you a date."

I knew something changed in my face when Jimmy said this, but he wasn't exactly the swiftest guy in the world. As a matter of fact, he was almost totally insensitive to everything except girls and partying and fast cars. We had gone over this at least twenty times, but it never seemed to sink into his skull that I wasn't a prospect for a double date, especially since that night with Lorraine. "No thanks," I said shortly.

"Hey, you can't hole up all the time. If you're not back here, you're in your apartment. Get a life, man!"

"Get somebody else, Jimmy."

He reached over and squeezed my shoulder. "Look, Ollie, it's been eight months since the last time we went out—and you ran out on me that time."

"Doesn't that tell you something?"

"So she didn't like you. She wasn't your type."

"Jimmy, look at me." I turned around and faced Jimmy squarely. I was wearing a Hawaiian shirt because the style was easy to get in extra-extra-large sizes. I hadn't bothered to get a haircut lately, nor had I yet shaved off the beard I knew was a failure. "What girl's going to want to go out with me?"

"You just gotta find the right one. There's gotta be one out there somewheres. After all, Ollie, you're smart. Hey, I bet you're the smartest dude in Memphis!"

"Girls aren't looking for 'smart.' They don't go to see Brad Pitt because he's smart."

Jimmy shook his head in disgust. I hoped he had given up. "All right, but I'm gonna find you a girl yet. See if I don't." He changed the subject abruptly, a way of his. "Hey, when you gonna get through with that program you've been working on for the last hunnerd years?"

"Finished it last week."

"No kidding! You never told me." He grinned broadly and slapped me on the shoulder. He was a toucher, always leaning on people, pinching their arm, or squeezing their shoulder. I didn't mind that, actually. "Come on now. You been keeping me in the dark. What is this great program that's going to make you rich and famous?"

I had never mentioned my program to anyone except Jimmy. Who could I talk to about it? I knew Jimmy would never understand the mechanics of programming, and I didn't know anyone who would. Even so, as he bounced and grinned in front of me, I thought about the satisfaction I had felt when I had finally mailed the program off, so I began telling him about it. "It's like nothing else on the market. I call it Film Maker."

"Film Maker? I *like* it! What's it do?"

"Well, it lets anyone who's the least bit computer literate make his own movies on a computer."

"Say what?"

"That's right. It lets you choose, first of all, your own setting. You can choose a desert, or set the scene on board a cruise ship, maybe a nightclub."

"Hey, that's neat!"

"Better than that, you can create your own actors."

Jimmy scratched his head and stared at me without comprehension. "Whatcha mean—create your own actors?"

"Well, there are stock models you can pick from. You can have an action hero like Chuck Norris. You choose Chuck, and you write him a part, and with my program he'll say the lines you write, and he'll do whatever you program into the scene."

Jimmy grinned broadly and poked me in the stomach. "Like, you can write a love scene and put any guy and any woman in it you like, and it'll come out like a movie?"

"That's right."

Jimmy began to walk around, and soon he was waving his hands. "Man, if that thing works, you're going to make a bundle, buddy! Don't forget your pal Jimmy when you're up there like Bill Gates."

"I won't, Jimmy."

Jimmy snatched up the computer and bounced out of the room. I knew he would have a thousand questions for me, and I regretted telling him as much as I had. But I'd needed to talk to somebody. I'd put every spare moment for the past three years into perfecting this program, and if it didn't work, I knew I'd want to go out and drown myself in the Mississippi River.

I pulled a Mac laptop over and began working on it, but I'd worked so much on computers I could shut my mind down and my fingers did the job automatically. What I really began thinking of was what I would do if I *did* make some money, as Jimmy had predicted. It wouldn't have to be a million dollars. Just enough to do something . . . well, *different*. Maybe I could go to New Zealand, or maybe Bora Bora. I thought about that for a while, and then I shoved it aside. I think my mind has got compartments in it like a desk, and one compartment is where I put all the dreams I've had that never work. It's pretty crowded in there, and this one would probably be one of them. I'd just like to make enough to get some new equipment, and maybe enough to quit this job and work at home on my programs full-time. That way, I wouldn't even have to come and face the world down here.

But it probably wouldn't work. It never does.

∞

I don't know why I always set the table when I fix a fancy supper for myself. No one would see it but me. I put a snowy-white linen tablecloth on the table and lit some candles. I set one place for myself of Noritake china, and the heavy silver flatware I liked—I've always hated flimsy stuff to eat with. Then I carefully folded the napkin as if I were a waiter at the Waldorf Astoria.

I went back to the kitchen and began to pull the meal together. As always I planned it down to the last bite. I decided on a Creole dinner with enough fat to bloat an African village. For soup I fixed chicken-okra gumbo and jambalaya, then avocado mold for a salad. One entree was never enough for me, so I cooked up baked Creole red snapper and a big platter of fried liver and onions. For vegetables I had a large bowl of hopping John and another of candied sweet potatoes. For dessert I made a platter of butterscotch pralines.

As I took the soup off the stove and poured it into one of the soup plates, I was thinking that there were only two times when I was really happy—when I was working on computers or creating a program and when I was cooking. I'd thought several times of going into cooking. Paul Prudhomme, the chef, wasn't as fat as me, but he proved you don't have to be skinny to cook well!

I set the soup down, took my seat, unfolded my napkin, and put it over my lap. I've always hated paper napkins. I won't have one in my house. Just another of my goofy ideas.

Before I could take a bite of soup, the doorbell rang. That surprised me, because I didn't have a lot of company. I wasn't expecting anybody at seven o'clock at night, but I got up, put my napkin down, and went to the door. When I opened it, I saw a man I didn't know. "Yes?" I asked, figuring he had the wrong address.

"I'm looking for Mr. Oliver Benson."

I was surprised, and I must have shown it, for I saw something flicker in the man's eyes. He was no more than five ten but very well dressed, wearing a royal blue linen suit, a white shirt open at the neck, and black, highly polished shoes. He had crisp, curly brown hair, warm brown eyes, and a good smile. I knew he must be selling something, but it was unusual for salesmen to come into our building.

"My name's Dane Fetterman," he said, handing me a white card, richly embossed, that said, *Dane Fetterman, Financial Planning and Management*, along with his phone number, fax, and e-mail.

"Wonder if I could speak with you for a few moments. I know it's inconvenient, but I think you might find what I have to say interesting."

I couldn't help smiling. "I don't need any financial advice. Don't have any money to invest."

Fetterman's smile broadened. "I think you're going to need someone like me. Just let me have five minutes, that's all."

I hesitated, but what else did I have to do? "All right, come on in."

Fetterman stepped inside, then stopped dead still, staring at the table, the white tablecloth, the candles. He turned to me, his brow wrinkled. "Hey, I've come at a bad time. You're having guests." He sniffed and said, "Your wife cooking supper? That smells great."

"I'm . . . not married. I do my own cooking." Suddenly I said, "Just a minute. I've got to take something out of the oven." I rushed back into the kitchen and pulled the salmon out of the oven, and after I put it on a plate with a cover, I went back.

Fetterman was standing with something like astonishment on his face. "You cooked all this just for yourself?"

"Yeah, I do that once in a while."

"Wish I could do that. Where'd you learn to cook?"

"Out of a cookbook." I hesitated a moment, and then something prompted me to say, "I always cook way too much. You're welcome to join me."

"No kidding! I mean, you're not just saying that?"

"No, really. You can tell me what you want to sell me while we're eating."

"What about we eat first and talk business later. Home cooking." He smiled broadly, and I noticed that he had a dimple on the right side of his cheek that made him look boyish.

"Sit down. I'll fix you a place."

"Hey, I'll do the dishes."

I set another plate out, and feeling somewhat foolish I said, "I've got some wine. I don't usually drink it, but . . ."

"Sure thing, Mr. Benson."

"Just call me Ollie. Everyone does." I got the wine, which I kept chilled for some reason or other. I don't know much about wine, but someone had told me that it was good.

When Fetterman looked at it, he whistled, "Well, you don't spare the horses when it comes to wine."

I opened it and poured us both a glass, and he lifted his, saying, "Here's to Oliver Benson. May great things happen to him."

His toast made me feel foolish. I knew he was out to sell me something, maybe life insurance, but I got tired of eating alone, and I could always say no.

As we worked our way through the meal, he commented on every bit of it. Dessert sent him into a feeding frenzy. It was my specialty: berry gratin, which included blueberries, raspberries, and blackberries mixed with cinnamon and granulated sugar and then topped with a mixture of plain yogurt, honey, and caramelized brown sugar. Finally I got us some espresso. I always grind the beans myself because I'm a coffee addict. I figure I might as well have the best.

We sat at the table, and he studied me for a moment and then looked down to his coffee cup as if he were looking into a crystal ball. I waited for him to make his pitch. He said nothing for so long, I finally asked him, "Why did you come to see me, Mr. Fetterman?"

"Hey, it's Dane. Well, you saw my card. I manage finances for people. What I've really come to talk to you about is computers."

Immediately I was interested. He began to talk about computers and programs, mentioning his favorites, and I could tell that he was pretty sharp. There were gaps in his knowledge, of course, but he knew his business. Finally he said, "You know, Ollie, when people come into money most people don't really know how to manage it. You read about these people who win ten million dollars in the lottery, then a few years later it's all gone. They don't realize that they could live forever on the income from that, so they go out and blow it."

"Well, I haven't won any lotteries. I don't have any money, and I'm not likely to have any. You can't make anything off me, Dane."

"I think I can." Fetterman grew very serious. His eyebrows drew together almost in a straight line, and there was tension in his features.

Uh, oh, here comes the hard sell. He'll want me to buy whole life, I guess.

"I've got a friend in California, Ollie, in Silicon Valley. Actually, he's a mole, my spy in the business there. He knows everything that's happening in the world of computer programming. He called me last night and told me about the program you sent to U.S. Online."

I stared at him, shocked. "But I haven't heard a word from them."

"You will, Ollie, you will!" He leaned forward, and I saw he was wearing a Rolex on his left wrist. He tapped his fingers on the table, his eyes shining. "Ollie, if you don't hear anything else, hear this. They'll try to steal your program."

"U.S. Online? They wouldn't do that."

"They'll probably offer you a million dollars. My friend's already told me that. That offer is probably in the mail right now."

I stared at him, watching for some sort of break in his expression. I didn't believe him. I've had too many busted dreams. "Well, *if* they offer me a million dollars, you can bet I'll take it."

"Don't!" Dane's response was so quick and forceful it shocked me. "If you take it, it'll be robbery, Ollie. Film Maker is the hottest thing to come down the computer pike."

"You know the name of it?"

"Yes, and I know what it does, and I know it'll work. Listen, Ollie, don't let them market it and don't sell it to them. Market it yourself."

"Why—that's crazy! I don't have the money to market anything, and I wouldn't know how."

"True, but I do. That's why I've come, Ollie. If you sign an agreement with me, I'll guarantee you that the bank will give us all the capital we want." He laughed softly and shook his head. His eyes were warm with admiration, something I had never seen before. "They'll be scared to death that we'll go to another bank."

"But—"

"I know—people are afraid of con artists, and they're everywhere. Anybody can come to your door and sell you gold bricks or wildcat stocks or swampland in Florida after showing you pictures of a beautiful beach. And I might be one of those fellows. I'm not asking you to trust me, not for one minute. All I'm asking you to do is this—when the offer comes, they'll try to rush you. They'll tell you that they've got other programs that they're looking at, and they've got to have a quick decision. Don't believe them. Don't even talk to them."

I felt like an actor in a play. This was all so unreal! "Dane, I wouldn't know how to talk to anybody."

"I know, but I do. You ever watch baseball?"

"Sure."

"Then you know all the big-money players have agents. Those guys play baseball, the agents handle the money. Did you read last week where a shortstop signed for 252 million dollars?"

I had read that story. "Yeah, I read it. It sounded almost obscene."

"I don't think so. A guy's worth what he can get. But those baseball players don't have time to haggle, and let me make a guess." He smiled and pointed his finger at me. "You'd rather be working on a new program than meeting some big shot and talking about deals."

I couldn't deny that. "Yes, you're right."

"Look," Dane said. "You're going to have to move fast. You don't know me. I may be the slickest con artist in the country. Tell you what, tomorrow you check into my firm, and you find out whether I'm on the level. I think you'll probably get a call from U.S. Online tomorrow, or one of their agents. They'll want to fly you to the coast. They'll send their own jet. But don't go. Don't jump in, Ollie. I've seen fellows like you with all the brains get eaten alive by the big companies. If you want me to handle you, that's fine. If you don't, that's fine too. But, Ollie, get *somebody*!"

Dane rose to his feet. "Now, that's all the business talk. I'm washing the dishes, and then afterwards you can show me how Film Maker works, if you're willing."

Was I willing? I would be willing to talk to Jack the Ripper if he would be interested in what I did in my computer room!

We spent two hours playing with the program. After Dane left, sleep was out of the question. I walked the floor and went over every word he had said. I've got a pretty good memory, almost total recall, and I tried to pick holes in his pitch. But each time I thought I spotted a red flag, I kept hearing him say, *Go check me out*. That sounded safe enough.

I went over to the computer and put a DVD in, Clint Eastwood in *A Few Dollars More*. I got a package of Doritos, some jalapeño dip, and a liter of Dr. Pepper. Soon Clint, lean and mean with a cheroot clenched between his teeth, was shooting people—but for once I didn't pay much attention.

∾

Fetterman's office wasn't as ornate as I'd expected. It was on the fifth floor of the Blaylock building, and the late afternoon sun was filtering through the window to the secretary's right. The chairs were all beige leather and stainless steel, and there were several pictures of horses on the walls. The secretary was a good-looking blonde with impossible eyelashes. She gave me a smile that must have set off the seismographs, and you would have thought that Mel Gibson had stepped into the office. "May I help you?"

"My name is Benson. I'd like to see Mr. Fetterman."

"Do you have an appointment?"

"No, but he asked me to contact him."

"Just one moment." She flipped a switch with a fingernail painted lime green. I noticed that the other fingernails were all different colors, and I wondered if that was the newest fashion. "Mr. Fetterman, there's a gentleman here to see you. He doesn't have an appointment."

"What's his name?"

She looked up at me, and I said, "Ollie Benson."

At once Fetterman's voice crackled. "Send him in right away, Diane."

"Right through there, Mr. Benson."

I thanked her and stepped through the door. I'd hardly had time to look around the room before Dane, who had popped up from his chair, demanded, "Did U.S. Online call?"

"Yes, early this morning."

"What'd they say?"

I shook my head, still in shock. "They want to fly me out to California. They said they'd have their jet pick me up whenever I like."

"Boy," Dane laughed with delight, "they *are* quick workers." He turned his head sideways and examined me. "What'd you tell 'em?"

"I put 'em off."

"Good. Now, did you check me out?"

I hesitated, then said, "I didn't know how to check you out so I hired a private detective."

Dane laughed and slapped his hands together. "Well, you're a quick learner. What'd he say?"

"It was a she. She looked like an old-maid schoolteacher, but she gave you a good report."

"She tell you about my being in the Mafia?"

I had to smile. "No, she said you were a reliable business-man. That means I can trust you, she said."

"Well, I'm glad I passed muster."

I'd made up my mind as soon as Miss Finley gave me the report. After all, what did I have to lose? "I guess I'd like you to help me, Dane."

"Great! I'll have my secretary draw up an agreement."

"I don't know anything about this. How much do I have to pay you?"

"Ten percent is the going rate for agents. Some get fifteen."

"Suppose I'll only pay five?"

"I'd take it." Dane laughed. "You don't understand, Ollie. Five percent of what you're going to make will keep me for the rest of my days. After all, I don't have a lot of expensive tastes. Just a Ferrari every now and then."

I suddenly felt good. Dane made me feel comfortable. "I'll pay whatever the others pay, Dane."

"We'll settle on ten, and since you're going to be my only client, you'll be seeing a lot of me."

"I'm going to be your only client?"

"I won't have time to fool with anybody else."

"All right. I don't know anything about business, Dane. I'm trusting you to take care of me."

Dane grew serious. He stood directly in front of me. "I know you don't, Ollie, and that's the part of my business I like most. I hope it'll work out so that this will be more than a business relationship. I'd like for us to be friends. I know that takes time, but I'd like to try."

I can't tell you in words what that meant to me. I'd never really had a friend, and here was one that had come out of nowhere. I swallowed hard, and, as silly as it sounds, if I hadn't done something, I think I would have got a little misty-eyed.

"I'd like that," I said. "I don't have all that many friends."

"Well, it's time you did. Now, the first thing is to quit your job."

"But—how will I live?"

"I'll open you an account today. We'll leave for the bank right now. I'll put five thousand dollars of my own money in your account. That'll be enough to hold you until we get airborne."

"You're going to give me five thousand dollars?"

"Not give, I'm going to lend it to you, Ollie."

"I'll have to give them a week's notice. They've been good to me."

"That's fine, but remember: Your job from now on is to come up with new programs." He shook his head and chewed on his lower lip. "I doubt that you'll ever top Film Maker, but you might. And I think it's what you like to do."

It was, indeed, and I agreed at once. My head was swimming, and then he said, "Tell you what. Why don't you cook supper again some night, just for the two of us, and we can talk."

"How about tomorrow?"

"Fine. Now listen. I'm going to be like a whirlwind today and tomorrow. I'm going to get in touch with those folks in California, then I'm going to hit some banks." He reached out and hit me hard on the shoulder with his fist. It stung, but I liked it. "Fasten your seat belt, Ollie, we're going where no man has ever gone before!"

CHAPTER
THREE

I had expected that living in California would feel different from living in Memphis—but it didn't. When the dollars had started rolling in, Dane had insisted that we move to California, and I'd agreed. Maybe I thought I'd find happiness on the beach, but it didn't happen.

Actually, as I looked down at the Pacific, I had a longing for Beale Street in Memphis. I looked at the Girard-Perregaux on my arm and, as always, was filled with a mixture of pride and shame. It was the first expensive thing I had bought for myself after the money started rolling in. I'd always thought that a Rolex was the most expensive watch made, but I found out that wearers of a Girard-Perregaux consider the wearers of a Rolex on about the level of sharecroppers.

For a couple of weeks after the really *big* money began to roll in, I went sort of crazy. For example, I flew to New York to be fitted for custom-made shirts. It was all Dane's fault, actually. I just mentioned that I'd never had a shirt that fit, and he found out about a place called Ascot Chang that custom-made shirts. He bought me a ticket, and two days later I was at 7 West 57th Street in New York getting fitted for shirts. The tailors there took thirty-one different measurements before they started making the shirts, and the guys that made it took twenty-four stitches per inch. But it wasn't all easy. I had my choice of 2,700 fabrics!

I saved so much money on those Ascot Chang shirts (after all, they only cost eight hundred dollars each, plus tax!) that I decided to get a whole new wardrobe. By the time I was all decked out in foppish attire, I'd spent a little less than the total budget of a developing African nation. It was worth it, though, because now instead of looking like a whale in my clothes, I looked like a *rich* whale!

Having a *lot* of money does something to your brain. By the time I got on the plane back to California, I was weighed down not only with Ascot Chang shirts, but with a Namdar diamond ring from Saks, two pair of Cartier sunglasses (one for formal wear, one for digging fish worms), a custom-made kissing alligator belt—the buckle set with rubies—and an American Bison computer case designed and crafted in Modena, Italy.

But when I got back to California with all this loot, I felt kind of—well, *let down*. Every time I looked at the Girard-Perregaux, I couldn't help thinking, *It doesn't keep any better time than my old Timex*. After all, you can only wear one watch at a time. Every time I looked to see what time it was, I thought about how the Sierra Club could have used the money.

I glanced at the Girard-Perregaux. Eight minutes after three. I leaned back in my chair and stared out the window. It was the penthouse condo, and I could see the beach down below with scantily clad women, and men as well, cavorting or lying there soaking up the sunshine. The sunshine was free, but to stay at a place like this and lie on the beach—well, it cost more than it should.

I stood up and went out to stand on the balcony. California was a wonderland. I'd read somewhere once that in Los Angeles Halloween is redundant. Jimmy, when I had left Memphis, had told me, *Everything loose rolls to California, buddy. Don't forget me now*.

I hadn't forgotten Jimmy. I'd sent him enough money to buy a new car. Cash to me didn't seem to be real anymore. It was like Monopoly money. Dane had been ecstatic about the way Film Maker had taken off. We'd marketed it ourselves and couldn't keep up with the orders. I couldn't even keep up with the *money*! I met with a CPA regularly, and he explained to me how he was investing it so that I wouldn't have to pay so much in taxes.

Now, looking out at the Pacific, I felt cheated. I'd always thought anybody with as much money as I had piled on top of me would be happy.

But I wasn't happy—and that scared me. All the clichés I'd heard, that money can't buy happiness—well, I'd never believed them. I'd always thought it *could*. The last few months had been like a dream. I'd been hounded by everybody. "The new miracle man," I'd been called. *People* magazine wanted a picture, which I refused to give them. Even Barbara Walters wanted to interview me. Dane had tried to get me to take advantage of some of these offers, but I just couldn't. We'd moved to the coast and leased this penthouse, but I didn't like it. I had no feeling of belonging, and was shocked to find myself longing for my little apartment back in Memphis. At least I'd had privacy there. Privacy is pretty hard to get if you're making millions and living in a place where most people crave publicity.

"What are you doing out here on the balcony? Why don't you come down on the beach?"

I turned around. Dane was wearing expensive sunglasses and had just the right amount of tan, while I was still as white as a slug.

How could I tell him I *couldn't* go out on the beach? I'd look like a beached whale. I went onto the beach late at night, when everybody was pretty well cleared out, and if anybody did see me, they couldn't see well enough to take in all the fat I was carrying around.

"You ought to go down. It's a great day. I just saw that actress who's in all the papers. She's right down there on the beach."

He pointed, and I looked. I'd never seen her in a movie—hardly knew her name. The movies I watched were mostly John Wayne and Clint Eastwood and the old Western stars. I had all their movies now, and I spent the nights going through them all.

Dane mixed drinks and brought me one. As usual, I took it, but I didn't drink it. He knew I wouldn't, but he never seemed surprised that I wouldn't drink. I'd explained that liquor made me sick, but he just kept bringing drinks that went to waste.

Throwing himself into one of the deck chairs, he began to go over some of the projects he had in mind. He asked me about the new program I was working on, and I said, "Well, it's coming along."

"You're a close-mouthed son-of-a-gun, but we're doing pretty well."

I sat beside him and felt the chair give under my weight. "Dane, I don't like this place. I'd rather be back in Memphis."

"Back in Memphis! You don't mean that. Memphis is nothing but Cleveland—without the glitter!"

"I know, but I was used to it."

Dane was silent for a time. Finally he sipped his drink and said, "I know what you need. You need a house. You need some privacy. That's the kind of guy you are."

I knew he was right. "Yes, that's what I need."

"Okay, we'll buy you a house. You can have any one you want. The only trouble will be choosing the right one . . ."

We found a house, all right. It was right on the coast, almost hanging over a cliff. It wasn't really the house itself that I liked so much—it was more the fact that John Wayne had owned it once. He hadn't kept it long, I found out, but at least he had lived here for a few months. It gave me a strange feeling to walk through the house and know that the Duke himself had been here, that he had walked with that odd, lurching gait of his right across every room.

But the house itself—well, I just wandered around in it. One room, of course, was my computer room. Dane had a man come in and set it all up with the latest furniture, ergonomic of course, and I changed most of the things around. It was the one room I felt comfortable in. The kitchen was enormous, with every device a cook could want. The bathrooms were huge, and the living room wasn't as big as the Rose Bowl, but it wasn't a lot smaller either—at least so it seemed to me.

We got it at a bargain. It only cost 6.3 million.

What was the matter with me? Here I was living in John Wayne's house, with every piece of computer software that I could think of and some that I couldn't, computers of every sort powerful enough to run Cape Canaveral, but I just blundered around. I did go out onto the beach once in a while, because it wasn't a public beach. I'd sit there and watch the waves come in, but when I went back to the house it just didn't feel right.

One thing I did during those first weeks was siphon money away from Jacob Lebnitz, my CPA. I'd go in and demand a big sum in cash, and he'd go crazy. Once I asked for a hundred thousand dollars, and he told me it would take awhile to get it, and it would create tax problems. I said, "That's your problem, Mr. Lebnitz," and insisted that he give it to me.

It had become a game. I finally got a million dollars together, in cash. Dane knew about it, of course, and it made him nervous. "Are you keeping all that money in the house?"

"I'm not telling." I grinned.

"If word got out, you'd have burglars lined up. It's a terrible idea, Ollie."

But I wouldn't listen to him, or to Lebnitz either. Actually I wasn't keeping it in the house. I was putting it in a Swiss bank account. Why? I guess it was because the money didn't seem real, and I had heard so many stories about rich people losing everything and winding up on the street. I did some research to find out how Swiss bank accounts work. Basically, they were simple. You gave them the money, and they kept it and invested it. If you wanted the money out, every account had a single number. If you knew that number, you could get the money. In other words, if I gave that number to somebody else, they could get it as quickly as I could. So I didn't write the number down anywhere. I just memorized it. I slept better at night knowing that if Film Maker failed, and I went bankrupt, and somebody took it over in a business deal, I'd have enough to live on the rest of my life.

But having a million dollars hidden away didn't make me feel better. I kept working on the new program, but it wasn't coming together. I wondered if I would ever learn to live any differently. I was as fat and ugly as ever, and nothing was going to change that. I knew I could get women—money does that for you. Dane had hinted at it, but the idea turned me off. So I just went on working on my programs, living in the Duke's house, and time seemed to run in one continuous stream.

∽

The noise of the combo filtered into the room where I had gone to hide out. Dane organized parties from time to time, and I had learned to live with them. People came, and I met them, but I was always on the outside. On this night Dane had tried his best to get me to mix, and I did try. But, as usual, nobody knew much about computers. They all wanted my money; I could see that in their eyes. They never mentioned it, not directly. There had been one man, a skinny guy with a foreign accent, and he had just mentioned, sort of accidentally, that he had the greatest movie script in the world and whoever produced it would get rich. I could tell he was waiting for me to rush forward and become that man, but I was rich already. I didn't know anything about making movies. Besides, he looked like a bank teller with cold eyes.

I stood it as long as I could, and then I went off to the TV room. I don't know what it had been designed for originally. It wasn't very large—no more than twelve by sixteen—but several overstuffed chairs in there fit me, and I sometimes watched my movies there. I had a computer there, of course. I sat down and began fiddling with it. As usual, I got lost in what I was doing, and I jumped when I heard a voice. "Oh, excuse me!"

I turned around and saw a woman framed in the doorway. She looked a little confused and then laughed. "I'm sorry. I was looking for the kitchen. I wanted to get a drink of water."

"There's a cooler right here. I'll get it for you." I got up, dispensed the water into one of the small paper cups, and handed it to her. As she drank it, I studied her in the dim light. She had brown hair and was trim and attractive. She was wearing a dress that seemed to make her look good, but I didn't know anything about fashion. "More?" I said when she finished.

"No, that's fine." She looked at me and said, "You don't like the party?"

"Not much."

"Neither do I. I don't know anybody. I don't even know the host."

I assumed that Dane had invited her. So she must be in show business or in the computer business. "I guess that's me," I said.

She turned and stared at me. "Oh, you're Oliver Benson?"

"Yes."

"I'm Marlene Wright."

"I'm glad to know you."

She smiled then and stepped a little bit closer. "I don't know what I'm doing here really. I came with a friend of mine."

I couldn't think of a thing to say to her. I was wearing expensive clothes, but they didn't automatically make me a social success. I said, "I'm not much of a host, I'm afraid."

"Neither am I. Congratulations. I hear your program is a great success."

"Yes, it's doing well." I tried to think of something to say and finally asked rather inanely, "Do you live near here?"

"Right down the road, Mr. Benson."

"Everybody just calls me Ollie."

She laughed. "If I had as much money as you, I'd make them call me Your Majesty."

She had an infectious laugh, and I smiled at her. "I don't think you would."

"Are you working on a new program?"

"Yes, I am."

"I like Film Maker. I play with it on my computer all the time, but I'm not very good with computers."

She lifted her eyes and saw the poster on the wall. It was a large blowup of Randolph Scott, the Western hero of the forties. "Randolph Scott, one of my first loves."

"That can't be. You're too young."

"Well, my father loved old Western movies, and I think he had every picture Randolph Scott ever made, so I got hooked on him when I was growing up. Look at him," she said and moved closer, staring up. "That lean jaw and those keen eyes. You just *know* he's going to do the right thing."

"I think I've got all of his movies. I collect them."

"Really! I'll bet you don't have any of Lash LaRue."

"Yes, I do," I said quickly. "Most of his."

"He was another favorite of my dad's."

We began talking about the old Western action heroes, and I was shocked to find out how much she knew. There are groups that meet throughout the country who collect old Western movies, and I had gone to one of those meetings in Memphis when Sunset Carson had come to address the group. He was older, of course, but it was still exciting. I told her about it, and she smiled. "I remember him. He was so lean and long."

The time seemed to fly by, and finally she laughed. "My goodness, we have been going on." She looked around and said, "Do you like your house?"

"No, not really."

She blinked with surprise. "You don't? Why did you buy it then?"

"Well, it was mostly Dane's idea—and I guess I really bought it because it once belonged to John Wayne. But I don't care for it much."

"Did you pick out the furniture and the paintings?"

"No. They all came with the house."

"No wonder you don't like the place, then. You wouldn't let someone else pick your clothes. A house is just as intimate a thing as the clothes you wear."

"Really? I never thought of that."

She smiled again. "Well, that's what I do."

"You build houses?"

"No, I decorate them." She mentioned several houses that she had decorated, but I didn't know any of the people.

"I have to know a person before I'll agree to do their house. I can't make them a house that will please them unless I know what they're like."

The idea was new to me. Of course, in my previous circle, people decorated with what they could afford, mostly from Wal Mart, not what would fit their personality. "Do you think you could do any-thing with this place?"

"Of course!" Marlene said, "but, as I say, I would need to know something about you."

"I wish you could."

"I'll tell you what. Maybe we can get together and talk about it, see if I'd feel comfortable decorating your house. If not, I could recommend someone good."

I had forgotten to be afraid of her. Usually I run like a scared rabbit from any contact with attractive women, but this one was different. "Maybe tomorrow," I said, afraid I was pushing it.

"Well, I'm busy all day tomorrow, but maybe tomorrow evening if it doesn't cut into your plans."

"I have no plans," I said quickly. "Hey—I like to cook. Maybe I could cook dinner for us."

"You cook? How wonderful!" She sighed and shook her head. "I watch those TV cooks, and it looks simple when they do it, but I either burn everything or something just as silly. Maybe I could watch you, and you could teach me a little bit."

"Sure."

"Okay. I'll see you tomorrow night. Say, six o'clock."

She put out her hand, and I took it. She was wearing a per-fume that wafted across to me, and her hand was warm and smooth and strong. She put pressure on my hand, nodded, and said, "I'll see you tomorrow, Ollie."

After she left, I thought about her for a long time. The party finally broke up, and Dane rebuked me for hiding away.

"I met a lady who says she decorates houses."

"Really? I didn't know we had an interior decorator here."

"She said she came with someone else. I don't know who, but she thinks she could do something to make me like this house better."

"Have at it, Ollie, you've got the money."

∾

I had a neighbor once who was full of folksy sayings. I heard him say once he was nervous as a long-tailed cat in a room full of rocking chairs. Well, that's how I was all day getting ready for Marlene to come. I knew it was foolish and silly, but I couldn't help it. I went to the store and bought everything I'd need for one of my best meals. I had decided on French onion soup, mixed greens, beef stroganoff, and chocolate mousse.

When I got home, I fussed over the right music on the stereo, but I had no idea what the right music was for her. She might like country-western music, which I didn't, except for the titles. I waited to start the meal because she had said she wanted to learn to cook. She was fifteen minutes late, and I felt everything in me settle into a deep pit. It was happening all over again. I should have known better.

But then the doorbell rang, and I almost fell down getting to the door. When I opened it, she was standing there smiling. She wasn't overdressed for the occasion, just a simple outfit—a light blue cardigan set and a black pair of slacks. "I'm a little late," she said as she came in.

"Not very. I haven't started cooking yet. I thought you might like to watch."

"Let me do part of it. Maybe I can cut up vegetables or something."

Fixing the meal turned out to be fun. She knew almost nothing about cooking, but she helped fixed the salad while I did the rest of the meal, explaining what I was doing.

"I can set the table," she said.

"The dishes are in that cabinet in there, and the tablecloth too."

"So—you do the cooking, and I'll decorate."

"Fine."

I finished cooking the meal, and when I went in, she had, indeed, made the room look bearable. She had put a white linen tablecloth over the dark mahogany table, added bright blue linen napkins folded into the shapes of swans, and had placed the plates, silverware, and crystal goblets into the perfect table setting. She had taken an arrangement of fresh flowers out of the living room, rearranged it, and placed it in the center of the table. She'd also added four crystal candleholders with bright blue candles, now lit and flickering in the darkness of the room.

I stared at the room and said, "How did you do that? When I do it, it doesn't look that good."

"Well, when I cook it doesn't taste that good, either. I'm starved."

We brought the food in together, and I hesitated. "You want some music?"

"I don't suppose you've got any Chopin."

I stared at her. "I've got everything by Chopin."

"Really!" She brightened. "How wonderful! Just any of it. I love it all."

"He's my favorite," I said.

"Not really! Well, he's mine too."

We sat down to eat, and the food did turn out well. For a small woman, she had a healthy appetite, and from time to time we would stop to listen to the music, and she talked about Chopin, how she admired him.

Afterward she wanted to help with the dishes, but I said there was a woman who came in the mornings and cleaned everything up.

We went into the drawing room, or whatever it was, and she was wandering around looking at the pictures. "I know this picture," she said. "It's from the Sierra Club collection."

"That's right."

She turned and looked at me. "Do you belong to the Sierra Club?"

"Yes, I do." I was shy about it, for I had been called a tree hugger once by Dane.

"So do I," she said. "I go to the meetings pretty often."

"I've never been."

"You haven't? Why, you should. Next time they have one in Los Angeles, maybe we can go together."

"That would be great."

I stood there awkwardly, not knowing what to do. She sat down on one of the modern chairs that I didn't particularly like. I don't know how she did it, but after I sat down across from her, she got me to talking. I think I talked more to her than I'd ever talked to anybody. She had a way of listening that was very attractive, sort of turned her head to one side and kept her eyes fixed on me. She had large eyes, very expressive, and she never once interrupted. I've never met a woman who could do that.

Finally I asked, "Have you thought about doing my house?"

"It doesn't take much of an interior decorator to know what you would like and feel comfortable with."

I stared at her. "You mean you know already?"

"Of course. You like Clint Eastwood and John Wayne and Randolph Scott and Sunset Carson. You like the Old West. What you really need, Ollie, is a contemporary Western decor."

"That sounds like an oxymoron."

"Not really. There's a lot of it around, especially in the Southwest. I've been thinking about you, and I have a book out in my car with some furnishings. Let me go get it, and we'll look at it."

She went out to get the book, and for the next hour we looked at pictures of rooms with Western settings, and I loved them. I never thought of such a thing! Of course, I couldn't have afforded it until now.

"Walk me through the house. I don't think there'll have to be any structural changes."

"Sure." I came out of that chair like a scalded cat, and we walked all the way through the house. She looked at every room, and finally, when we wound up back in the drawing room, she said, "Something could be done with this place, Ollie, and it wouldn't be frightfully expensive, not that that matters to you."

"So you'll do it?"

"You understand," she said cautiously, "I'll be underfoot. I have to be. I only take one or two jobs at a time, so you'll have to put up with me."

I felt something turn over in my stomach or my heart or somewhere, but I managed to say, "That—that'd be all right."

"It might interfere with your work," she said. "It's not something I can do alone. It works like this. I'll get an idea, but I'll have to talk with you about it. You'll have to try it on, more or less."

"That's all right," I said quickly. "I've got lots of time. Will you do it for me?"

"If you'd like, Ollie."

"When do you think we could start?"

"Right now. Let's take this room . . ."

∾

For the next few weeks Marlene was in the house every day. We spent hours looking at pictures, and twice we went to Los Angeles where I got dizzy looking at furniture and drapes, but she seemed to be having the time of her life.

I didn't get anything done on the new program I was working on. I guess it was inevitable that I would fall in love with her.

I never thought it would happen to me. Naturally I had adolescent dreams of sex, and as a man I had wanted women, but this was different. That sort of thing was pure sexual fantasy, but I longed to be around Marlene just to be with her, to listen to her, to watch her eyes. At times I was even able to forget what I was, and during those weeks I told her more about myself than I'd ever told any other human being. We went to a meeting of the Sierra Club, and I found myself, at her mild urging, giving fifty thousand dollars to save the whales—or the turtles, I can't remember which.

Of course, nothing would come of it. I knew that. She didn't say much about her past life, but she did mention once that it had not been pleasant. "My family had money," she told me once as we watched an old Clint Eastwood movie. We had both seen it before, so we ignored it to chat from time to time. She seemed disturbed and said, "We had money—and we had misery. That's when I got cured of the idea that money brought happiness."

"You're right about that, Marlene. When I didn't have any money, I thought that was a sure way to be happy. I guess everybody thinks that."

"I suppose so, and most people die without learning any different, but I didn't." She shook her head and said, "I don't really like to talk about it. It's not a happy story. I have nothing to do with them anymore."

She liked to walk on the beach after dark, as I did, so we spent a lot of evenings down there after working on the house, just walking along. She always took her shoes off, and so did I, and rolled my pant legs up. When the surf was high and crashed over us, she didn't mind getting wet.

Well, as Dickens says, "It was the best of times, and it was the worst of times." I was having the best time I'd ever had in my life, and yet I knew that it was all going to end. I dreaded finishing the house because I wouldn't have any excuse to keep Marlene around me anymore. I tried to slow it down as long as I could, but eventually everything was done. The carpenters, the paper hangers, and the painters were gone, and it was a wonderful house.

Marlene was very pleased with it and took me for a tour, though I'd watched every stage of it. She took my hand and led me into the bedroom. Gesturing at the spacious room, she gave my hand a squeeze. "Does this *feel* right to you, Ollie?"

"I love it!"

The ceiling was high and the bed was enormous! It was designed especially for me by a famous craftsman named Jerome Siddons. He collects old wood, then paints it with what he calls his "funky finish," a mixture of green, red, and brown. He sands it down then works on it until it has a rugged chipped-paint look. He uses rusty branding irons for braces instead of new polished steel. He also works tarnished silver conchas into the wood. He made all the other pieces too, like a beautiful steer-head bench made of aged, bleached wood. It was big enough to hold me up, and it seemed to *belong* there. That was true of everything in the room—it blended in as if it couldn't possibly have fit into any other room.

"It's a great room," I said. "I feel so comfortable in it."

"You should, as much as you paid for it. Come on, you'll have to brag on me a lot more."

I did brag on her, a lot more! The dining table was made of driftwood, carved around the edges into buffalos, and the chairs were in a keyhole style, the seats padded and covered with dark maroon leather. Over the table a beautifully crafted glass-and-copper chandelier was decorated with Indians wearing full headdress racing around the edge.

On one wall was a genuine Remington painting—which Marlene had advised me not to buy. "It goes perfectly with the room," she'd sighed, "but it's too expensive." I'd said, "Buy it!" and her delight had been reward enough for the money.

We went through the entire house, and finally Marlene said, "Well, I think we deserve one great banquet to celebrate the house. Are you happy with it, Ollie?"

"I feel at home in it, Marlene. I've never felt like that about a house."

She smiled and reached out and put her hand on my chest, saying, "Then I'm happy." She was wearing a white sleeveless top and a pair of cotton denim jeans that clung to her. At that moment I remembered a fragment of poetry that I'd read. I didn't remember the poem or who wrote it, just the phrase, ". . . I knew a woman lovely in her bones."

That was Marlene to me, in a way that no other woman had ever been. She was fine-boned, and the smooth roundness of her sholders and the curves of her body were enough to keep me speechless. Finally I managed to say, "It's perfect, Marlene— just perfect!"

"It pleases me so much to hear you say that, Ollie." A small dimple appeared at the left corner of her mouth and light danced in her eyes. "We'll celebrate—my treat! Tomorrow night we'll have our own banquet. We'll do the town!"

"I–I'd rather stay here. We could cook and watch a movie."

"All right, Ollie, if that's what you want . . ."

∽

The next night, as usual, I cooked and she helped me. We were rather quiet. I was quiet because I was sad—something was ending for me. Finally, after dinner and listening to music and walking one more time around the house, she said, "I've got to go."

"So soon?"

"It's really very late."

I walked her to the door. She turned to me, and I said, "I hate for all this to end, Marlene."

She stared at me with an odd expression. "You know, I've got to change my brand of toothpaste or my deodorant."

"What?" I could not understand what that meant.

"All this time we've been together, Ollie, and never once have you tried to kiss me."

I could not have been more stunned if she had smashed me in the forehead with a hammer. Of course I'd wanted to kiss her, to touch her, but I had been too afraid, and I was still afraid—afraid that if I did touch her, it would all be over forever, and she would turn away with the revulsion I'd seen in the faces of other women. Finally I managed to say, "I've wanted to."

"Why haven't you?"

"Because I'm ugly and fat."

And then she came to me. She put herself against me and put her arms around my neck. I felt the soft contours of her body, and it stirred me so much that I was embarrassed. I put my arms around her, still afraid that I would frighten her off.

"Ollie, I've learned two things. First, it's not what a person has that counts. I've had money, and I know how worthless it is in buying happiness. The second thing I've learned is that what a person looks like doesn't really matter. It's what's on the inside—and inside of you, Ollie, is a very sweet and gentle and wonderful person."

She was leaning against me, and my head swam. Her perfume was like a drug, and I kissed her roughly, knowing that it would probably be the last time.

But she didn't run away. She stood, her arms around me pulling me ever closer, and when I did lift my head, she still held me tight. "Well, that makes me feel a little better," she laughed. "I thought I had gone ugly or something."

"No, never that, Marlene." I still could not believe what she had said. "You don't mind that I'm fat?"

"I mind things that are inside of people, Ollie. You're the sweetest man I've ever known. The only one I've ever known, really, that didn't try to take advantage of me. To me, that's what's wonderful."

She pulled away then, and I said quickly, "Can I see you again?"

"Of course you can. Whenever you like."

She left then, and I stood there stunned. I thought about what she had said, wondering if it could be true. She was so beautiful, and I was so hideous! I whispered aloud, "Maybe the money will make up for what I am . . ."

CHAPTER
FOUR

After Marlene kissed me, I went a little bit crazy. Oh, I didn't run down the streets dressed like Dracula or anything like that—although in Los Angeles very few would have noticed! What really bothered me was that I couldn't work. There's never been a time, since I got my first computer, that anything's ever been able to stop me from spending every available moment at a keyboard.

But that one kiss did it. Of course, I'd never had a woman and had never expected to have one, and just the idea of having her was enough to set me off. When I tried to work, all I could think of was Marlene!

A week passed, and I amused myself by wheedling money out of Jacob Lebnitz, the CPA. He had warned me that there was danger in transferring things into cash. Banks, I discovered, even made an official notification to the federal government if you withdrew over a certain amount of cash—or even if you put a certain amount in. I never could understand that. What business was it of the IRS if I wanted to deposit fifty thousand dollars in cash?

With the money, I bought a lot of Rolex watches. I'd write a check for them at one place and then go sell them at a big discount at another jewelry shop for cash. I'm pretty sure they thought I stole them, but I didn't care. Anyhow, the money came in, and I kept squirreling it away in my Swiss bank account. I knew there was something abnormal about that. I'd read about one woman who starved to death in a rathole of a house, and when they went through her things they found she had over a hundred thousand dollars in cash.

This business of squirreling away money scared me a little bit, but so did the idea of poverty.

Another thing I did was ask Dane about getting in shape and losing weight. Of course, I'd already tried everything in the world. I must have tried fifty different diets, and I'd bought, at one time or another, every sort of weight machine made. I'd use them for a week or two or maybe even a month, and then I'd let them gather cobwebs in a corner and finally sell them for next to nothing. There's not much market for secondhand weight machines.

But Dane was enthusiastic. He took me down to his health club, and I signed up. I bought some workout clothes as big as circus tents, of course, and Dane stayed right with me. I'll give him that. For almost a week I met him every day. I found out that he was an expert at martial arts, and he thought that would be more interesting for me than just running on a treadmill or using a stair-climbing machine.

He bought me one of those loose-fitting suits where your opponent can grab you by the front and throw you into the air, but I don't think even Dane could have thrown me into the air. He was quick and strong, but moving me around was like moving a Mayflower van.

Surprisingly enough, I found out that I had good reflexes. Of course, he could have killed me at any time, but the first time I parried one of his blows, he was shocked. "Hey, man, you're *fast*! You'll be great at this. It's all in reaction, and yours are great."

But it all came to nothing. I just had too much to lose. If I'd only needed to lose fifty pounds, I might have succeeded. But I needed to lose nearly two hundred pounds, and that was the impossible dream. So after a few days I missed an appointment, and then another, by telling him I was just going to work on the machines.

I didn't though. A few times I went in, and I'd get on one of those stair-climbing machines and huff and puff, and some young girl would come in who weighed a hundred pounds, and I'd watch her as she'd run the machine at full speed while I was still on the first level.

All this time I was really thinking of nothing but Marlene. I was so bad off that I couldn't even watch my old John Wayne movies anymore.

She'd been busy with a house, so I'd only seen her a few times. We went out to dinner, and when I took her home I wanted to try to kiss her, to tell her I loved her, but I didn't have the nerve. I think one more rejection, especially from her, would have shoved me over the edge.

What made all this worse was that I couldn't talk to anybody. I thought about calling Jimmy, but he would have said something like, *Man, you got enough bucks, she'll crawl into your lap.* I didn't need that.

One night, after we went out to eat, we watched *Casablanca.* At the end, when Bogart was walking off with Claude Raines after giving up Ingrid Bergman, I would have given anything to tell her what I was feeling. But she started talking about saving the whales, and something about an Alabama beach mouse. I like to save redwoods and whales, but I don't care how many mice people kill. I guess I'm not a genuine tree hugger. She went home, and I stayed awake all night thinking about her.

The next day Dane came over to find out how I was doing on the new program, and I couldn't hold it in any longer. I was so desperate I finally said, "Dane, I can't work, I can't even think!"

"What's the matter?" he said. "Are you sick?" He looked alarmed.

I said, "No, it's—" I couldn't say it, and he came closer and looked up at me. "What's wrong? You sure you're not sick?"

"No," I blurted, "it's Marlene. I'm crazy about her, and I don't know what to do."

Dane blinked with surprise. He stepped back and studied me for a moment, then said, "I think I knew that."

"How? I never said a word."

"I've seen you watch her," he said quietly.

I walked across the room and slammed my fist into the wall. It hurt, but I didn't care. My throat choked up, and I was afraid I was going to start blubbering.

Then I felt Dane's hand on my shoulder. He pulled me around and put his hands on the back of my neck. "Look, give it a try, Ollie. What can you lose?"

"You don't know what it's like, Dane. I've never had anything to do with women. Why would she look at me? She's beautiful and smart."

I couldn't say any more, and I guess Dane knew it. "Look, let me tell you something, Ollie. I've been waiting for the time when some woman would try to get to you, and believe me there have been plenty. They've tried through me. Most of them had dollar signs in their eyes as big as that sign that says Hollywood, and a guy like you would be a prime target for one. Never had a girl, suddenly they're after you. They're smart. They know how to make the moves. So, I checked her out pretty closely."

"What do you mean you checked her out?"

"You were getting close to her, and I saw that you liked her. Well, I'll tell you one thing. She's not after your money. Her family had plenty of that. She's still got a bundle."

"We never talked much about that."

Dane shook his head. "She's a strange woman, Ollie. She could have had a dozen men." He grinned and said, "Believe it or not, I even tried to put the moves on her myself." When he saw my stare, he laughed and said, "She's just not interested. She likes ecology, and I have no interest in that. But you do, and she likes those corny movies, just like you. Look, I think you'd better let her know how you feel. You're not going to find any better than her. If she says no, then it's no. But who knows? Like I say, she's marching to the sound of a different drummer, pretty much like you are."

I couldn't believe what I was hearing. "I can't take a chance. At least this way I can see her once in a while, but if I ask her to marry me, and she says no, she'll slam the door in my face."

"What good does it do you looking at her? It's like a kid in a candy store with no money in his pocket. Don't torment yourself, Ollie." He slapped me on the shoulder again and said warmly, "Look, I wouldn't steer you wrong. You either need to get her out of your system, or get her, period. Take a shot, Ollie."

∽

For two days I thought about what Dane had said. Finally I knew I had to at least give it a try. I wasn't losing any weight. I was gaining—because when I worry, I eat. I was like a fellow up on a diving platform afraid to jump off. There's no way to take a dive like that a little at a time. It's all or nothing. So I made up my mind to ask her.

That night she came over, and we talked about the Sierra Club awhile. I didn't pay much attention to her. My palms were sweaty, and I knew I was about to go off that high board. We were sitting on the couch listening to Chopin, and finally I couldn't stand it any longer. She was sitting beside me. I looked at her, swallowed hard, and said, "Marlene, I know what I am. I've got a mirror. I can't expect you to feel anything for me, but there's something I have to say."

That should have been enough to make her get up and run out of the room screaming, but she just sat looking at me. When she didn't answer, I said, "I don't know anything about women, you know that, but I love you, Marlene, and I guess I always will. Is there any hope at all for me?"

She was watching me with a steadfast gaze, and her eyes were wide open. She didn't say a word, and I thought that she was trying to find a way to let me down easy. When she didn't speak, I turned away from her and clasped my hands together. "I shouldn't have said anything," I mumbled.

And then I felt her hand on my arm. I felt the couch stir, and then she reached out and took my hand. "Ollie," she said. And when I turned around, I saw something in her face I hadn't seen before. She was having difficulty speaking, and finally she got it out. "I was very much in love once. It was like nothing else for me. I loved him so much I would have killed myself if he had told me to, and after what happened, that might have been better. I found out he didn't love me at all. He was seeing another woman, my best friend, and they were laughing at me. And when I caught them, both of them just laughed." Her hand tightened on me, and she looked away. I saw she was biting her lip hard. I couldn't say a word.

"I swore I'd never let another man hurt me." And then she turned around, and her lips were trembling. "But you'd never hurt anyone, Ollie. I didn't think there were any good men in the world—but you are. I–I'm not sure I love you, but I know I trust you."

Hope blossomed in me then. I can't think of any other way to put it, and I turned to her and pulled her around. "Marry me, and I'll lose weight. I promise! I can make myself into something you'd be proud of. You can help me, Marlene." My voice was unsteady, and I knew it, but when a man doesn't have hope for nearly twenty-four years and finally it comes, it's hard to handle. "I know you don't love me as much as I love you—but maybe some day you will."

And then Marlene smiled. She had a beautiful smile, and she reached around and put her arms around me and pulled my head down, and I kissed her. She was all sweetness then, and I was trembling all over. I was so big I was afraid that I'd hurt her, but she held me tight and kissed me as I'd never dreamed a woman could kiss a man. She drew back, and I saw that there were tears in her eyes. "I never thought I'd want to live with anyone, but all right, Ollie, I'll marry you." She laughed and put her hand on my cheek. "And we'll live happily ever after, just like the books say."

I kissed her again, and then she drew back, and I said, "I hope you don't want a long engagement—or a fancy wedding. I hate those fancy weddings."

"Whatever you say, Ollie."

CHAPTER
FIVE

"... and so they got married and lived happily ever after."

That's the way the romances end, pretty much—in the movies and in old romance novels. To tell the truth, by the time Marlene and I had been married a few weeks, I was beginning to believe it was true.

It's hard to explain what those first weeks were like. Of course, on our wedding night, I didn't know any more about making love than I knew about Etruscan pottery. I must have been the most nervous bridegroom who ever went to the wedding bed.

But Marlene made it easy for me. I was aware that she was not a virgin. So, when I went to her that night, she was the aggressor, not me. I was probably the most clumsy husband who ever lived, but she didn't seem to mind.

And things got better in that respect as the weeks rolled on. I learned a little bit about women, and actually got to be rather proud of myself. I went around with a foolish grin on my face until Dane laughed at me, saying, "You don't know how different you are, Ollie. Marriage is good for you."

It was. I was happier than I'd ever been in my life. Of course, that wasn't hard, since I'd never been happy. We went on a fourteen-day Caribbean cruise, and everything was fun. I even learned to dance a little bit. For such a fat slob, I'd always been fairly light on my feet, and I picked up the new steps easily. At the ports, I always crammed my pockets full of money so I could buy Marlene anything she wanted. When we got back home, it practically took a van to move the things she had bought.

Back in California, I tried to work on the new program. But I was so besotted with Marlene, I knew I wasn't doing my best work. Fortunately Film Maker was producing more income than we would ever need. Still, Dane kept after me. "You never know," he'd say, "what's going to happen. You need to make it while you're hot."

While I worked on programs, Marlene and I did a lot of work with the Sierra Club—at least we sent a lot of money. She was always bringing books in about new problems; men were tearing up the world and destroying it quicker than one could imagine.

I tried once to talk to Dane about things like that. I had just read an article and had gotten interested in it. One day I said, "Dane, do you ever think about what happens to you after you die?"

"I don't believe in pie in the sky."

"I'm not talking about your soul. I'm talking about your body." He stared at me, puzzled, and I hurried on. "You know, they put material in a hermetically sealed container, then encase that in a concrete-and-steel structure. It weighs more than a ton, and they bury it underground."

Dane said, "Are you talking about toxic waste?"

"No, I'm talking about you. That's what they'll do to you when you die."

"Where's all this leading?" Dane said.

"Look, we're ruining the earth as quickly as we can, and bodies don't help. Cremation isn't much better. When you burn a body, it produces carcinogenic dioxins, trace metals, hydrochloric and hydrofluoric acids, sulfur dioxide, and global-warming-inducing carbon dioxide."

Dane laughed. "I didn't know I had so much in me."

"Things have got to change, Dane. We're ruining the planet."

"So what do you plan to do with bodies?"

"Well, they've got a different system catching on in Great Britain. It's called the Green Burial Movement. People are buried in a simple shroud or in a biodegradable coffin made out of recycled newspapers. Graves are marked with trees, and cemeteries double as wildlife habitats."

I continued, but Dane simply stared at me, and when I finally finished, he said, "I don't care what you do with me when I die. I'm interested in what happens to me while I'm alive."

So Dane wasn't into ecology. But I didn't give up.

Marlene had a room fixed up with some exercise machines: a stair-climber, a treadmill, and a weight machine. I hated all that stuff, but I didn't object to swimming. I had always been a good swimmer—all that fat floated pretty well, of course. So, instead of going into the workout room, I would swim in the pool. I didn't lose any weight during those first two months, because the more I would burn off, the more I would eat.

I ate when I was in a crisis, and I ate when I was happy—a real no-win situation!

I didn't meet many people during those days. I didn't want to; Marlene was enough for me. The neighbors weren't too friendly. I did meet one couple, a Mr. and Mrs. Finley who lived just down the road from us. I was coming back from the mailbox once when they came by in their jogging outfits. They didn't exactly stop, but as they jogged in place to keep their pulse rates up, we introduced ourselves. He was a retired engineer, and I found out pretty quickly that he wasn't interested in the Sierra Club. He invited me to go golfing, which I declined, since I hated it.

"You ought to be careful swimming in that pool by yourself," Mrs. Finley said. She was a wiry woman, muscular, with blue hair. I stared at her, and she laughed. "Oh, I met your wife at the store! She told me about your late-night swims. Better not swim by yourself. You could have a heart attack or a cramp and drown."

"I'll be careful," I said.

"It's not a good idea to drink before you swim either," Mr. Finley advised.

"Oh, I don't drink."

He winked at me. "I don't drink anymore either." He laughed and said, "I don't drink any *less*, of course." He thought that was terribly funny, and as they bobbed off, I could hear them laughing.

I later mentioned them to Marlene, and she said, "I'd hate to go on a two-week canoe trip with them. I met them at the store. She's very nosy."

"They knew all about my swimming."

"They wanted to know everything about you." She smiled and ran her hand down my neck. We were lying in bed together, and just that touch stirred me up. "Everybody's interested in the *wunderkind*."

"They seem to think I drink."

"They drink, and they think everybody else does. Never mind them," she said.

ω

May came, and we were rapidly approaching our two-month anniversary. I'd been picking out a present for Marlene at the jewelry store. The jeweler told me that some stones were more expensive and precious than diamonds, so at his advice I was getting her an emerald necklace, designed specially for her.

Dane came by one day and tried to get me to go down to the fitness center with him. "You need to get more into the martial arts. It'd make a new man out of you."

"Given up on that, Dane. I'm hopeless."

"If you'd just stick with it, you'd like it."

"No, I wouldn't. It's one of those things I hate at both ends, the beginning and the end. Besides, I've got to go to a meeting."

"Where you going?"

"Marlene and I are going to Sacramento. There's a conference sponsored by the Sierra Club there."

Dane grinned. "What are you doing? Saving the Alabama beach mice again?"

"This time it's serious, Dane. Did you know that fishnets are killing dolphins out there by the thousands? We're going to put some teeth in the law to make those fishermen use different nets."

"Okay, that's cool. When are you leaving?"

"Tomorrow. We'll be there for our second month's anniversary. Thought I'd make it kind of a second honeymoon."

Dane grinned. "Okay, you two have a good time."

ന

I just can't make it, Ollie, I'm so sorry."
I had gotten up that morning and packed my things, but Marlene stayed in bed. I cooked breakfast, and she put on her robe and got up but couldn't eat anything. Her face looked puffy, and she shook her head. "I've got a flu bug or something, Ollie."

"We'd better call the doctor."

"No, it's viral I'm sure, and they can't do anything for that. I'll just have to stay in bed and take aspirin and tough it out."

"Well, I'll stay with you."

"Oh, Ollie, you've looked forward to this conference! You go on, and you make tapes of all the meetings, and then when you come back, you can play them for me. It's important."

I didn't want to go without her, but she insisted. So finally I came over and kissed her good-bye. "I hate to leave you like this, Marlene."

She smiled wanly. "I'll be all right. You go on and have a good time. Be sure you tape all the meetings."

"I'll do it."

I left the house and got into my Mercedes. Marlene had tried to get me to buy a Dodge Viper, but I couldn't even get into the thing. And if I had gotten in, I couldn't have gotten out. She loved it, though, which was okay with me. I bought it for her, but the Mercedes was more my size. I parked it at the airport and got onto the plane. I flew first class, of course—just as cheap as buying two regular seats. Not that I had to worry about money, but old habits die hard. I still found myself looking for bargains in shoes and things like that.

The flight attendant came by and offered me a cocktail. I got her to bring me some tomato juice instead. Then I opened up John Grisham's latest book and put myself into it.

I got off the plane in Sacramento, took a cab to the Radisson, and settled in.

ω

I enjoyed the first two days of the conference, attending meetings on all the subjects I was interested in. The third day was just summing up, so I decided to fly home early. I called the airport and had no trouble booking a flight for a late-night arrival.

I'd called Marlene both nights, and she'd said she was getting better, but I thought I'd surprise her this time so I didn't call.

The flight was uneventful and boring—but it beats the alternative, I guess. When we landed at Orange County Airport, I felt good again. I drove the Mercedes over the speed limit as soon as I was clear of the city.

I couldn't wait to get home! For a man who's never known a woman's love, it's a lot like drink, or what I think drinking would be like. You just can't get enough of it.

I had gotten a lot of letters from women offering themselves to me. I showed them all to Marlene, and we laughed over them. Once she said, "If you ever get rid of me, you'll have no trouble filling my place."

"Yes, I would," I had said quickly. "No one could take your place, darling."

"You're sweet, Ollie."

Things like that made me hope that she was falling in love with me, even though there was no reason she should. Still, I tried to be as good to her as possible.

It was after midnight when I pulled up to the house. We had a first-class security system, and you could only get in by opening the gate with a special electronic device. They opened silently, and I pulled the car into the garage, parked it, and, as always, I put the key on the shelf. I had lost several keys, and this had become a habit with me. I pulled my suitcase out of the backseat and went into the house. I was fairly sure Marlene would be asleep, so I tried to make as little noise as possible as I moved up the stairs to our bedroom on the second floor.

I heard voices. I thought, *She's watching television.*

I got to the door, reached out to take the handle—and froze.

It was no television I was hearing. It was the voices of a man and a woman, the kind of sounds people make when they're having sex. A thought ran through me, *Maybe it is just a television program—although I didn't know Marlene watched movies like that.*

And then I recognized the man's voice.

Dane Fetterman.

And suddenly I knew the truth.

Something happened to me then that had never happened before. Anger flamed within me. I had hardly ever been angry at anyone in my life, but the thought of Dane and how he had been such a "friend" to me burned.

I opened the door. There was a light on in the room. They were in bed together naked.

I heard myself bellowing, shouting something garbled, and I ran toward them. If I'd had a gun, I'd have shot them both, but I had nothing.

I saw Dane roll out of the bed, and I raised my arm to strike him, but he was much faster. I caught a blur as his arm made a quick arch, then the edge of his hand struck me in the temple, and the world was filled with purple and orange sparks. I felt myself falling. There was another blow, and I fell into an enormous black pit where there was no sight and no sound.

CHAPTER
SIX

I came out of the darkness with a rush. One moment I didn't know a thing, and then my eyes flew open and I saw Dane standing in front of me. It all came back—the ugly sounds and sights that I knew I would never forget. I had no idea how long I had been out. I was lying on the floor looking up at him. I sat up, then got to my feet. He had pulled a gun from somewhere and was pointing it at me.

I was staring at the gun, hypnotized by it, when Marlene appeared from my right. They were both dressed now. She was wearing a green dress I had bought her a few weeks ago, and she was brushing her hair as calmly as if nothing had happened. I stared at her, unable to believe that this was happening, but it was.

"Well, you woke up," she said.

I felt something damp on my head. I reached up, touched it, and found I had a cut.

"Don't worry about that." Dane smiled. "That's the least of your worries, Ollie."

"Let's take him downstairs now," Marlene said.

Something about the way she spoke frightened me. *Take him downstairs*. She was speaking about me as if I were a piece of furniture! She saw me staring at her and laughed. "Poor Ollie, you don't get it, do you?"

I wanted to answer her, but they were both smiling in a way that frightened me even more.

"All right," I said. "I'm not very swift, but you two have been having an affair."

Dane laughed and let his arm drop, but the gun was still in his hand. "Having an affair! You're slower than I thought, Ollie. We were together long before either of us ever met you."

Something in his eyes chilled me, but at the same time my mind was working as fast as a computer. It all came together, and I swallowed hard. "You planned all this before you ever came to me?"

"Sure did. Marlene and I planned it together."

"Poor baby. You weren't hard to fool," Marlene said. Then she shook her head impatiently. "Come on downstairs. We've got to get moving."

Dane lifted the gun and said, "Downstairs, Ollie."

"What for?"

He lifted the gun until I was looking right into the bore. His voice grew icy. "I said get downstairs!"

I stumbled out of the room, and both of them followed me. I went down the steps, my mind in a whirl. There was something going on here even worse than my wife having an affair with a guy I thought was my best friend.

"Into the rec room," Dane said and shoved me with the pistol. I stumbled forward, and when we entered the room, I turned around. Both of them were staring at me.

"Look," I said, "I don't know what this is all about."

"Shut up." He had pulled a chair away from one of the tables; now he shoved me into it. "Put your hands behind you."

I obeyed. He handed the gun to Marlene. "If he moves, shoot him," he said. His tone was no different than if he had said, *Pass the salt, please*, and Marlene pointed the gun directly at my head.

Dane moved behind me, and I felt him tying my hands together.

I began to beg, "Look, Marlene, I know you never loved me, but—"

"Loved you? What woman would ever love *you*, you fat pig? It made me sick having to go to bed with you! I almost had to go out and vomit."

Her face was calm, but the words were vitriolic. I couldn't think of a thing to say. Everything was going to pieces.

Dane walked back to her and took the gun. He slipped it into his pocket and shrugged. "Sorry about this, Ollie, but it's the only way."

Fear shot through me. "What are you going to do?" I said, my voice hoarse.

Marlene smiled slightly. "Why, you're going to have a tragic accident, dear. You know how I've warned you about drinking and then getting into the pool."

"You know I never drink!"

"Oh, but the neighbors know you drink, and they know you swim sometimes afterward."

I remembered the neighbors who had stopped me out by the mailbox, and it dawned on me that she had spread that story. This was clearly no spur-of-the-moment thing, and I still couldn't believe it was really happening. But the ropes cutting into my wrists told me that it was.

I took a deep breath and tried to keep my voice as even as possible. "Look, it doesn't have to be this way."

"I'm afraid it does, Ollie," Dane said casually.

"You want the money. That's right, isn't it?"

"That's right, Ollie. We want the money."

"Well, you can have it. You know me, Dane. I never cared anything about money. This house was your idea. You can have it all. I'll sign over my rights to Film Maker to you."

"And then if you changed your mind, once we let you go, what then?" Marlene said.

"I wouldn't change my mind. Just let me live."

"Sorry, Ollie." He ran his hand over his hair. "Remember that story? 'The Short Happy Life of Francis Macomber'? Well, this is kind of like that. The short, happy life of Ollie Benson. But—" He turned and went to stand beside Marlene. "You don't have to worry about your dear wife. I'll watch after her. She won't be a widow for long, I don't think."

It was unbelievable the pain I felt. I had been such a fool!

Marlene said, "It was like shooting fish in a barrel."

"Look, Ollie, somebody was going to take you. It might as well be us."

"Let's get on with it, Dane," Marlene said.

Dane moved across the room and came back with a fifth of whiskey. He grabbed my hair and said, "You can take this the easy way or the hard way, Ollie. It doesn't matter. You're going to get drunk either way." He grabbed my hair, yanked my head back, and lifted the bottle against my mouth. It struck my teeth, and he forced it down between them. I tried to struggle, but he was too strong for me. I tried to cry out, but the whiskey poured into my throat. I swallowed involuntarily, coughing and choking, and he kept it there what seemed like forever. Finally he removed the bottle and released my hair. "Actually, you won't feel a thing, Ollie. You'll be so drunk by the time I put you in the pool, you won't suffer a bit."

I don't like to think about what happened next. I began to cry. I was scared to death, and the whiskey acted almost at once. I hadn't eaten anything since leaving Sacramento, and the whiskey bit at my stomach like fire. Very soon, the room seemed to be moving around. They were watching me, and I was crying and begging, and twice Dane came and made me swallow some more. I tried to close my throat, and a lot of it ran down my face and neck, but I swallowed even more of it.

I couldn't focus my eyes. I heard Dane say, "Come on, we've got some things to do. This has got to look right." His voice sounded far away, and I heard their steps as they left.

I had never been drunk before, but I knew there would never be a better chance of escape than now. The liquor was working too quickly; soon I'd be unconscious. I struggled to get my hands loose, but Dane had tied them tightly. I tried to stand up—impossible. I threw myself to one side, and the chair fell over. I was able to slip my arms out over the top, but then I was so dizzy that I couldn't get up.

They had left the light on, and I knew they'd be back soon to force-feed me more liquor. I struggled against the ropes that cut into my wrists, and I yanked at them until they burned like fire.

I don't know how it happened. In the movies, the one who's tied up always finds a sharp object and is able to cut himself loose. All I know is that I was lying on the floor crying, fighting the ropes, and suddenly I felt them loosen. Maybe Dane couldn't tie knots as well as he thought. I yanked frantically at the knots, and suddenly my hands were free. I pushed myself up on my hands and knees. The room seemed to whirl, and I shut my eyes. "Got to get out of here," I muttered. I got to my feet and immediately almost fell down again. It was like someone was spinning the room at high speed.

I staggered to the wall, held on, and tried to think.

I looked at the door. *Can't go out that way. They're out there somewhere.* The only other exit was through the window. I tried to lift it, but it was locked. I felt along the top till I found the lock; it was frozen. I pulled at it until my fingers felt like they were bleeding, and finally it gave way. I pulled the window open. I couldn't stand. I just leaned forward and went through the window, taking the screen with me. It seemed to make an enormous crashing noise. I fell on the pavement outside and got to my feet. I had to hold onto the wall.

But I couldn't run. I was too drunk. I couldn't move without holding onto something, and I knew that if they heard the noise, they'd be right back.

The car. You've got to get to the car . . .

I groped along the wall on the east side of the house. The garage was on the west side. Three times I fell flat. I was sick now, but I scrambled along, crawling until I crossed the back of the house, expecting any moment to hear Dane or Marlene's voices or to feel a bullet stopping me.

When I turned, I saw that the door to the garage was open; I had forgotten to shut it. I got up and staggered into the garage. I felt on the shelf for the car key. My hand hit it, and it fell to the pavement. I almost cried with fear then but went down on my knees. I couldn't find it at first. Finally, my hand touched it. I carefully picked it up and staggered to the Mercedes. (I always backed the car into the garage, and it's a good thing, because I could never have backed it out!) I was so drunk by that time that it took every bit of my concentration to get the key in the ignition slot. Finally I did, and the engine caught as soon as I turned the key. I held onto the wheel and stepped on the accelerator—harder than I had thought, for the car leapt with a scream of rubber against the pavement.

They know where I am now!

I shook my head, but the world was still whirling around. I ran off the pavement into the grass, swung back, and then the gate was before me. There was no question of opening it with the electronic remote—I didn't even know where it was. So I hit the gate, and there was a wrenching sound of metal tearing.

I was thrown forward and hit my head against the windshield, but the car never completely stopped. I kept my foot on the gas pedal and ricocheted down the driveway to the highway.

Everything I did was an overreaction, and when I jammed on the brakes to keep from plunging past the highway, I stopped the car completely. Fear ran through me then, and I blinked rapidly, trying to clear my vision. I was seeing everything double, but in the darkness I could at least make out the streetlight. I turned on my headlights, stamped on the accelerator, and shot off into the night.

Everything that happened after that was like something in a surrealistic movie—out of focus and grotesquely twisted. I kept the car in my lane as well as I could, but I don't know how I avoided hitting someone. I was so drunk that every move I made was wild and out of proportion. I passed several cars, one of them so closely he must have had to drive off the road. I didn't even stop to see what happened to him.

Thinking was impossible. All I could do was react. I knew that Dane and Marlene would get into her Viper and come after me, so I fled for my life. Several times I thought about turning off the main road and trying to hide, but I couldn't turn the thought into action.

I drove on and on, and the alcohol seemed to stay with me. I had no experience with whiskey and didn't know how long I'd be drunk. I tried to think about what I should do. Obviously I would have to go to the police, but would they believe a drunken man?

Thinking was too hard, so I just concentrated on getting as far away from that house and from those two as I could.

I drove for three hours. I had no idea how far I had come, and only a muddled idea of direction. By that time, some of the first effects of the whiskey had faded away, but I was growing tremendously sleepy.

I glanced down at the gauges; I was nearly out of gas.

The stretch of road I was on was lonely, and at this time of night there was little traffic. I thought that somewhere up ahead was a national forest, and one thing I didn't want to do was to run out of gas. My nightmare was being stuck beside the road and seeing that red Viper come up beside me, and Dane and Marlene getting out.

Up ahead I saw a convenience store. I pulled up to the gas pump. I just sat for a moment, trembling all over, and suddenly I felt sick. I knew I had to vomit. I rolled out of the car and stumbled toward the restroom. I barely managed to make it inside before I threw up in such convulsions I couldn't believe it.

I washed my face and went out. There was a man standing outside—a middle-aged fellow who looked like a working man. "Are you all right?" he said.

"Yeah, I got sick."

He came closer. "You don't look too good." He moved closer still and shook his head. "Buddy, you don't need to be drivin'. You've been drinking, haven't you?"

"I—yes, a little."

"Not a good idea. That road up there twists and turns through the mountains, and if you go off the road, it's a long way down. You could kill yourself."

"I've got to get away. I can't wait here."

"Well, you know what's best for you. But I wouldn't try it."

I was sick and weak, and I couldn't think. "Could I hire you to drive me?"

"Where you going?"

"A little town about fifty miles up the road." I had no idea whether there was such a town.

"Well, I'd expect to be paid."

"Fine, but I've got to get gas first."

"You get in the car. I'll gas it up."

I got in on the right side. I closed my eyes and heard the sound as the man put gas in the car. He knocked on the window.

"Got to have money to pay for this gas." He had a round face and wore a baseball cap of some kind shoved back on his head.

I got my billfold out and handed him a couple of twenties. He said, "I'll be right back."

I leaned back and closed my eyes. The world was still spinning even though I had gotten rid of the whiskey. *Why would anybody deliberately do this to themselves?* I wondered. I never have been able to understand the fascination of drink, and at that moment it seemed insane.

The man got in and started the engine. "Okay, buddy?" he said.

"Yes, I'm fine."

"Just lay back there. What's the name of that town?"

"Ah—Bradley."

"Okay, you just take it easy, and I'll get you there."

The car started, and I felt myself falling to sleep. The car moved quietly, and all I could think of was, *I'm safe for now.*

I drifted off several times, and finally fell into a deep sleep. I had tried to get Marlene out of my mind, but I knew I never would. She had hurt me worse than the drowning would have hurt. She had made me believe in her, and now I didn't think I would ever believe in anybody again.

The crunch of gravel under the tires awakened me. I sat up and shook my head. "Why are we stopping?" I looked beside me; the driver's seat was empty.

Suddenly my door opened. I had been leaning against it, and I rolled out and fell, my hands hitting the gravel. "What—what is it?" I cried. I got to my feet.

There was a bright moon out, and I saw the man's face clearly. His voice sounded different now. "Give me your money," he said.

I stared at him, unable to believe what I was hearing. "Look," I said, "I'll give you my money, but I need the car to get away from here."

"Give me your billfold."

I reached back, got my billfold, and handed it to him. He stuck it into his pocket and said, "Now, give me that fancy watch you've got on your arm."

I took off my watch, handed it to him, and he said, "I'll take that ring too." I had to struggle with the ring. It was five karats and had cost fifty thousand dollars. He tried it on his own finger. I started to walk away, but he grabbed me and turned me around again to face him. He was very strong. He said, "Sorry, buddy, I'm takin' this car."

"All right," I babbled, "take the car. Just let me go."

No answer. Suddenly, he shoved me backward, hard. I had not noticed, but we were on the edge of a tremendously steep cliff. My legs hit the corrugated steel barrier and I fell over, striking the back of my head on something hard. I cried out, but then I was falling, rolling over and over, and every time I rolled some part of my body hit the sharp rocks. And then my head hit again, hard, and that was all I knew.

CHAPTER SEVEN

At first the sound was thin and far away, but then it swelled and got stronger. I didn't know the voice or the tune, and I kept my eyes closed as I listened to the words:

> *I am a pilgrim and a stranger,*
> *Traveling through this weary land;*
> *I've got a home in yonder city, O Lord,*
> *And it's not made by hand.*

The singer was accompanied by a harsh jangling sound that I didn't recognize at first, but then it came to me—a banjo.

> *I've got a mother, a sister, and a brother,*
> *Who have gone to that sweet land.*
> *I'm determined to go and see them, good Lord,*
> *All over on that distant shore.*

My eyelids were heavy, and I struggled to open them—but when I did a lightbulb hanging in the center of the room threw its light into my eyes, and I quickly shut them again. I tried to move, but a spasm of pain ran through me that made me catch my breath. The singer went on plunking on his instrument:

> *As I go down to that river of Jordan,*
> *Just to bathe my weary soul,*
> *If I could touch but the hem of his garment, good Lord,*
> *Well, I believe it would make me whole.*

The fragrance of coffee laced the air—along with other odors, but nothing else seemed familiar. Finally I opened my eyes enough to see an old man sitting near the wall. He wore a threadbare checked shirt and a pair of faded bib overalls and was playing a banjo, but when I groaned he got up, put the banjo down, and came to stand over me.

"Well, now," he said in a thin, creaky voice. "Looks like you've decided to live a mite longer." He had silver hair worn long and an old-style cavalry mustache. "What's your name, son?"

I tried to speak, but my lips were dry as dust. The old man had sharp eyes, a faded blue. He picked up a glass of water and reached down and pulled my head up. It sent pain all through me, but the cool water was the best thing I'd ever tasted. I gulped it, spilling some down over my neck, and after I'd taken a few swallows, he said, "Take it easy now. You can have all you want—but a little at a time." He set the glass down, then put his eyes on me again. "I need to know your name, boy."

"My—my name's Ollie Benson."

"Well, Ollie, I'm Eli Burke. Now lemme see can I get you set up." The old man leaned down and put his arms around me. He pulled me up to a sitting position, and the pain took my breath away. I hurt everywhere! He helped me until I was leaning against the headboard. I just lay there trying not to cry out with the pain.

"You reckon you could eat somethin' on your own hook?"

Suddenly I felt ravenous, and I said hoarsely, "Yes, I'm starving."

"You just lay still, son, and I'll whip you up somethin'."

The old man walked to a small woodstove. Next to it sat a rough table with one chair drawn up to it and a wash pan on it; over that, wooden boxes fastened to the wall held canned goods and sacks of sugar. I stared down at myself and tried to turn my body around, but the pain was so bad that I gasped. The old man turned around and said fussily, "You be still. You got some ribs cracked or maybe broke. I ain't decided yet which it is."

I knew he was right. On my left side especially, just to touch the rib cage was painful. I even had to breathe slowly, for when I took a sharp breath it was like getting bayoneted.

As the old man worked at the stove, clattering pans, I looked around the cabin, which had only one room. Its door was open, and I could see the trunk of a large tree and an expanse of green grass. The two windows that pierced the logs were both open, and pale sunshine slanted through them, motes dancing like tiny fragments of light. Near the foot of the bed sat a wooden chair with a cushion. Curled up on the cushion was a cat, and a large hound slept under the chair. Beside the chair was a small table covered with a stack of books, an ashtray, and a pipe. A single bulb—the one whose light had hurt my eyes—glowed feebly overhead. I traced the wire and saw that it ran to an automobile battery on a shelf on the wall, evidently the extent of electronics in the old man's shack.

But the most obvious element in the small room were the books. Books everywhere—on the floor, in overflowing boxes stacked on top of each other, and on shelves that ran all the way to the ceiling on two walls—magazines, old newspapers, paperbacks, hardcover copies. I couldn't see the titles of any of them, but clearly the old man was a reader.

I waited until he came back with a bowl in one hand, a spoon sticking out of it, and a piece of toast on a tin plate. He squatted beside me and handed me the bowl. "See can you get this down."

I took the bowl, and he grinned. "Hope you like your oatmeal with goat milk and honey—'cause that's what you got." I gobbled it, and when I looked up the old man was still grinning. "Like feedin' time at the zoo. Here, gimme me that bowl. We'll let that settle, and I'll get you some more pretty soon." He pulled up a three-legged stool, sat beside me, and peered into my face. "I been feedin' you like a baby nigh onto two weeks. I reckoned you was goin' to die, but you didn't. Couldn't take nothin' but liquids, and I sure got tired of spoonin' it down your throat."

"Where—where is this place?"

"It's in the backwoods. Far back as I could get."

"In the national forest?" I knew there was national forest land throughout much of these mountains, but the old man shook his head.

"Naw, this here ain't no government land. Belongs to a timber company, but they done give up on tryin' to make any money off it. The timber ain't worth it, too hard to git out. Fellow came by once and seen my place and told me to git, but I never. He never come back neither."

"Could I have more water?"

"All you want." Burke handed me a full glass of water, then leaned back and studied me as I drank. "I wasn't right sure what to do with you. I don't have much to do with folks. I keep to myself out here in the woods, but I reckon you'll want to get word to your people about gettin' hurt." He tugged at his mustache, then observed, "Reckon they think you're dead by now."

For a moment I thought about who to get in touch with. I thought of Jimmy, but we weren't really that close, and what could he do? Obviously, I couldn't contact Dane and Marlene; the memory of how they'd tried to kill me was bitter. I had no family, no friends. I shook my head. "No, Mr. Burke, I don't have any family, and I'm between jobs."

The old fellow seemed to be one of those men who had retained strength and agility even into his later years. He was tall, a little stooped, but the white T-shirt he wore revealed stringy muscles, and he didn't have an ounce of fat on him.

"Nobody at all you want me to get?"

"No, not really."

"I guess you're like the fellow in that song I was singin'. Just a pilgrim and a stranger in this here world."

How right he was. "That's pretty much it," I said. "Could I have a little more to eat?"

"Sure." The old man got up and went to the stove, and I heard the spoon scraping the pan. I watched as he added some honey and milk and stirred it up. "This here oatmeal is good for a fellow. I eat it every day."

I ate the oatmeal slowly and thanked him for it. "How'd I get here?"

"Oh, I was out huntin', and I found you right at the foot of that big cliff. You must have fell off from the top. The highway goes along it."

"That's what I did, Mr. Burke."

"Don't know no Mr. Burke. Just Eli's fine." He brushed his mustache back with two hands and nodded. "I had myself quite a time gettin' you here. You're a mighty big feller and I couldn't pick you up, so I took my Jeep in with a trailer, let the trailer down, and winched you up." He laughed silently and shook his head. "Kind of like winchin' a big sow hog, no offense."

"How'd you get me into this bed by yourself?"

"Well, that was a hummer of a problem, but I done 'er!" Burke grinned and nodded at the thought. "I backed the trailer up to the front door, and I used a come-along to git you into the house. First few days you slept on the floor. I knowed that bed you're on wouldn't take your weight, so I had to shore it up. Then I took my hoist that I use to pull the engine on my Jeep and rigged it to one of them beams up there. Got you all tied up and moved the bed. Then I hoisted you up, put the bed under you, then let you down." Burke seemed pleased and said, "You're a big feller, but I got kind of interested in the job. Hope your feelin's ain't hurt, bein' pulled around like a sow at killin' time."

I was hurting too bad to take offense at anything. I was just grateful to be alive. I handed him the bowl, and as I did, I noticed that I had shrunk somewhat. My stomach had always been like a balloon. It was still large but smaller than I'd seen it in years. Living on nothing but whatever liquids he fed me had one good effect!

He went to the stove and poured something out of a kettle into a large cracked white cup. I took it and said, "What is it?"

"Sassafras tea. It'll purify your blood."

I drank it. It was good, though I'd never tasted anything like it.

"I'll fix up some stew for supper tonight. I reckon as how you can handle some hard grub now."

Eli's words faded, and the cup grew very heavy in my hand. I tried to speak, but I was suddenly and totally exhausted. I felt him take the cup, and he said, "Here, you'd better lay back down, son." As my head touched the pillow, I went to sleep at once.

 confin

When I awoke again, something was pressing on my chest, and I felt something soft moving against my mouth. It scared me for a moment, but when I opened my eyes, I found myself looking into the golden eyes of a huge white cat. She reached out and touched my mouth so gently I could hardly feel it.

"Take it easy, Betty." Eli had been sitting beside my bed, and he took the cat and put her on the floor. "She wakes me up like that." He got up and walked over to the stove. "Well, son, you sure sleep like the dead. I'm finishin' up this stew. I call it black bug stew."

I managed a smile. "I don't care what's in it. I could eat anything."

"Well, this one ain't got no bugs in it. Just call it that because when we used to go huntin' we fixed a stew out in the woods with no top on the pot. And once in a while a big black bug would just hit it and sizzle. We et it anyway. Never hurt me none."

I'd always eaten a lot, and now was, according to Eli's timetable, two weeks behind on meals. I struggled up to a sitting position, and when he came over with a bowl of stew, he warned me. "This here is pretty hot. Don't burn yourself. You've got enough bruises without addin' to 'em."

I took the stew and forced myself to eat it very slowly. While I ate, he pulled the three-legged stool up and sat and watched me. "You're gettin' plumb whiskery. I'm gonna have to maybe give you a shave."

"Doesn't matter." A thought came to me, and I stopped eating long enough to ask, "Do you have many neighbors?"

"Ain't got nary a one. People think this is a national park so they don't come huntin'. Once in a while a tree hugger will come in just lookin' around, but they don't mean no harm."

I ate another bite of the stew. It was delicious. It had some kind of meat in it that was very tender, carrots, onions, and seasoning.

"What kind of meat is this?"

"Squirrel. Good, ain't it?"

"I don't think I ever ate squirrel before."

"Well, that ain't your fault, son. You was raised wrong." He got up and picked up a pipe from the table. He knocked it out against the floor, reached into his pocket, opened a worn leather pouch, and dipped the pipe down in it. He packed it, and as he came back and sat down, he pulled a match from his shirt pocket, struck it on his thumbnail, and got it going. "Tobacco's a filthy habit, but I got to have it. Man needs to keep one bad habit, I always say. Suppose I had to repent all of a sudden, and I didn't have a single sin to repent on? Wouldn't that be a caution?"

I couldn't help but smile at Eli's theology. "I don't guess I have to worry about that."

"Why, a young feller like you couldn't have too much on his conscience."

I finished the stew, and he handed me an apple. "Try your teeth out on this. Eat the peelin'. Good for you."

The apple was delicious, and I forced myself to eat it slowly. "What's wrong with my leg?"

"Well, I thought it was busted, but you was out so bad I could do all the punchin' around I wanted to, and I couldn't feel no bones broke. But, Lord, every time you moved that leg, you cried like a stuck pig, so I thought I'd tie it up and put some splints on it so you couldn't twist it so bad."

Eli puffed on the pipe and the purple smoke drifted lazily toward the ceiling. He reached over and touched my head. "I had to sew up that head of yours too. Half your scalp was fallin' off."

I reached up and sure enough I felt the stitches. "What'd you use to sew it with?"

"Just some fishin' line I had. It wasn't too bad."

"How did you learn to do that?"

"I grew up the rough way. We had to do a lot of doctorin' ourselves."

"Why didn't you take me into town, Eli?"

"Don't rightly know. Reckon I should have, but I don't like to go to town in the first place. Don't like hospitals. I thought I could take care of you here. Maybe if you had gotten worse, I would've took you."

I was glad that the old man had kept me here, and said so. "I'm in your debt. I've been a lot of trouble."

"Why, it give me somethin' to do, Ollie. You sure there ain't nobody I can call? I can go into town and phone anyone you want."

"No, I don't have anyone, Eli."

Eli puffed at his pipe and then with his left hand tugged at his mustache. "Neither do I," he said quietly. "Reckon we're two of a kind."

∽

I held the straight razor in my hand with a bit of apprehension. I had never shaved with one before, and it looked like a dangerous weapon. I was sitting up in a chair, and Eli had pulled the small table that usually sat beside his chair over close and then brought me a basin of steaming water, a washcloth, and some soap. I had washed my face, and at his advice had soaked it for a long time with a steaming towel. Then he picked up a shaving mug with a brush in it, worked up a lather, and said, "I reckon you probably use an electric razor."

"That's right."

"Never could stand them things. Here, let me lather you up."

The soap was strong smelling but fragrant as he put it over my face and on my lower jaw and neck. When he had finished, he extended the razor and said, "You want to do it or do you want me to?"

"I guess I'll have a try."

"Here, lemme hold the mirror for you."

I held the razor and looked into the mirror. It was the first time I had seen myself in the four weeks I'd been at Eli's. I was shocked—my face wasn't as round. The flesh had melted away, and I could begin to see the bony structure underneath, something I didn't remember ever seeing. I didn't look like myself at all.

"Just hold that straight against your cheek there and bring it down. No sudden moves, now."

I brought the razor down and felt it pull at the beard. I moved very slowly, and Eli coached me. "When you get better with it, you can turn that razor with a leetle bit of an angle. Cuts a heap better. Also can cut your face off with it if you slip."

I managed to shave very well, only nicking myself once, but that was a good one right under my chin. Eli waited until I had finished and said, "That cut's a bleedin'. Here, you'd better let me dab it with this."

"What's that?"

"It's a styptic pencil, son. Stop movin'." He touched what looked like a white crayon to my face, and it stung, but he held it there until finally he nodded with satisfaction. "That'll hold her, I 'spect. I just use a piece of toilet paper myself, unless it's a bad un."

I rinsed my face off and felt much better. I ran my hands over my cheeks, and I felt the thinness of them. "You done lost a bunch of weight, son," Eli said. "I don't 'spect your clothes would fit you now."

I smiled, and he raised one eyebrow quizzically. "What's funny?" he asked.

"What's funny, Eli, is that I've tried everything in the world to lose weight. Fifty different diets and all kinds of exercise and nothing worked. Then I fall off a mountain and nearly kill myself and I'm losing weight."

Eli smiled gently. "You look like a different fella. Not a bad-lookin' one either. I 'spect it's pretty hard to haul that extra fat around, ain't it?"

"It's not just hauling the weight around, it's what goes on inside."

"What do you mean by that?"

I heard myself speaking of how hard it was to be obese. I told him how it made me turn in upon myself. "I've never really been able to function, Eli. I saw myself as a ridiculous fat man."

Eli listened, sitting there on the kitchen chair. He said nothing for a time, but finally he said, "Well, we all got our problems."

He had never said much about himself, but I was curious. "What about you, Eli? Don't you have any family?"

"I don't even know, son. My daddy got kilt in a loggin' accident. I never knowed him. I grew up hard on a hill farm in Missouri with more rocks than dirt. I remember my mama with seven kids tryin' to make it. It's a miracle we did. She died when I wasn't but fourteen, and the rest of us had to make out best we could. Nothin' easy about scratchin' a livin' out of a hill farm in Missouri."

His voice had grown soft, and he had picked up the banjo. He ran his hands over it but did not play it. He told me he had made it himself and taught himself to play out of a book. I thought he would say no more, but he looked up, and I saw old memories cloud his eyes. "The war come along, and I went into the Marines. I was pretty tough, but I wasn't tougher than Vietnam. Most of the fellers I served with didn't make it back, and when I come home, I was too mean to live with anybody. Nearly killed a fellow in a fight. Just a simple little fight, and if they hadn't pulled me off him, I would of kilt him sure as the world."

He grew very still, then said, "I had a boy once."

"Did you, Eli?"

"I named him Jefferson Davis." He shook his head, adding, "I never liked Yankees, so I named him after the president of the Confederacy."

He fell silent, but I was curious. "Where is he now, Eli?"

"He's gone, son."

"And your wife?"

"I never married her—and that was a mistake. Should've done it. She wasn't a good woman, but then I wasn't a good man. We lived together for three years after I got out of the Corps, but she died when Jeff was born."

Eli crossed the room. He opened the drawer of a battered pine chest of drawers, removed a small box, and sat down again.

He fished through it, then handed me a black-and-white snapshot. "That's me and Jeff," Eli said, tapping the picture. "He was just nineteen then."

The young man had an open, guileless face and a sweet smile. "Fine-looking boy, Eli."

"He's buried out there under that big walnut tree." Eli saw my surprise and shook his head. "Jeff and me moved out here after I retired from the sawmill. He hated town worse than I do. Took a job for a spell drivin' a delivery truck, but he hated it. Finally he just quit and we lived on my Social Security check. He loved the woods, and him and me, we made out fine." Eli fell silent, then said, "He loved to climb trees, Jeff did. He'd climb the tallest tree he could find, clear to the top, and set there for half a day, just lookin' at the country."

"How did he die?"

"Fell out of a big tall pine. Broke his neck."

"I'm sorry, Eli."

"Well, he went quick, doin' what he loved. Most don't get to go like that." Eli took the picture and stared at it. "Nobody even knowed when he passed. I laid him out and buried him. Didn't want nobody to come around tryin' to make talk." He went through the box, showing me his boy's driver's license and Social Security card. "This is all I've got of him, but I'll see him pretty soon."

Tears came to my eyes, and it was a moment before I could answer. "I'm sure you will, Eli."

I felt a surge of pity for the old man, and I knew that, indeed, as he had once said, we were a lot alike. We were both loners; neither of us had any friends or family. His life seemed so lost— but then so did mine.

The days passed, and I got better. My leg was sore, and I had to use a pair of crutches at first that Eli had made for me out of some saplings. He was good at carving things. He had carved animals out of native wood, and I was amazed at how good they were. I told him once that he could sell them, but he said, "Ain't interested in selling nothin'. Don't need anything, and that's the way I want to keep it. Seems there's a shame in buyin' and sellin'."

I was getting around well enough now that I could help Eli a bit, washing what few dishes there were. Eli had a garden, and I could get out and hoe it for a short time. I had never spent much time outside, but I soon learned that Eli knew all there was to know about the animals and the plants. He treated himself with herbs that he found in the woods, and he tried to treat me too, but I resisted most of the time.

Eli got a Social Security check once a month, and he drove to town in his old CJ-5 Jeep to get it. While there, he would pick up any supplies he might need.

When he went that month, I felt lonely. I had been there a month and a half and now was walking with just a slight limp. Somehow I'd lost my taste for Twinkies and other junk food. I ate lean meat and vegetables, and for sweets just honey on toast. It became a game, watching the weight fall off me, and I did all the work I could to speed the process.

My leg and my scalp were healing fast, but the one thing that had not healed was my memory.

I had decided that Dane and Marlene were not going to get away with what they had done. I had never hated anybody before, but I made up for it now. Night after night, lying on my bed, I'd think about them, hating them. I didn't say anything about it to Eli, but it ate away at me all the time. I knew I would do something to them for what they had done to me, and the more I thought about it, the more bitter I got.

Eli had left early in the morning and was back by noon. He unloaded the groceries. He had brought me some sweets. He didn't eat them himself, but, as he said, most folks had a sweet tooth.

"I picked up a bunch of old newspapers too. I thought you might like to read 'em some."

For the next several days, I did read those newspapers. I read them slowly, in order, for no real reason. I was totally uninterested in politics, so I skipped most of that, but read the human interest stories.

It was on the third day after he brought them back that I was leafing through one of the papers and came upon a picture. I stared at it, unable to believe it. It was a picture of Dane and Marlene standing beside a grave. The headlines said, *Wunderkind Wife Grieves Over Her Lost Genius.*

I couldn't believe what I was reading. I was being buried, but I wasn't dead!

The story simply said that Oliver Benson had been killed in a car wreck. It went on to speak about the work I'd done and the success I'd had. All I could think was, *How could this happen?*

I searched backward through the papers and found another story that I had missed. It simply said that my body had been found in a wreck at the bottom of a canyon. The Mercedes had gone over a cliff, crashed at the bottom, and exploded into flame. The body had been so badly burned that it had to be identified by the ring and the watch.

As I sat there in the silence of the cabin, I tried to pull all this together.

They think I'm dead. The guy who pushed me over the cliff must have been wearing my ring and my watch when he crashed. They'd have no reason for thinking it wasn't me. Marlene inherited all the money, and now Dane is comforting my "grieving widow."

I said nothing about it to Eli. But for several days I reread the story and thought about how things had worked out. The moon-faced man who had robbed me had, obviously, changed everything. He was in a grave with my name on the tombstone, and I was free to do as I pleased without having to worry about Dane and Marlene coming after me.

And the thing I pleased to do was to get my revenge on the two people who had betrayed me.

CHAPTER
EIGHT

Maybe I'd been thinking too much of that man's body buried under a stone with my name on it. Whatever the reason, I dreamed I was in the ground, and someone was throwing dirt in over me, which pressed down on my chest with a horrible weight. I tried to call out, tried to move, but the weight just seemed to be getting heavier. Terrified, I tried to dig my way out.

Then, groggily, I emerged from the nightmare and, without opening my eyes, knew that I was lying in the narrow bed where I'd lain for the past few weeks. All the same, though I was awake, I still felt a weight on my chest. I opened my eyes and found myself looking into Betty's golden eyes. That blasted cat was sitting right on my chest, staring into my face. Relief washed over me. I didn't care how many cats were on my chest as long as I wasn't being buried alive.

Betty considered me for a time and then lifted her right paw and reached out for my face. She touched my eye very gently with that soft pad, and I closed it. When she moved her paw, I opened my eye again and stared at her.

"Would you please get off my chest, Betty?" I whispered, but all she did was reach out and touch my eye again. Evidently she was fascinated with the way it opened and shut.

I stroked her soft fur, and she began to purr, setting off that miniature motor deep inside her somewhere. She was a beautiful animal. I had never noticed her lying on Eli's chest this way.

He had grinned and said, "You got a way with females." He had no idea how his innocent remark cut me!

Turning my head, I saw that Eli was gone. Pushing Betty off and ignoring her protesting meows, I swung my feet over the side of the bed, pleased that most of the pain had gone from my right leg. The bruises had faded away, and Eli had taken the stitches out of my scalp awhile before, so I felt pretty good. I got to my feet, limped over to the kitchen table, and saw a note under the sugar bowl. *Gone to run the trotline. Be back at noon.*

I looked down at my wrist out of habit, but there was no watch there, of course. I thought about my watch being burned when the Mercedes had exploded in a fiery ball, and a shiver went over me. That could have just as easily been me, but somehow I was still alive.

Eli kept a bottled-gas stove to cook on in the summer. The woodstove could be used for cooking too, as well as to heat the cabin, but in summer it was too hot. I lit the gas stove with a kitchen match, poured water into a kettle, and then decided to put on a record. I'd listened to all of Eli's records a lot. He had a large collection of old seventy-eights from the forties—Vaughn Monroe, Dick Haymes, and the old crooners, mostly. He ran the record player from the same battery that powered his electric lights; he kept it charged with his Jeep.

The cabin was soon filled with the voice of Patsy Cline, a country-western singer I'd never heard of before but whom Eli thought a great deal of. She was singing about some man who had done her wrong, which pretty well summed up country-western music as far as I could tell. I had never listened to country music much, though I'd grown up in the South. My taste ran in a different direction. But I loved some of the titles. One of them was, "If I Told You You Had a Beautiful Body, Would You Hold It Against Me?" Another was, "If Your Phone Don't Ring, It's Me." Another, "I Paid for Those Shoes That Walked Out on Me."

By the time the coffee water was boiling, I'd had enough of Miss Cline, so I put on Frank Sinatra doing "Stardust." As I poured the coffee water into the dripolater, I wondered how a man could sing so well and be such a thug. I felt a bit guilty enjoying his music so much and yet despising the man who mistreated women and committed about every other sin in the book.

As the coffee drained, making a slight gurgling sound, I sat and thought of artists who had been hoodlums. Paul Gauguin, for instance, who was, according to the experts, a genius—but who abandoned his wife and children. There were plenty of other examples of people who performed well and found public acclaim but were terrible in their private lives. The NBA provided a long list—men who were paid millions of dollars for playing brilliant basketball but spawned illegitimate children like salmon. Having a big bank account didn't protect a man from being a scoundrel.

When the coffee was ready, I poured a mugful and then limped over and sat in the one easy chair. I was reading a Travis Magee detective story by John MacDonald. There were about thirty of them out, all with a color in the title and all pretty much alike. But as I read, it occurred to me that Travis Magee, MacDonald's detective hero, was tall and lanky, and beautiful women fell in love with him after just one look. Surprised, I realized that Travis Magee was just John Wayne wearing a trench coat. He was another of those lean, mean heroes whose posters I'd plastered over my mirror for so long. For some reason this spoiled the book for me, and I placed it back in the bookshelf and decided to cook up dinner for Eli.

I had been helping a bit with the cooking already, but this time I thought I'd do more. Eli had brought in a bunch of greens he had picked out in the woods. For some reason he called them "greasy greens." I picked out all the dirt, debris, and damaged leaves, then chopped them up and tossed them into a pot of salted water, adding a big chunk of ham. Then I chopped up an onion, added a liberal dose of pepper sauce, and set the pot on the stove to boil.

I'd watched Eli make what he called "hoecakes," and they seemed simple enough. I took out the bag of cornmeal, checked it for bugs, dumped some into a pan, heated some milk, and made round cakes about a half-inch thick. I threw them into the skillet, browned them on one side, turned the cake over, and that was it. I ate the first one and found it good, as always. Maybe I'd been wasting my time on fancy French dishes, I mused. Hoecakes were about as good as anything I'd ever cooked.

I got ambitious and cut up the two squirrels Eli had shot and dressed the day before. I diced some salt pork, put the pork in the skillet, and then as it cooked, added the squirrel and cooked it all until it was brown. I kept adding a little water, simmering it, and tossed in whatever I could find—some ketchup, some chopped onions, and several kinds of seasoning. I had no idea what to call it, but it smelled good as it simmered on the stove.

Pete, Eli's big hound, was lying in the middle of the floor, his head up, his eyes watching my every move. I always threw him some scraps, and I did so now. He caught in the air the chunk of meat I tossed him, and waited hopefully for more.

"No more for you, Pete. You can't afford to get fat."

And then, just to be sure I'd make Eli happy, I cooked some grits. He ate grits with every meal—breakfast, lunch, and dinner. And sometimes at night when he got hungry, he'd just make himself a bowl of grits, put butter and salt on it, and eat it with a spoon.

Cooking didn't require a lot of thought, so my mind drifted, as always, back to what was happening to me. When you die and get resurrected in a cabin, it does tend to make you think a little bit.

The thing that puzzled me the most was that I didn't even miss my computers. You have to understand that, since I got my first computer, I hadn't missed a day sitting in front of one. I suppose you might say a computer was my idol, for I did everything except kneel in front of it and give thanks. I have no idea how many hours I'd spent working on my computers, but it was in the several thousands.

Even so, since I had awakened in Eli's cabin, it was as though computers did not exist. We had no television, and the only electronic items other than lightbulbs were the old record player and an old Philco radio that we listened to sometimes. Eli listened to preaching from Del Rio, Texas, and I listened to the news. But no computers—and life went on without them. Maybe I'd go back one day, but for now I was in sort of a twilight zone, and it was as if that which had controlled my life for so long had ceased to exist.

Another big change was the weight loss. Eli had no scales, of course, but I had lost, I guessed, at least sixty to seventy-five pounds. That may sound like a lot to normal people, but it left me well into the obese range. Still, it gave me a strange feeling to look down and see my feet. I hadn't seen them for years except by bending way over and holding up my leg. Now just to look down and see my toes was startling, as if they belonged to someone else, and I was always caught off guard when I saw them.

And when I shaved, my face had changed so much that it was like a stranger looking out of that mirror right into my eyes. The color of the eyes were the same, and the hair was the same, but everything else was changed. My real face had been covered by a balloon of fat for so long that neither I nor anyone else had any idea what I really looked like.

Most of all, there was the eerie feeling that kept coming back that I was dead. I dreamed about that body, or the ashes of it, burned to a crisp and buried somewhere. And on the tombstone, or maybe on a plaque attached to the urn, was my name. I suppose Jimmy might have mourned me, and the few acquaintances I'd had in Memphis, but I had no family. So—now I was nobody. I didn't exist. It's hard for me to put into words, but Ollie Benson was dead, and I was a walking, breathing man who had no identity.

As I finished cooking the meal, I tried to put these things out of my mind. I had found some old Johnny Mercer records and played "Accentuate the Positive" three times in a row, wondering how Johnny had come up with the lyrics to that one.

I heard Eli coming back, whistling as usual. He always whistled a hymn called "Tempted and Tried," and when I looked out the window, I saw him stop beside the big pine tree out front. He reached into a sack and hauled out an enormous catfish. He picked up a rusty hammer and a big nail from a bench and nailed the catfish by the lower lip to the tree. He came into the house. "Had good luck," he said. "Got a whopper." He saw the food and nodded. "Well, you got dinner ready. Let me wash up, and we'll lay our ears back and fly right at it."

As soon as Eli washed, we sat down. He loved Dr. Pepper, which I thought tasted like cough syrup that had gone bad, and he drank it warm straight out of a can. Just popped the tab and put them down. I shuddered as he drained one before even starting to eat, then unpopped another one. "You ought to drink more Dr. Pepper, son. It's good for your innards."

"I'll just have water."

Eli bowed his head and, without waiting, fired off a grace. The way he said grace was amusing and yet touching, praying for the food by name. "Thank you, Lord, for the grits. Thank you for the salad. Thank you for the squirrels and the hoecakes—and heal my friend Ollie here. In the name of Jesus. Amen."

The last part of his prayer caught me off guard, but he just began eating. As we ate, Eli spoke of his time with the Marines in Vietnam. I knew that many veterans who had gone through that time didn't like to think about it, but Eli spoke of it freely.

"There was one of our fellers that mined gold while he was there," he said, taking a sip of the warm Dr. Pepper.

"Mined gold? How could you mine gold there? Didn't know there was any in Vietnam."

"Oh, he mined the mouths of those Viet Cong we killed. He went out lookin' for 'em and knocked their gold teeth out. Had a whole leather bag full. Carried them around his neck. I expect before he got through he had thousands of dollars' worth of them things."

"Wonder what he did with the money."

"Didn't do nothin'. He got kilt. We was just sittin' around eatin' breakfast one mornin' and a sniper put a bullet right through his skull. He fell over dead as a hammer. Poor fella! He didn't know the Lord either. He's in poor shape right now, I'd guess." He was silent for a moment as he thought of that time, then he said, "That was a good lunch. We'll have us some catfish for supper. I'll go out and clean 'im."

I followed and watched Eli clean the fish that he had nailed up. He just skinned it with a pair of pliers; it was like stripping off a pair of gloves.

I'd noticed that Eli always carried an old pistol—a forty-five automatic, he said—even just to run the trotlines. He said it was for snakes, but that thing would have stopped an African buffalo, I think. I said, "You know, Eli, I've never shot a gun in my life."

"You ain't! Well, now that's peculiar."

"You suppose I could shoot your forty-five?"

"Don't see why not. I've got plenty of ammunition. I like to practice myself a bit. Let me go put this fish away where the flies won't get it, and we'll go out and blaze away."

A few minutes later, he emerged from the cabin holding a box of shells in his hand. He handed it to me, and I opened it. "These are big bullets," I said.

"You don't want to fool around, Ollie. There ain't no sense carryin' a little thirty-two or even a thirty-eight. They just kind of make a feller mad when you plug 'im. But you hit him with one of these, why, son, the argument's over!"

We stood out in front of the cabin. Ollie put some cans on a low-lying tree limb. He came back and said, "See can you hit one of them." He showed me how to hold it in my right hand, bracing my wrist with my left. I pulled the trigger, and it sounded like the world had blown up!

"Well, you didn't kill nobody that time. Just fire off the whole clip."

I shot at the cans until the gun was empty, finally managing to knock one off.

"You ain't a bad shot, Ollie, for a first timer. Most of them shots would have hit a feller."

He shoved the fresh clip in, turned sideways, and began firing. The earth was one long roll of explosions, and the cans began flying off. When he had finished the clip, there wasn't a single can left.

"Wow!" I said. "You're a good shot!"

"Had lots of practice. That's 'bout all I do for entertainment. Here, you try another clip."

We fired away until the whole box of shells was gone, and Eli nodded with satisfaction. "You're just a natural shot, Ollie. Some fellers can shoot up enough shells to kill half the world and never hit nothin'. Some just pick up a gun like you done and can hit with it."

I was pleased with my performance and thought about it as I went back to the cabin. An image formed in my mind of Marlene and Dane being hit by one of those blunt .45 slugs. It gave me a queer twist of pleasure, and for the first time in my life I understood what evil really was.

∾

Firing that forty-five had done something to me. Later that afternoon, Eli was taking a nap across the room from me, and I was sitting down reading with Pete, Eli's blue-tick hound, coming over to nose me every once in a while. He liked to have his head scratched, and I scratched it while I read the book. But I wasn't paying much attention to what I was reading. I was playing a little game with myself—and not a very pleasant one.

My hatred for Marlene and Dane would sometimes seem to die down, but then it would burst forth again, stronger than ever. I've never hated anyone before, and it frightened me. Since firing that gun, I had been getting a great deal of pleasure picturing myself just walking up and shooting Dane and Marlene right in the face. I would act it out in different ways in my mind. Sometimes I would picture them eating at an expensive restaurant, and I'd just walk in and say, "Hello, Marlene," and shoot her. Then I'd smile and say, "How you been, Dane?" And then I'd blow him away. Other times I would sneak into their house and catch them in bed having sex. I'd just stand over them and smile and shoot them.

Of course, one side of my brain told me that I was bound to get caught. I'm not smart enough to get away with murder, but I'd have all the money. It would belong to me then, and I could buy my way out of the worst of it. It's hard to put twenty million dollars in a gas chamber! I could even get a smart lawyer and convince the jury that I was insane and get away with it.

In any case, I found myself enjoying the little scenario—and that bothered me.

∾

Time went by, and I listened to country-western music and Tommy Dorsey and read detective stories. Late one night I was reading a book called *Great English Poetry*, just a battered old hardcover that Eli had picked up somewhere. There was a poem in it by William Blake called "A Poison Tree." I had never read Blake before, but the poem, for some reason, frightened me.

I was angry with my friend;
I told my wrath, my wrath did end.
I was angry with my foe:
I told it not, my wrath did grow.

And I watered it in fears
Night and morning with my tears,
And I sunned it with smiles
And with soft deceitful wiles.

And it grew both day and night,
Till it bore an apple bright,
And my foe beheld it shine,
And he knew that it was mine—

And into my garden stole
When the night had veiled the pole;
In the morning, glad, I see
My foe outstretched beneath the tree.

I don't know why that poem scared me. Maybe because I realized that I was actually capable of murder. I'd never been able to understand how anybody could take another human life, but I understood it now.

With an effort I pushed those thoughts away and made up my mind not to let such evil nest in me.

I put the book down and turned the light off, but I couldn't go to sleep. After a while I started thinking that maybe I would just take the money out of my Swiss account and make another life. I could buy this place from the timber company and stay here with Eli. I could make it nice. Put in a real inside bathroom—which would please me!

∞

As the days ticked themselves off, I had recurrent dreams—sometimes of being buried alive, sometimes of Dane and Marlene laughing as they planned my death. So despite my attempts to put all that behind me, I amused myself by thinking of ways to kill them. After all, just *thinking* about it wasn't going to hurt me.

One night after supper Eli was reading a World War II book about the Nuremberg Trials. He shook his head and looked disgusted. "They shouldn't of kilt them war criminals."

I was surprised at that. "Don't you think they deserved to die?"

"Sure they did—but dyin' was too easy for 'em. Should of kept 'em alive and let 'em live with what they was. Make life pretty hard on 'em. When you kill a feller, why, it's only a minute's pain, and then he's out of it. It ain't right."

I paid little attention to Eli's remark at the time, but it had sunk in, and it kept coming back.

It was three days after this that something began coming together in my mind. It began, I think, with a single thought: *Eli's right. Killing Dane and Marlene would be too easy for them. I need to make them suffer for a long time.*

That was the beginning. I don't know what sort of mind I have that puts things together like it does. It takes a special combination of brain cells, I suppose—and a perverse one—to do things like that. Just as it takes a special combination to write a symphony or a great novel.

I began playing with it as if it were a computer program. I would try this little piece, and if it didn't work, I would throw it away and try another. This went on for several days. All the time I was living with Eli, listening to Dodger baseball games, learning to cook real Southern, and Eli never realized what a bloody man he was living with. I thought of a line I remembered from *Hamlet*: "One may smile and smile and be a villain."

Slowly something began to come together. It was hazy, but it got clearer as time went by. I began thinking things like, *I could come back from the dead. Marlene would still be my wife. I could kick Dane out, then divorce her.* For a while I considered it, but it wasn't enough just to kick them out. I wanted them hurt worse than that. And I hadn't yet thought of a way to prove that they'd tried to murder me.

Always, when I worked on a program, I had a strong feeling about how it was going. Sometimes things wouldn't work at all, but I just knew somehow that I would figure it out. And I knew it would come all at once instead of in little pieces.

And it did. It came together with three elements. The first one came when I put on a pair of pants that Eli had brought me from town—from Goodwill, I suppose. They had fit me when he brought them home, but now when I put them around my waist, I had to hold them up. I had lost another fifty or sixty pounds, I guessed. I picked up the mirror and saw that I had lost more weight in my face too. The man who had been hidden inside of me looked nothing at all like Ollie Benson. No one would ever recognize me.

That was the first piece. The fact that, if I kept losing weight, I could walk right up to Marlene and Dane, and neither of them would know who I was.

The second piece came when I was reaching in the drawer for something, and there lay the driver's license and Social Security card of Eli's dead son, Jeff Burke.

Then, like it always did, the parts came together. *He's dead and buried and nobody knows it. His Social Security account is active. Here's a driver's license and a birth certificate.*

Those were the first two pieces. Nobody knew me. I had a ready-made identity.

And the third piece was that I had nearly two million dollars to do it on in the Swiss bank account.

I went out at once and made my way down to the small river. I could walk now almost without limping. I sat down beside the stream and put my feet into the water. It was a beautiful day with an azure sky and white, puffy clouds overhead. I could hear birds singing.

The silvery bodies of a school of minnows in the stream moved all together in some way I could never understand. I watched those minnows change direction, move, pause at exactly the same time.

And then without warning the whole thing came together in my mind. It had happened that way with Film Maker. I had struggled with parts and pieces, and one day the whole thing had fit together in a single instant.

I would do exactly the same terrible thing to Dane and Marlene that they had done to me. I knew they'd be living high— on my money—and I knew that they were both rotten at heart, so I had no reservations at all about my plan.

First, I'd leave this place and make myself into a different man. I would look different, talk different. I would know things that the old Ollie Benson would never know. I would change everything about myself. Somehow I would become the kind of man I'd always envied—tall and lean and tan and confident.

Then I'd move into their circle, wherever they were. I would establish myself as a rich bachelor—and here I laughed out loud. I would make Marlene fall for me. I would win her away from Dane, and I'd steal all the money. Dane would be left without anything. And then I would throw Marlene out without a penny, and laugh at both of them for being such fools—exactly as they had laughed at me when they planned to kill me.

I sat beside that small stream putting it all together, and I knew that I could make it happen. I'd played charades a few times, and I was pretty good at it—acting out things. Now I was going to play a game of charades with the two who had taken away everything I had.

CHAPTER
NINE

I was surprised to discover that creating a plan to destroy two human beings wasn't a great deal different from creating a software program. In my mind, I was able to set aside completely the moral element of wiping out two lives—after all, didn't they deserve it, after what they'd done?—and look upon Dane and Marlene simply as two of the ingredients I needed to achieve a desired end. It never occurred to me that the Nazi monsters who designed the plan to murder millions of Jews operated in this same way. I remember reading that one of the men who operated the ovens at Dachau boasted about the efficiency of the place.

For several days, as I made plans, I was quieter than usual, and once Eli asked if something was troubling me. I just gave him a smile and said that things were fine. In my mind, at that time, I'm sure I meant that. Don't ask me how a mild-mannered man who couldn't stand to hurt anything living could contemplate destroying two lives with no more compunction than I felt. Within three days I had completed the rough outline for what I intended to do. I dreaded telling Eli, but I had a plan for him as well that I knew he would like. So, on Thursday evening after supper, while we were listening to recordings by Bob Crosby, I said, "Eli, I'll be leaving in the morning."

I expected him to show some surprise, but he simply turned and fixed his gaze on me with an expression I couldn't read. "I hate to hear that, Ollie. I was hopin' you'd stay here."

"I would, but there's something I have to do."

Eli gave me a strange look, but finally he shrugged his shoulders saying, "I hope it turns out good for you."

I don't know what I'd expected, but I felt disappointed that he hadn't tried to talk me into staying. I felt that things were incomplete. Also, oddly, I felt a need to explain what I was going to do to someone. I couldn't tell Eli about my plans, of course, but the desire was there.

After the record ended, Eli moved the needle and turned the machine off. He picked up his banjo and sat in a straight-backed chair. He began playing quietly enough, and pretty soon he started singing some hymn that I didn't know. It wasn't a fast hymn like Eli usually liked but rather slow. I listened to the words carefully.

When peace like a river attendeth my way,
When sorrows like sea-billows roll;
Whatever my lot, Thou hast taught me to say,
It is well, it is well with my soul.
It is well, with my soul,
It is well, it is well with my soul.

Eli ended the song, and for a while he sat there simply rubbing his hands over the old banjo. Finally he looked up and said, "I heard a preacher one time tell about how that song came to be writ. A fellow named Spafford wrote it. Him and his wife, they lost their son and decided to take a vacation. Spafford couldn't get away so he sent his wife and his four daughters to England on a ship. He told them he'd be over in a few days, but they never made it. The ship went down. Most of the passengers got drowned. Miss Spafford, she made it to shore somewhere in Wales, and she sent her husband a cablegram that said, 'Saved alone.'"

Eli looked up at me then, and the silence filled the room. I could hear the crickets outside making their symphony, and Pete started scratching, thumping his leg on the floor. Except for that it was quiet for a long time.

"That's a sad story," I said.

"Yep, it is. Spafford got on a ship, and when they was crossin' the sea, the captain pointed out where he thought the ship went down his wife and girls were on. He looked at that place, and he went back to his cabin, and he wrote that song, 'It Is Well with My Soul.' It takes a man pretty safe and sound in the faith to do that. He must have knowed God real well."

"I suppose so."

The story had laid a chill on me, and I said, "I guess I'll go to bed. I want to get an early start tomorrow."

"Good night, son," Eli said. "You sleep good."

ᘜ

Despite Eli's words, I didn't sleep well, and I got up the next morning feeling almost ready to change my mind. Eli fixed a good breakfast—pancakes, eggs, and grits, of course, along with some leftover biscuits that were still good. We ate without speaking much, and when we got ready to go, I stroked Betty's fur. She looked at me with those huge eyes of hers and I said, "Good-bye, Betty. You take care of Pete and Eli."

We went outside. I had a sack with some shaving things and some of the old clothes Eli had bought, even though they didn't really fit anymore. Pete followed us outside to the Jeep, and I scratched his shoulders, and he reared up and put his front paws on me. I pulled his ears and told him good-bye, then got into the Jeep. As we drove down the dirt track, I turned around and looked at the cabin, thinking, *That's more of a home than I've ever had.*

The Jeep was too noisy for us to say much while we were riding. I thought about how safe I'd been while I was staying with Eli. I knew things wouldn't be that easy from now on, and when the Jeep moved out of sight of the cabin I felt as if I were in a burial vault and the door had slammed shut.

When we got to the small town, Eli said, "You want out at the bus station, son?"

"That'll be fine." I had no intention of taking a bus, but I had to get out somewhere.

Eli pulled up in front of a shabby-looking bus station, and I got out. Eli reached into the pocket of his shirt and came out with a couple of bills. "You'd better take this, son. You're going to need some cash."

I took the money, touched by his gesture, and saw that it was two tens. "Thanks a lot. I'll send it back to you."

"Never mind about that. You just take care of yourself, boy. I'll think of you."

I put my hand out, and when Eli took it, I felt the strength of his grip. As old as he was, he was still a better man than most. "I'll never forget you, Eli," I said.

His wise, old eyes considered me pretty thoroughly then, and I knew I was being weighed in the balance. He knew more than he was letting on, or so I felt, but then he released my hand and nodded. "You just trust the good Lord, son, and you'll be all right." He gunned the engine and whipped the Jeep around in a U-turn. I watched him until he was out of sight, and then I was alone in the world.

I went inside the bus station and asked if there was a pay phone. A tall man sweeping the floor said, "There's one in front of the Dew Drop Inn. Right over there across the street."

"Thanks."

I left the bus station feeling the man's eyes on me. I must have made a pretty sorry sight with my leftover clothes. I had shaved, but my hair was simply hacked off with a pair of shears, and the boots had floppy soles. I went into the Dew Drop Inn and laid down one of the tens. "Could you let me have some quarters?"

"Reckon so." The speaker was a short, heavy man with curly brown hair and sharp gray eyes. He gave me four quarters, the rest in dollars, and I said, "Thanks a lot. I appreciate it."

Leaving the Dew Drop Inn and feeling conspicuous, I went to the phone attached to the side of the building. I put in the coins and dialed the number I had memorized. A neutral voice said, "Yes, how may I help you?"

"I want to have some cash brought to me."

"What is the number of your account, sir?"

I gave him the number, and there was a moment's pause. Fear came over me then because I thought, *What if he won't give me the money?*

But the voice came back, the sort of a voice that seemed to have no body. He asked me the amount I wanted, then asked, "Where would you like the money delivered, sir?"

I gave him the name of the small town and said, "I'll be waiting in front of the Dew Drop Inn on Main Street."

"The expense of delivering the cash will be deducted from your account, sir."

"That's fine. How long will it be?"

"I couldn't say. I will dispatch a man right away."

"How will I know him?"

"He will be in a black sedan, and he will pull up right in front of the Dew Drop Inn. Identify yourself using your number, and you will receive the cash."

"Thank you."

I hung up the receiver and then felt at a loss. It might take an hour for the money to come, or maybe half a day. I walked up and down the street for a time, then walked back to the Dew Drop Inn and sat down. There were four customers inside, all men, and the owner came over and asked what I'd have. I wasn't really hungry, but I had to order something. "Coffee and some sort of roll."

The owner nodded and brought back a white mug of coffee and a Danish on a white saucer. I nibbled at it slowly and drank the coffee. I had two refills, then paid for the food and left a dollar tip. I walked outside and saw across the street, right down from the Dew Drop Inn, a hardware store with a wooden chair in front. I went inside and asked the lady behind the counter if I could sit awhile in the chair outside. She gave me an odd look but said, "That'll be all right, I suppose."

"Thank you very much." I went out and sat down to wait.

Almost exactly two hours later, when I was stiff from sitting in that chair, I saw a black Cadillac coming down the street. When it slowed and pulled up in front of the Dew Drop Inn, I got up at once and hurried toward it. By the time I got there, the door had opened, and a tall, thin man with an olive complexion and a black mustache had gotten out. He was wearing a dark suit, a white shirt, and a maroon tie. He didn't speak; he just waited for me.

"Do you have something for me? I'm Ollie Benson."

"Names aren't necessary. All I need is a number."

He had eyes absolutely black, as though there were nothing behind them. He made me nervous, but I gave him the number. He pulled a card from his pocket, read the back of it, and asked me to repeat it. I did, and his eyes came back to take me in. "Very well, sir." He opened the car door, reached inside, and turned back to me with a brown briefcase in his hand. He handed it to me, and without another word got into the Cadillac and drove away.

The briefcase felt heavy. It had no markings on it, and there was no lock—just a simple clasp. I held it up flat, opened it, and peered inside. It was full of money, more than I had ever seen at one time. I shut it quickly, then realized I couldn't go around looking like a bum. I glanced at the Dew Drop Inn and felt a sudden impulse. I walked inside, but the manager didn't look overjoyed to see me. I sat down, and he grunted, "What'll you have?"

"I need to buy a car."

Suspicion flared in his eyes, and he said, "A car? What kind of car?"

"I know this looks a little odd, but I've been on a vacation and lost my outfit. I want to buy a nice car to drive back east in."

Disbelief was still mirrored in the owner's eyes. "My brother-in-law owns a Lincoln dealership over at Middleton. Think that'd be good enough for you?"

"That would do. How could I get over there?"

"You don't look like you could buy a new car."

I laughed at him. "Haven't you ever heard about paupers that have millions of dollars? Maybe I'm one of those."

The owner was staring at me, and finally he smiled. "All right. I'll call my brother. He'll come over and get you, but he's kind of rough. If you're puttin' one over on him, you won't enjoy his reception."

"Tell him I like Town Cars. Either that or a Navigator would do me pretty well."

The owner went into another room to make the call. When he came back, he said, "My brother's sendin' one of his sales-men over to get you. You know what those things cost?"

"I have no idea."

"I seen that guy in the black car give you that briefcase. It looked like Mafia stuff to me."

I was feeling rather light-headed, and I scowled at him. "Best not to mix in business like that. A fellow can get in big trouble."

"Hey, I was just kiddin'!"

"It's all right. Just forget you saw me."

I waited twenty minutes, and a car pulled up. I said, "Remember, best not to talk about this."

"Hey, I won't say nothin'."

Amused, I met the salesman, whose name was John Hamish. I could see the disappointment wash all over his face when he saw me, but I said, "Don't worry. You're gonna make a sale today."

I bought a Town Car for the sticker price. Didn't even argue. I had gone into the restroom and transferred money to my pockets. When it came time to pay, Hamish stared at the new bills. "You're payin' cash. That doesn't happen very often."

"You do take cash, don't you?"

Hamish smiled. "As long as they're not counterfeit, I do."

I drove out of town in my old rags of clothes but in a brand-new Town Car with only thirty-two miles showing on the odometer. As I left there, I knew that I'd started on a road I couldn't see the end of. But I'd started, and now I knew I'd never turn back.

CHAPTER
TEN

California gets bad press. Jimmy always called it "the land of the fruit and the nuts." But as I drove toward the big city, I didn't feel that way about it at all. It was the first of May, and God was in his heaven and all was right with the world. The sky was a pale blue and hard enough to strike a match on. I left the windows of the Town Car down and smelled the rich earth and the clean smell of evergreens, and the breeze was warm and comfortable. It seemed wrong for the world to be so beautiful when I was headed toward a rendezvous that would culminate in the ruination of two lives.

I had a sudden thought that maybe I was getting hardened—like the men who operated the ovens at Buchenwald and Auschwitz. Maybe some of them had families, and I wondered what they would say if one of the kids asked, "How did your work go today, Papa?" Did they laugh and talk about how production was well ahead of schedule?

I had learned to shove such thoughts into the closet we all keep for storing unpleasant things. As I drew nearer the city, the highway fanned out and vehicles streamed by. I wondered where they were all going, each one headed toward his own particular destiny. I studied the faces of the people in the vehicles I passed. Most of them had dead faces and looked as if they were on their way to their own funerals. I wondered if there was a name for this disease, and decided that if there was it was called *civilization*, or perhaps the *American disease*.

The Town Car purred under the pressure of my foot, and I began to think of how I would handle my mission. I remembered the old television program *Mission: Impossible*, and the words of the narrator came back: "Your mission, should you choose to accept it . . ." And although I had made up my mind that nothing would prevent me from wiping Dane and Marlene out, it came to me that I had other choices. I had enough money to leave the country. A man could live like a king on the money I had—say, down in Belize—but I pushed those thoughts away and began to think of not whether I would wipe out the two who had wronged me but of how I would do it.

One thing I knew: I would have to break all the routine of my past life, and that was likely to be hard. Most human beings find satisfaction in following a set routine. I put on my right shoe first every time. For no real reason, I always started shaving on the left side of my face.

It occurred to me that routine gives us some kind of comfort, but my old life was buried now, and I determined to put on my left shoe first and start my shave with the right side of my face and break other conventions that had been written into my life by years of habit.

Still on the interstate, I passed a suburb, saw a mall, and quickly took an exit. The clothes I had on were clean but ragged, and I still had to find a place to live. No one would rent a home or apartment to a guy dressed as I was, so I circled the mall looking for a place to buy more presentable attire. I was depressed by the mall itself. I had always hated malls. To me they represented the very worst in American life.

I threw myself into the traffic pattern and passed the obligatory shops until I came to a Sears. That was the place for me. I went to the men's department, but I was still too large for almost all of the clothing. The lady who had come to ask if I needed help suggested rather daintily, "Perhaps you would like to try the large men's shop. They would have your size, I think."

I took her advice, went to the large men's shop, and bought enough clothes to do me. The clerk, a tall, well-built man with a bored expression, helped me all he could. He used that special smile that people use when they don't believe anything they're saying. I had seen it a lot.

I got back into the car and drove on into the city. I had never really scoped out Los Angeles before, and I had no idea where to start. I drove aimlessly, feeling like an ant in a very busy anthill. All of the activity around me discouraged me, and finally I decided that I would have to have help. I got an address from a phone book and finally found my way to a real-estate company that specialized in rentals. The woman gave me one glance, and I knew I had been put through the little economic computer in her mind, and then she began to interview me.

"What price apartment were you thinking of?"

"Something very expensive."

The woman's eyes flew open, and something humorous crossed her features. "Well, we can help you there. Almost everything in Los Angeles is expensive."

"I want a place very close to a good fitness center. And I'll need a furnished apartment. Aside from that, you can be my guide."

Mrs. Taylor glanced at me suspiciously, but still her fingers flew over the keys of her computer, and she came up with four possibilities. "Would you try these four? And if they don't work, we'll try something else, Mr. Burke."

"Thank you." I got up. At the door, I glanced back and saw her watching me with an air of disbelief.

∾

I hired a taxi to take me to the four locations—actually only three, for I chose the third one. I tipped the cab driver twenty dollars, which made his day, then I drove my car back to the apartment. There was a special parking area and one of the slots would be assigned to me, I was told.

I was tired, but I asked the manager of the building where I could get some groceries. It was close enough to walk, and I passed a computer shop on the way. For a moment I felt a strong desire to go in and buy one, but I had already settled that. Computers were not to be a part of my life until my mission was accomplished.

I bought a sackful of groceries then went back to the apartment. When I stepped inside, I felt a strangeness, almost like Robinson Crusoe cast onto his desert island. The apartment was very nice, two bedrooms, a large kitchen, a living/dining area—which was good, because I would be spending months in it.

I cooked an eight-ounce ribeye and a baked potato, and served it with one roll and two-percent milk. I gobbled it down and was still hungry. I had yogurt for dessert, and then I sat there thinking of food, mostly of Little Debbies.

"No Little Debbies for you, Davis Burke," I said. I had started calling myself by that name to get used to it. Taking on a new name is a hard job, for already I had discovered that moving into a new identity is more difficult than moving into a new apartment.

I washed the dishes, which didn't take long, then walked around the apartment. I hung up the clothes I had bought and then walked to the window and looked out for a long time. I was on the sixth floor. I watched the traffic below, cars and trucks going by in both directions, people walking, all seemingly in a hurry to get somewhere. Every one of the people I saw had some master plan for their life. Most of them had as many problems as characters in a soap opera.

Finally I sat down at the table, took out a pen, and began to jot down elements of what I had come to call "The Master Plan." I had always been methodical in approaching jobs, and I wrote down the three major problems that had to be overcome if the master plan was to work:

I. Appearance

II. Speech

III. Personality

For a long time I sat there staring at those three items. There wasn't anything I could do about my height, but aside from that I had decided that almost everything else could be changed. Weight loss, of course, was the most significant thing. Hair could be changed. Color of eyes—contacts would take care of that. Color of skin—sunlamps, or here in California just lying out on the beach.

I thought about speech, how to sound different. That was beyond me, but there were people who could change that. I didn't know where they were or their names, but I would find them, and Davis Burke would sound very little like Ollie Benson. Personality—well, one thing was plain: If Ollie had been a frightened introvert, Burke would have to be something entirely different. Marlene and Dane would be moving in fast company, and I would have to be faster than any of them if I were to succeed.

For a long time I sat looking at that list, making notes. Finally it came to me that I was a little bit like Professor Higgins in my favorite musical *My Fair Lady*. He had taken a cockney girl with terrible language, terrible appearance, terrible everything, and made her into a beautiful, cultured young lady. I had always loved that movie. And now it was time for me to transmogrify myself. I like that word *transmogrify*. I wasn't sure what it meant, but I knew that Ollie Benson was going to have to be transformed into a completely different person.

I got up still hungry, and knew that this was going to be a way of life for me. I walked downstairs, went to a newsstand,

and stood before the magazines. I picked up a copy of *People*, thumbed through it, and realized that I didn't know who half of these people were—but they were the beautiful people everyone had to know about. I bought *Cosmopolitan* and *Vogue*, so that I could catch up on what women were thinking, then added a copy of *Robb's Report*. I had seen it before—a sort of a Sears and Roebuck catalog for billionaires. It had amused me to look through it and find out that you could buy islands in the South Pacific and become king, as Marlon Brando had done.

Back at the apartment, I stood before the elevator, lifted my hand to punch the button—and sensed that something was wrong with that. I looked around until I located the sign that said *Stairs*, then resolutely walked over to it, opened the door, and started up.

I had to stop four times to catch my breath. It seemed a hopeless proposition, but I had known it wasn't going to be easy. Finally I reached my floor, went into my room, and then plopped down on the couch gasping for breath. I turned on the TV and surfed the channels until I found a Western starring Johnny Mack Brown. Nobody even remembered Johnny these days. He had been all-American at Alabama, and then had played a soft-spoken cowboy hero with a nice smile.

I watched the movie for a while and then turned it off. I went into the bathroom and showered.

When I stepped out of the shower, I glanced into the mirror, and immediately my mind went back to my old life when I had covered up mirrors with posters of Clint Eastwood. Now I forced myself to look, and said, "You might as well get used to looking, Davis Burke, because you're going to have to look until you get sick of it." I had lost weight while I had been with Eli, but I was still a globby mountain of fat. The idea of ever looking different seemed remote, but as I grabbed a towel and began to dry off, I knew that no matter how long it took, sooner or later I would be transmogrified.

CHAPTER
ELEVEN

I didn't sleep much my first night in the new apartment, accustomed to the hard bed and the flat mattress in Eli's cabin. The air-conditioning clogged me up, and early in the morning I had gotten up, turned the air off, and opened all the windows. I knew, of course, that in Los Angeles I was letting in air that had the purity of smokestack emissions, but I ignored that and managed to toss and turn until a little after dawn.

I dressed and had my breakfast, which wasn't exactly the equivalent of a Roman emperor's banquet. I ate a bowl of bran flakes and one banana and tried to make it last as long as I could. At least my appetite had been conditioned by eating Eli's cooking. As I sat trying to make the fragments of bran flakes and slices of banana last, I realized that the real battles lay here. There were probably over a hundred diets on the market, and I had tried most of them at one time or another. The new ones were simply rehashes of the old ones. They could all be trusted to achieve one result: whatever weight you lost, you would gain back in about the same amount of time.

It was too early to go out so I poked around the apartment, then read the newspaper from back to front trying to pick up on what kind of a world I was living in. The usual tribulations. Social scientists were forever scrambling around looking for the formula that would make everything all right. They would never find it, of course, and neither would the physicists or the politicians.

The thought came to me that, while most statistics are lies, one of them is absolutely true. The death rate is still one hundred percent. It always would be. It didn't seem to me, as I sat there, that it made much difference whether an Indian put an arrow into your liver or a crazed militant blew up the building you were sitting in. Death was death, and the fellow that figured out a way to eliminate it would make a bundle.

I went to my suitcase and picked out the old newspaper containing the story of my funeral. I read the text again and sat looking at the picture of Dane and Marlene standing together. Dane had his arm around Marlene—who was grieving, or so the text would have you to believe. The picture fascinated me. What bigger and better things had they moved on to from that moment frozen in time?

I put the clipping away and left the apartment. A bunch of sparrows were fighting over a few crumbs in the street. I stopped for a moment and watched them kicking and pecking and remembered an old line of poetry: "If birds in their nest agree, then why, oh why, can't we?"

The fitness center was only eight blocks away, so I ignored the Town Car. I walked as rapidly as I could, and after one block I was puffing. After three blocks I was almost staggering. By the time I got to the fitness center, I was sucking for air and about to pass out. I stood outside until I was able to breathe almost normally, and then stepped inside.

I had been in fitness centers before. This one was more ornate than most. The lobby could have been lifted from an Oriental potentate's palace: white marble on the floor, a mottled darker marble on the walls, skylights allowing yellow sunlight to filter down. I walked to the desk, where a young woman sat watching me. She was young, no more than twenty I would guess, and had the Hollywood tan—which probably came either from a lamp or out of a bottle. Her lips had been enlarged. No one had luscious lips like that without a little help, and her eyes had been given a sultry look by Maybelline. She gave me a bright smile, saying, "Well, good morning. You're up early."

"Yes, I am. Too early for you?"

"Not at all. Won't you sit down? My name is Tammy."

"I'm Davis Burke."

"Glad to see you, Mr. Burke." She paused for half a second, undoubtedly while figures flicked through her mind. "Are you interested in a membership?"

"Yes."

"Well, here's a brochure you might like to look over."

I took the brochure and flipped through it. She watched me carefully. I looked up and said, "Sounds good, but I'll also need a personal trainer."

"Oh, we can take care of that."

"I want the very best," I said.

"Of course. I have several. Would you prefer a man or a woman?"

"A man."

She smiled, and her capped teeth glittered. "You're not a male chauvinist, are you?"

"When it comes to trainers, I guess I am."

"I know one man. He has several clients here, but he's rather expensive."

"That's not an issue, Tammy."

"When would you like to start?"

"This morning."

That surprised her. "Well, I like a man who knows what he wants. We have several plans here. Are you married? We have a family plan."

"Not married."

She started to list the different plans, and I said, "Just give me the whole nine yards."

"Well, I can certainly do that. We would prefer to have a month in advance."

"I'll pay a year in advance." I took out a roll of bills and peeled off a few; she stared as if hypnotized. I'd discovered that money has that power over people. She took the money reverently and placed it in a drawer. She stood up. "Let me show you around, Mr. Burke."

"Davis is fine."

"Davis then."

The tour was thorough, but I saw nothing I hadn't seen before. There were all of the Nautilus machines, barbells, and a line of treadmills and stair-climbers. The swimming pool was impressive—Olympic-size with ten lanes. No one was in it at this hour, and the water glimmered a pale turquoise. I followed Tammy through the racquetball courts, took a quick glance at the indoor track that looked down on a full-sized basketball court where two tall, limber black men were going one-on-one. The sound of the basketball thumping on the floor made a hollow ringing, and Tammy said, "They're both professional basketball players." She said their names, but I didn't know them since I didn't follow basketball.

We walked outside to the tennis courts where two couples were playing, lobbing the ball back and forth. Turning to me, Tammy said, "What do you think?"

"It looks fine. What about the trainer?"

"The one I have in mind for you is a little bit . . ." She hesitated over a word, then shrugged her shoulders. "Picky, I guess you might say."

"Picky in what way?"

"Well, he doesn't take just anyone."

"What are his criteria?"

"I don't really know. It's not money. He does a lot of work with people who really can't afford him."

"He has to like you? Is that it?"

"No, I think you have to convince him that you're serious."

"I'm serious as income tax, Tammy." I grinned. "Take me to him. Is he here?"

"I think he has an appointment. If you'd care to wait, we have a lounge and TV."

"Thanks. I'll wait."

She took me to the lounge, showed me the coffee and soft drink machines and the bank of magazines. I thanked her.

"I'll come and get you when Trey comes in."

"Trey?"

"That's his name—Trey Jackson."

"I'll be right here."

I watched her walk away. She had one of those girlie walks. I don't know how else to explain it. It made a statement. I picked up a copy of *National Geographic* and read a story about how gorillas are a threatened species. The pictures made me sad. I had always been on the side of the animals in their conflicts with the human race, when it came down to that, and a picture of a mother gorilla holding a baby got to me. I stared at the picture a long time, worrying about gorillas. At other times, I've worried about whales, snail darters, the Alabama beach mouse, and cheetahs. Now I closed the magazine, opened up the current copy of *People*, and slowly turned the pages, studying the strange species that was documented on its pages. They didn't seem to me to be as pretty or as noble as the gorillas.

"Mr. Burke?"

It was a male voice, calling me. By that time, I had immersed myself in the current issue of a magazine apparently written for sixteen-year-old girls. The main thrust of it seemed to be clinical instructions on how to satisfy the sexual needs of a male partner. Ah, sweet mystery of life, where have you gone?

I tossed the magazine down, struggled to my feet, and turned to face the man. "Yes, I'm Davis Burke."

"Trey Jackson."

I waited for him to give me some sort of sales talk, but he just stood there, loosely and at ease, watching me. He was about two inches shorter than I was, and obviously in tip-top physical condition. He had that perfect body you see in swimmers or aerialists at the circus. He was not bulky but was heavier muscled than most men. His skin was the color of dark honey, but his features were aquiline. His eyes were dark brown, and I couldn't read a thing in them. Seeing that he was not going to initiate a sales pitch, I said, "Tammy tells me that you take on a few clients. I need a trainer, as you can see."

"What do you want, Davis?"

I noticed that he didn't bother calling me "Mr. Burke" and that he was rather abrupt. Tammy had been right. He was not knocking down doors to find clients.

"Well, obviously, I need to lose a lot of weight."

"Why?"

"Why!" His short, monosyllabic question puzzled and even angered me. "What do you mean *why*? It's obvious enough, isn't it? I'm killing myself with all this fat."

"That's been going on a long time. Why have you suddenly decided to do something about it?"

"I haven't suddenly decided. I've been trying for years, but nothing works."

Trey Jackson seemed almost disinterested. "What makes you think I can help you?"

"Well, that's your business, isn't it?"

"More or less."

I laughed, liking the man. "I wish you'd quit trying to give me the hard sell, Trey. I don't respond to those tactics."

Jackson smiled slightly but shook his head. "I don't have a lot of time to waste. I can only handle so many clients, and I only take those that are serious."

"I'm serious."

"Are you?" Shrugging his shoulders, Jackson said, "Everybody's serious when they start a program. They go to a doctor, get scared, rush out, and either buy a bunch of expensive exercise equipment or they come to me. Most of them wind up selling their treadmills at a yard sale after using it to gather dust in the bedroom."

I knew this was the man I wanted, but it was obvious that I was going to have to convince him.

"You're a hard man, and that's what I want to be—a hard man. And I know you're telling the truth. I bought the machines and they didn't work. I tried every diet I heard of and they don't work. But I want to be able to look in a mirror without hating myself. I want to buy a single plane ticket instead of two. I want to be a normal human being."

"Lots of folks want that, but it costs too much for most of them."

I was almost stunned by his resistance and a little angry. "Why are you a trainer if you don't want to help people?"

"I *do* want to help people. Most people just don't want to be helped."

"Well, *I* do, and I'm telling you I'll do anything you tell me to do until I can get into a pair of slacks with a thirty-six-inch waist."

Something in the way I spoke must have caught Trey's attention. He stood there poised on the razor's edge, and I could see it in his eyes. "How long have you been obese?"

"Long time. Most of my life."

"I charge fifty dollars an hour."

"That's fine," I said quickly.

"You want to come in three times a week?"

"I want to come in every day."

Trey laughed. "I've heard that before. You won't last. Three times a week is plenty if you do it right."

"No, I want to come in every day."

Trey Jackson studied me, then said, "Well, you put on a good show, but let me tell you, I can't do it for you, Davis. I can tell you what to do and I can show you, but you have to sweat it out for yourself."

He had angered me a little, so I said, "Can't I just hire a member of a minority race to do it for me?"

Jackson's eyes opened wide, and I could see anger rush through him, but then he said, "All right, Burke. You got to me, but now I'm going to get to you. Come on. Let's go get started."

"I didn't bring any clothes."

"You can go get some later. I want to weigh you and check your fat."

I followed him into a room where he put me on the scales.

"Two hundred and ninety-eight."

"A few weeks ago it was four hundred and six," I told him.

He looked at me quickly. "How'd you lose it?"

"I had an accident and I couldn't eat for a while."

He took a pair of calipers, grabbed the fat around my waist, and closed the calipers on the roll. He wrote the figure down and then measured my height.

"An even six feet," he said. "You need to lose a hundred pounds."

"At least."

"You realize that eating has as much to do with losing weight as exercise. It takes both of them."

"You tell me what to eat."

"I'll send you to see a lady. She'll tell you what to eat, but she won't follow you around and snatch the Hershey bar out of your hand when you're about to eat one."

"Little Debbies."

"Whatever. She can't make you not eat, and I can't make you exercise. It's all up to you."

"I'd like to make it interesting for you, Trey."

"Interesting? What does that mean?"

"Let's go on a bonus system. I'll pay your regular fee, and every time I lose five pounds, I'll pay you five hundred dollars."

I had surprised him. He laughed. "That's a bargain, but I'll get that money out of you if I have to cut your leg off. Now, go get some equipment."

"What kind of equipment?"

"Clothes, man, clothes! Doesn't matter what they look like, but I want them to be comfortable. You'll have enough problems without tight pants cutting you in two."

∞

I came back for my first appointment the following morning dressed in loose-fitting sweats.

"I thought you wanted to get in shape. Come on! Lift that weight."

I was lying flat on my back, pushing the barbell. Trey had selected a reasonable enough weight, but by the time I had done one set I was already quivering with fatigue. On the second set I nearly gave up, but he taunted me until I kept at it. Now I was straining and pushing, but the blasted bar wouldn't move.

"Come on. This is the one that's going to do you some good. The one you can't make is the one you got to make. You trying to get out of paying me that bonus?" He grinned.

I struggled and finally managed to shove the bar up the final two times, and he helped me ease the bar into its rack. I lay there panting for breath, and he stood watching me. Finally he looked at his watch and said, "We got a long way to go. I'll see you tomorrow—if you come back."

"I'll—be—back!"

"Maybe you will tomorrow, but you won't make it, Burke."

"Have you ever been wrong?"

"Lots of times."

"You're wrong again. I'll be here at ten o'clock in the morning."

It took all I could do to shower, get dressed, and stagger home. I walked it, and by the time I got to the stairs the temptation to take the elevator was overwhelming. I took the stairs one at a time, and I mean that literally. I would step on one and bring the other foot up. It took me half an hour to get to my floor. My hands were trembling so that I could hardly hit the lock with my key. I closed the door and started for the bedroom. When I got to the bed, I simply collapsed on it and lay there for almost thirty seconds before I went to sleep.

CHAPTER
TWELVE

I woke up and started to get out of bed, then let out a yelp like a wounded coyote. I fell back in the bed. After lying there for a few moments, I pulled myself up more cautiously. I felt like I had been beaten with a boat paddle, but after two weeks of enduring Trey's tortures at the fitness center, pain had become, more or less, a normal condition. I got out of the bed moving slowly, shaved, and then got dressed.

By the time I had breakfast fixed, I was able to move without screaming. The breakfast was scrumptious: a whole egg, three slices of turkey bacon, two pieces of buttered toast—that is, buttered with something that was supposed to be like butter but was not—a small glass of orange juice, and lots of black coffee. I ate as slowly as I could, making each bite last as long as possible, just one of the little tricks of the trade. Thinking about food had become my avocation. I had never realized what a big part food played in my life, but I had certainly learned it now. I woke up thinking about food, thought about it all day, went to sleep thinking about it, then dreamed about it. But aside from that, it didn't bother me much.

I plopped down on the couch with a huge cup of decaf, used the remote to turn on the TV, and watched the news. It was all pretty bad. I wondered what it would be like to watch a station that handled nothing but good news. Probably have a pretty short broadcasting day.

As a network anchorman with pampered hair, a sincere voice, and insincere eyes told me how to feel about things, I thought back to how my life had been before I encountered Dane Fetterman. Getting up, eating a huge breakfast, going to work, coming home, cooking, and playing with my computers. That had been it. It had seemed horrible at the time. Now, though, it at least sounded regular, and I didn't have to work my tail off at a gym under Captain Ahab, the nom de plume of Trey Jackson. It had been a pretty easy life, and the more I thought about it, the more I considered leaving town, flying to the Caribbean, and buying a beach house. I could eat all I wanted, do what I pleased, and no more exercise.

Temptations are subtle, and they catch you at your weakest moment. Now, every morning was my weakest moment. It gave me some sort of sensuous enjoyment to just think about living that kind of life instead of the one I was living now. In Memphis, I might have been a little better off than a lifer in a federal prison, but it hadn't seemed like it at the time.

Even as I was lulling myself into insensibility with dreams of such a life, suddenly I saw Marlene and Dane right there before me on the screen.

It was like getting a bucket of cold water thrown right in my face. I sat straight up and listened as a woman began to speak about the new life of the couple.

"Most of you have been influenced," she said in a high-pitched, bright voice, "by Film Maker. It has proven to be the most widely used entertainment computer program ever invented for the public. Most of us have been able to take our favorite movie star and make them do anything we like.

"Many of you remember the name of the man who gave us this wonderful gift—Oliver Benson. You also remember that Ollie, as he was called by his dearest friends, perished in a tragic automobile accident some months ago."

At this point a picture of me filled the screen, and a chill ran along my spine. Until I changed my appearance by losing weight, I'd have to disguise myself somehow. It was unlikely that anyone would take me for a wealthy dead man, but I didn't intend to take any chances.

The woman's voice grew brighter as she dusted me off and turned to face Marlene and Dane who were sitting at a table wearing swimming suits. They both looked wonderful, tanned and fit, and tried to look pained when the interviewer mentioned my name.

"But life goes on, and we have a happy ending to a sad story. Marlene, you found a new life. Would you care to tell us about it?"

"I can't speak about Ollie. That's just too hard," Marlene said. Her lips quivered a little, and I was astonished at what an actress she was, although if anyone should have known that, it was me. "When I lost Ollie, I lost the whole world. I went completely to pieces, but if it hadn't been for Dane here, I think I would have lost my mind." She reached over, and he took her hand and held it. She gave him a smile that would have toasted bread.

"Well, Dane, I understand you two did find a life after you lost Oliver Benson."

"Ollie was the best friend I ever had," Dane said. He was keeping a stiff upper lip and obviously having a hard time of it. "Marlene wasn't the only one who had a hard time, but things have a way of working out. You know," he said thoughtfully, "there's a power up there that watches over us, I think, and we were so grieved, and neither of us knew what to do. But then . . ." He put his arm around Marlene and drew her close. "We realized that we could have a life together."

"How wonderful! And you've been married how long?"

"Just a week. We are actually going on an extended honeymoon right after this interview," Marlene said.

She looked down for a moment as if overcome, and then looked up, smiling bravely. "We've lost Ollie, and we'll never forget him, but as long as Dane and I are together, there'll always be an Ollie Benson in this world, in our memory."

As I listened to the stupid woman interview them, I felt cold chills. It was a strange feeling, as if an older and crueler Ollie Benson had been born within the jolly fat man.

"Going on a honeymoon? Well, enjoy it," I said softly, then got up and left the apartment.

As I drove across town, I was so filled with cold rage that I ran a red light and almost plowed into a white Jaguar right in front of me. When he heard my brakes squealing, he turned around and glared at me. He made an Italian hand gesture, and I managed to smile, saying, "Have a nice day."

The last thing I needed was an accident, so I forced myself to be cool as I drove to the address I was looking for. I had gone to some trouble to find a good speech and diction teacher, and now when I pulled up in front of a beach house that wasn't as large as the Taj Mahal but wasn't a great deal smaller either, I sat there for a moment and studied it. "Speech and diction teaching must pay pretty well," I muttered. I got out and walked up to the front door and rang the bell. As I stood waiting, I wondered how much the place had cost and whether it had brought happiness to the people who had bought it.

The door opened, and a woman stood looking at me. She had on some sort of silver pants and a gold lamé shirt. She was in her mid-fifties, I guessed, although I think she had a little help. It's not natural for someone middle-aged to have no forehead wrinkles. Botox is the latest miracle.

"I'm Davis Burke. I called earlier. You're Miss Dubose?"

"I'm Carmen Dubose. Come in." She turned and walked away, and I stepped inside, closed the door, and followed her. She led me down a short hall and then to the right into an overly large room. Three sides of it were covered with glass, letting the sun in, and all kinds of modern art adorned the walls. The floor was carpeted in a rug so thick that if you fell over, it would feel like falling into bed.

"Have a seat. Mr. Burke, is it?"

"Yes."

"Will you have a drink?"

"No thanks. This is a beautiful house."

"Not mine. It belongs to a banker from Sacramento."

"Oh."

"The only reason I live with him is because of his house. That and the fact that he doesn't come here more than a day or two a month. What do you want?"

The question was abrupt, and she stared at me with a cold light in her greenish eyes.

"I want voice lessons."

"You're an actor?"

"No, not at all. I just want to do some things different." She stared at me, and I said, "I'm losing weight, trying to do a *makeover*, I think it's called."

"Well, you need one," she said, then laughed. "You'll have to excuse me, Mr. Burke. This hasn't been a good day for me. Do you do drugs?"

The question caught me off guard. "No, I don't, Miss Dubose."

"Well, I do." Without apology, she walked across the room, took something out of a drawer, then came back. She spread some white powder on the glass coffee table, took a razor blade, and arranged it into a nice line. She took a straw, stuck one end of it in her nose, leaned down, and dragged the other end of the straw across the white powder, which promptly disappeared.

"Sure you don't want a snort?"

"No, thank you. I'm fine."

She took the cocaine with no more embarrassment than if she had taken a sip of water. I hadn't gotten around much in California, especially with the movie-making people, but I had heard that they kept drugs out at their parties for guests to sample as you might sample punch at a Christmas party.

"Well, I need money, and I'm not cheap—at least not about money." She smiled. Even as I watched her, she changed into another person. I had never seen cocaine used before, and it shocked me how the hardness evaporated. She became softer, more vulnerable, and a warm smile touched her broad lips. "So tell me about it. I'd like to help you if I can."

"Well, Miss Dubose—"

"Carmen is fine."

"Well, Carmen, I'm going to be moving in different circles, and I need to change everything about myself. I'm in that process right now. But I don't know how to change the way I talk. How does one do that?"

"One hires me." Carmen smiled. She reached over and patted my hand and said, "What part of the South are you from?" She laughed. "Your Southern accent is charming, but I assume it's what you want to get rid of."

"Yes."

"I've done this for many people, especially young women who come from the South and want to get into movies. The first thing to know is that there isn't a lot I can do about the timbre of your voice—the tone. And I wouldn't think you'd need to. You have a very nice voice, not too deep. A man with a big, deep baritone voice isn't all that much in demand, and high tenors are great for opera but not for speaking. Your voice is very nice."

"That doesn't sound too hopeful."

"Oh, I don't mean to depress you. I think we can do something that will please you very much. You must remember that you've been using your own voice for how long, twenty-five—thirty years?"

"About twenty-five."

"Well, one thing that you can do is to learn to speak with an accent."

"You mean German or French?"

"No, not for you. You don't have the Nordic look or the French look either. I would suggest either English or Australian. Canadian is much easier, but it doesn't change enough. I would suggest Australian."

"Is that very hard to learn?"

"Anything is hard that you've been doing all your life and you decide not to do anymore. But I assume you are losing weight as part of your makeover."

"Well, yes, I am."

"Is that easy?"

"No, very hard."

"It's hard because previously you ate what you wanted and did what you wanted. Now you can't. It's the same with diction. But I can help you. The simplest thing is to work on the way you pronounce words. What do you call a garment that a man sleeps in?"

"You mean *pajamas*?"

"Yes. The way you pronounce that one word would tell anyone that you came from the South."

"How did I say it?"

"You said pa*jah*mas, with a broad A. Anyone from north of the Mason Dixon line would call it pa*jam*as, as in strawberry *jam*. How do you say the name of the animal that goes around on four legs saying 'bow wow'?"

"You mean *dog*?"

"You're calling it *daieog*. That's a diphthong, the voice sliding up and down with the vowel. Most Yankees would pronounce it *dahg*, with one syllable. What do you call the place where you go to check out books?"

"The library."

Carmen laughed. "That's a dead giveaway. You called it *lyeberry*, leaving out the *R*. You've got to change your *R* up to a different position."

I ran my hand over my hair. "I don't even know I'm saying these things."

"No, but I do. It will only take two sessions to get through those. We can start today if you like."

"I'd like that."

"I've done this so often that I've got it all printed out. I'll get it for you."

We spent the better part of an hour going over the words, and when we were finished, Carmen said, "I want you to watch all the Australian movies you can, like *Crocodile Dundee* or *Gallipoli*. And I want you to listen to some tapes." She left the room and came back in a few moments with some tapes in a shopping bag. "We can go as fast or as slow as you want to."

"Fast is good for me."

"Well, this is Tuesday. Come back Thursday. By that time I want you to practice what these tapes do and learn to say them over and over again."

"I appreciate your taking me on. Here, let me give you a check."

"I get two hundred dollars a session," she said coolly. When she saw I didn't flinch, she said, "I didn't ask enough, did I?"

"Maybe there'll be a bonus at the end."

I gave her the check. She glanced at it, then put it on the table. She stood and walked to the door. "Do your homework, Davis," she said, then smiled and put her hand on my cheek.

"I'll give you a reward if you do well." I couldn't think of a thing to say, and she laughed. "I can't believe it—an innocent male! But don't worry, darling, I'll find some way to defile you." She laughed again, then stepped inside and shut the door. As I went back to the car, I wondered if there were any normal voice teachers—but I doubted it.

∞

I listened to the tapes for hours. I knew that a new voice wasn't something I could put on as you put on a different shirt. I had to speak the same way *all* the time. Once I went into action with Dane and Marlene, it would have to be flawless. Much of it was learning to use different words like *lift* for *elevator* and *windscreen* for *windshield*. And then, of course, the abbreviated "g'day" for "good day."

I listened to the tapes over and over again. They were recorded by a man simply speaking about different things under different circumstances. I realized very quickly that the melody or rhythm of the Australian dialect would be the most difficult thing, but I worked hard at it and I must have watched *Gallipoli* twenty times. It's a terrible movie, an anti-war film, but I soaked in the speech of the actors and when it got too grim I could always watch *Crocodile Dundee* for laughs.

∞

Why you talking so funny, Davis?"
I had just picked up a barbell and was prepared to do curls with it when I saw that Trey was staring at me. "You trying out for a play or something?"

"Well, something like that."

I began to do the curls, but Trey wasn't satisfied. "Has this got something to do with losing weight? Looks to me like you're trying to change everything about yourself."

"Most of it needs changing."

Trey stared at me and shook his head. "Why you doing all this?"

"Because I don't like the old me. I want to change the way I look, the way I talk, and just about everything else about myself."

Trey waited until I had done one set and put the barbell down. Then he said, "When did you decide to do all this?"

"Fairly recently."

Trey had a way of looking at a fellow that made you feel kind of guilty for some reason. "Look, Trey, you see what I look like. Fat as a hippopotamus. Couldn't have any normal life with a woman. Who would want to marry a blimp?"

"What does that have to do with your voice?" he asked critically.

"Just don't ask questions. You don't know what it's like, Trey, being fat."

"Something like being black, I'd guess," he mused, and he laughed. "Difference is you can stop being fat, but I'm going to be black until they bury me."

"It's not the same thing," I said.

We kept on doing weights, and he was quiet for a while, then said, "I had two Miss Americas for clients—not at the same time. There they were, the two most beautiful women in America, according to the judges, and you know what, Davis? They didn't like the way they looked. They were always trying to do something to their faces or their bodies."

"I don't understand that."

"I didn't either. Some of the happiest people I've known were pretty homely. You'd better be careful," he said. "It isn't what's up front that counts. It's what's inside."

"Are you preaching at me, Trey?"

"Me? No. I'm just saying be careful."

"You just get me into a size thirty-six waist, and I'll take care of the inside."

Trey must have seen that he had crossed a line, because he changed the subject. "I think we'll cut back on the weight lifting some."

"Why? I'm losing weight and getting stronger too."

"Yeah, but any idiot can lift weights and build all kinds of chunky muscles. If the object is to lift the front end of a car or make the girls say 'Oooh,' that's all right, but they aren't the best kind of muscles to have."

"What's the best kind?"

"Well," he said thoughtfully, "you want a muscle structure that'll help you move very quickly. Quickness, that's where it all lies. You always need to keep in mind, Davis, what the body was designed for. I think it was designed for running long distances, and climbing trees, and carrying weights. So you need to work in a way that'll help you do that. Besides, most exercise is too hard on the body."

I looked at him in surprise. "But you *have* to exercise."

"Sure, but too many deep knee bends will ruin your knees in time. Too many push-ups—same thing. Weight lifting selects muscles and makes them big and bulky, so that's not all good. So instead you take to jogging on hard surfaces. But if you do that long enough, you'll hurt the rest of your life. Stretching is a lot better. We haven't got into that yet."

"Stretching?"

"Sure. Watch cats sometimes. They stretch a lot. They twist and bend. We're going to get into that pretty soon. You don't lose as much weight, but it limbers up your body, loosens everything up."

"I don't have time for that."

"I'd like to know what your big hurry is," he said. "But I got my standards."

"You may have to lower them for me."

"No, you may have to find another trainer."

I glared at him for a moment and then laughed. "All right. Tell me more."

"Who are the most perfectly conditioned people in the world?"

"I don't know. Who?"

"Dedicated, professional dancers, circus fliers, tumblers, combat rangers. Every time you get close to one of those people, you can hear their motors humming. Lots of lung capacity, and the whites of their eyes almost always a blue white."

"It would be easier to get contact lenses."

"Yeah, you're funny and all that, but now I've got a personal interest in you. You're going to start doing more stuff that's good for you. Come on," he said. "We'll start now."

"We aren't through with the weights."

"You've done enough of that. Come on."

He took me to the racquetball court and handed me a racquet. "Hit this against the wall," he said.

"I'm not into tennis."

"This isn't tennis. This is racquetball."

"Just hit the thing against the wall?"

"Yeah. Then when it comes back to you, hit it back again."

I took the ball and whomped it. When it bounced back, I batted it again. I kept it up, and finally Trey said, "Now, you let me hit every other ball. I'm going to make you reach a little bit."

He wasn't kidding! He put the ball just enough out of my reach that I had to lunge for it. In two minutes I was panting and gasping for breath like a fish thrown out on the shore. I kept it up though, until he stopped. I stood there dripping sweat and staring at him, trying to make it look like I could breathe.

"You got reflexes," he said.

"Everybody's got reflexes."

"No, not like you got. I gave you some pretty tough things there. You never played this before?"

"No. Never did."

"Here. Stick your hands out palm up, both of them."

I stared at him and then shrugged. I put my racquet down and stuck my hands out palm up. He put his hands right on top of mine and said, "Now, I want you to slap the back of my hands as hard as you can."

"Which one?"

"Any one you can."

I didn't know what he was doing, but I moved my right hand and caught his right hand right on the top. I saw his eyes open wide, and he looked up at me without a word. "Do it again," he said. He put his hands out, and I tried again. This time it was harder, but I caught just a piece of his left hand with the tip of my fingers.

"Again."

Pretty soon I was hitting the top of his hands at least every other time.

"Here, put your hands on top of mine." He stuck his hands out palm up, and I did. "Now, I'm going to slap your hands. You jerk away and keep me from it."

When I felt his hands leave mine, I jerked mine back and he missed. "Nah, nah, you missed me!" I grinned.

"Try that again."

He was fast, but I made him miss half the time.

"What does all this prove?" I said.

"It proves that you've got fast reflexes—very fast. Not many guys have been able to match me in this game."

"Well, if life ever becomes a contest of hand slapping, then I'll have a chance."

Trey wasn't laughing. He was staring at me hard. "I've never seen a fellow so quick, except professional athletes. Next time you come we're going to start you on karate."

"I don't want to do that stuff."

"Remember what we agreed on? What you want don't count. It's what *I* want that counts. I think you'll be good at it," he said, ignoring me. "Martial arts is about reflexes. Most sports are. I ran the slowest dashes of any guy in the backfield for the Rams. You know how I kept my job? I wasn't the fastest on my feet, but I was the quickest. You got to out-quick 'em." He stared at me, then said, "You're up to something, Davis. Something I can't figure out. Be glad to listen if you ever want to tell me. Now, go home."

I showered and went home, but as I was showering I was thinking, *I can't be a friend to Trey, and he can't be my friend. You have to trust people, but I don't trust anybody—not anymore.* I toweled myself off thinking about that, and when I was dressed, I combed my hair and stared at my face in the mirror. It was thinner now, not just a ball of fat. I hardly knew the man I was looking at. There was nobody in the room with me, and I whispered out loud, "Maybe after I settle with Marlene and Dane, I can start trusting people."

But I knew there was something wrong with that.

CHAPTER THIRTEEN

I reached up to get the brush for my hair and something happened that had never happened in my life.

My pants fell off!

I mean it. I always tried to look skinnier by wearing tight pants, which is a mistake, I know. But now I stood staring down at my pants gathered around my feet, pulled them up, and realized that they were at least two inches too big. I stepped out of them, walked over to the scale, and stepped onto it.

Two hundred and eighty pounds—I'd lost twenty pounds!

Trey had warned me not to go to the scale every day. It was like going to the mailbox looking for a check. It just irritated you. So I hadn't stepped on it since I started working out, two months earlier. I knew I had lost some weight—I was moving easier and could climb the stairs now without gasping. Now I stared down at the pants and realized that this was a victory like D-day. I still had eighty pounds to go, but I knew now that it could be done, not just out at Eli's cabin but in the real world.

I fastened my belt, and it gave me great satisfaction to pull it back to a notch that had never been used. I went into the kitchen whistling and fixed breakfast: grapefruit, oatmeal, toast with blackberry jelly, and juice. I sat down and ate it slowly. I had learned two things about eating: eat slowly and eat often. When Trey told me that, I thought it was wrong.

"Eat often?" I said. "That's how I got fat."

"Don't eat *big* often. Eat *little* often," he said. "Just a bite or two of something. Half an apple. Just something to keep your jaws working."

So I'd done that now for two months. I kept all kinds of fruit around, and I had learned that you could buy candy bars that had practically no calories in them. They tasted pretty much like Sheetrock, but it was something to eat. At least it worked better than fasting.

As I cleaned up the kitchen, I remembered asking my doctor back home in Memphis about diet pills. He was a big fellow himself, and he had stared at me in disbelief. "Diet pills!" he spat out. "If diet pills worked, do you think I'd look like this?" So much for diet pills!

As I moved around the apartment cleaning up, I spoke out loud. Didn't matter what I said, but I practiced the Australian dialect. I had it down pretty well, I thought. Carmen thought so too. I had been there twice a week every week, and she had tried to defile me in every way she could think of, and some that shocked me. I hadn't found it too hard to resist her, though.

As part of my makeover, I'd decided to take dancing lessons. I had an appointment at ten, so to kill time I tried to watch the video of a currently popular movie. It was probably bad enough to win an Academy Award. The critics all loved it, which meant it had to be bad. As a matter of fact, I'd come to hate most movies and *all* situation comedies.

I gave up on the movie and picked up a book on Australia. I had given myself a course in Australian history and geography, and I read something every day about that country. It made me want to go there. It sounded like a great place.

Finally I got up and changed clothes. I had bought some new clothes that made me look less like a Goodyear blimp, but before I put them on I tried something.

I'd bought a pair of slacks with a thirty-six-inch waistline. I hadn't even tried them on, of course, because I knew that I couldn't get into them with a shoehorn. But now in the privacy of my bedroom I slipped them on and pulled them up. There was no way I could zip them up, of course, and I stared down at them. "One of these days, buddy, you're going to zip nice and easy, and I'm going to wear you out of this room."

I took them off, put on some of the newer clothes I'd bought, and left the apartment.

∞

The dance studio wasn't busy that early in the morning. My teacher proved to be a young woman named Caitlin Marlow. She was a good-looking girl trying to look too much like Marilyn Monroe. She said, "Let's have something to drink first. Coffee? Soft drink? You can tell me what you'd like to learn."

"Coffee for me," I said. I didn't know exactly what I did want, so I said, "Have you been doing this long?"

"Oh, I'm just between jobs. I'm an actress."

"Really! Have I seen you in anything?"

"Not unless you look quick." She smiled and named a couple of movies that she'd been in very briefly. "I want to be an actress more than anything in the world. I always have."

"Why do you want that?" I said, genuinely puzzled.

She looked shocked at the question. "Why, it's everything I want."

I tried my smile out on her. Somewhere along the line I was going to have to go to charm school or its equivalent. That was part of my plan. Now I said, "Well, I didn't think of that, but now that I think of it, all stars are happily married, grow old gracefully, and are very happy."

"Oh, you're too hard on them."

"Well, how many Hollywood stars do you know who have held a marriage together?"

"Well, let's see. There's Jimmy Stewart."

"He's dead."

"Yes, he is, isn't he? Well—" Her list of happily married Hollywood stars, long-term at least, was very short, and finally she grew embarrassed and said, "Do you dance at all?"

"Not at all."

"What kind of dancing do you want to do?"

"I want to do whatever people are doing right now."

She laughed. "They're not into dancing much. Just kind of moving around. Well, come along. We'll start with just a little of the old-fashioned stuff, just like Clark Gable and Princess Grace."

Actually I had danced a little bit, and she gave me a few instructions. She put on a record I recognized. "That's a Tommy Dorsey," I said.

"I like to listen to the old ones once in a while. You weren't telling me the truth, were you?"

"About what?"

"About not dancing."

"Not enough to amount to anything."

"Well, you're doing very well. You know you move very well for a—" She broke off.

I was able to finish it for her. "A fat man?"

"I–I was going to say *big*. Some people can't dance a bit and never will, but I can tell I won't have you for long."

"Well, I don't even know what kind of dancing to learn. I haven't been in the mainstream."

"I'll teach you a little bit of everything. The newest dances are the easiest. People just stand on their feet and do what they please."

"A sign of the times."

"I guess so."

∽

I was gasping for breath, but when I looked over at Trey as he returned my serve, he was breathing hard too. It was the first time I had ever seen him do that. He seemed to be made of rhino hide and steel wire, and he apparently had concealed oxygen tanks. But he was huffing and puffing now, just a little bit.

"Hey, you out of breath, Trey? You want to take a rest?"

"You go hang!" Trey gave me a hard look, then laughed. "You're gonna beat the old man some day. When you do, you're out of here. I don't like to lose."

I doubt that I could ever beat Trey at racquetball. He was just too good for that. But it made me feel good that I was making progress.

"Come on. I got a present for you," he said. We left the racquetball court. I followed him into the dressing room, and he reached into his locker and pulled out a sack. "Get into these."

I took the sack and pulled out what was inside. "What's this?"

"A martial arts outfit. Put it on. I had to guess at the size, but they're all supposed to be loose anyhow."

I clambered into the white, loose-fitting outfit, and by the time I was finished Trey was wearing his. "Come on. I intend to hurt you bad."

"I hate martial arts movies," I complained.

"So do I, but in moderation it's good for you. I don't know what you're trying to make yourself into, Davis, but it never hurts to be able to take care of yourself."

I followed him into a room I hadn't been in yet. It had pads on the floor, and Trey began to speak very slowly, as if I were retarded. He threw me over his shoulder in slow motion, and he did it so easily I might have been made of foam rubber. Then he speeded it up. He would tell me what he was going to do, and then he would do it before I could even move. "You're real quick. You'll catch on to it."

By the time we got through I was puffing, but I sensed he was doing me a favor. "Does this stuff really work?"

"An expert can whip you quick, and an amateur can kill you without meaning to, so I'm not going to give you much of a chance to do that. But as a means of self-defense, everything in this sport is based on a wrong assumption."

"What do you mean?"

"It's based on the idea that your opponent is going to play by the rules."

"And they don't?"

"They do in a regular match, sure, but if you meet somebody out in the alley, forget it! The same thing is true of boxing. Lots of good boxers get their brains scrambled in a brawl. They know how to block a left, but when somebody picks up a bottle and breaks it over their head, they're not trained to prevent it."

"It doesn't sound like studying martial arts does much good."

"It has its uses. Good physical training. You see these movies where they beat up on each other and take blow after blow? Davis, the average man is so unaccustomed to pain that if you break his nose, he'll cry about it for an hour. He won't be thinking about the next karate move."

"It's getting late and I haven't eaten. Can I treat you to dinner?"

∞

At the steakhouse, Trey ordered fried chicken and biscuits. I stared at him. "That's full of fat grams."

"I grew up on ghetto food—moon pies and R.C. Cola. It might hurt you white folks, but not me."

I cautiously ordered a six-ounce steak, a salad, and a baked potato. When it came, I ate all of the salad and steak, and half of the potato.

I watched Trey devouring the fried chicken and biscuits. It was disgusting! He'd make a little hole in the top of the biscuit, fill it full of white gravy, and then scarf it down. "How can you eat that stuff and stay in shape?"

"Well, what I'm doing is *maintaining*. I'm right where I want to be. It's kind of in balance, you might say. If I eat too much today, I can eat too little tomorrow. But don't you go trying it. You ain't maintaining, you're trying to get there."

I had been half-watching two women across from us. "I think those women are after you, Trey."

"Why should they be different?" Trey grinned.

"Aren't you interested?"

"No."

"Are you married?"

The answer came quickly, sharp and cold. "Not anymore." The door was closed, and I fumbled around drinking my coffee to cover up my discomfort.

"You married?" Trey asked.

"No. Never was."

The conversation had taken a wrong turn. I paid the check and we got up and left. We walked along the streets. It was early summer. We had worked out until late, and now it was dark. I heard a man's voice and looked up to see an older man in an ill-fitting suit. He was holding a Bible in one hand and making gestures with the other. A street preacher. I'd seen them often enough in Memphis, and they always embarrassed me. I would cross the street to avoid getting close to them.

This man was a little different. He was in his fifties, I guessed, a small man whose hair was salt-and-pepper gray. He looked like a working man, and I was surprised when Trey stopped to listen.

I stopped with him. When I glanced at him, Trey's face revealed nothing, but then it never did. I began to listen to what the man was saying, and just as I did, he opened his Bible and began to read.

"'For if you forgive men when they sin against you, your heavenly Father will also forgive you. But if you do not forgive men their sins, your Father will not forgive your sins.'"

I recognized the passage; it came from the Sermon on the Mount. I stood listening as the preacher continued to speak about the importance of forgiveness. It made me uncomfortable and I wanted to go, but I felt Trey move. I looked at him. He had turned to watch four young men coming across the street. Two of them were black, one was Hispanic, and one was white. I'd seen street gangs often enough on the streets of Memphis to recognize them. They were laughing, and I heard one of them say, "Look, let's go see what the preacher says."

One of the blacks reached out and grabbed the preacher's Bible. "What you got there, preacher, a Bible? Maybe I ought to take over the preaching here."

I felt Trey move, and he stepped forward and said in a dangerous voice, "Give it back."

The black whirled and stared at Trey. His pupils weren't normal; he was high on something. "You ain't gonna take sides with white bread here against a brother, are you?"

Trey took another step forward. "Give the Bible back to the man, or I may have to chastise you, brother." He made the word *brother* sound like an insult. The hood kept the Bible in his left hand and came around with a blow that would have destroyed Trey, but something happened. It happened too fast for me to see it, but suddenly the kid was down, struck by a blow he never saw.

At once there was an outcry of rage, and the three others charged in against Trey. It happened so fast I could only stand there. Trey moved fast, but one of them had come around behind

Trey with something on his hand—brass knuckles, I thought, the first I had ever seen. He raised them to hit Trey in the back of the head, and without thinking I grabbed him and threw him down. He came rolling to his feet and headed straight for me.

I had never been in a fight in my life and knew that there was no way I could keep him from half killing me with those brass knuckles. I managed to block the blow, then reached out and put my hands behind his neck. I jerked his head forward, ducking my head at the same time, and felt something snap as his nose hit my head. He was screaming and beating at me, but I had a good hold on his throat, and I continued to beat his head against the top of my skull. It hurt but not as much as getting hit in the face with brass knuckles.

And then somebody was pulling me back, and Trey was saying, "All right, he's had it, Davis. You don't have to kill him."

I stopped and looked down at the face of the kid I was holding by the throat. His eyes were rolled up, and his face was bloody. Blood was running from his nose and his mouth, and when I let him go, he fell bonelessly to the street.

"Come on. Let's get out of here," Trey said. The other three were stirring, holding themselves and staring at us. Trey grabbed the preacher's arm and said, "Come on, dad, let's get out of here."

We moved down the street, turned the corner, and Trey drew a deep breath. "This is a dangerous line of work you're in, preacher," he said. "Go find you a church somewhere."

The preacher stared at Trey. He was holding the Bible in both hands, and shock was in his eyes. "I can't do it, son. Jesus sent me here to the streets to preach his Word."

Trey shook his head and started off. I pulled some money out of my pocket, peeled off a hundred, and handed it to the preacher. He looked at it, then said, "Thank you, brother. May the Lord restore it to you a hundredfold."

I caught up with Trey. He was walking rapidly, and it was all I could do to keep up. Finally he slowed down, took a deep breath, and expelled it. He said, "You did real good, man. That kid would have had me, I think."

"First fight I was ever in."

"I hope it's your last." He was quiet for a while, and then he said, "I kind of lost it back there, Davis. I had a brother get killed in Detroit by a gang member like that. I went after the guy who did it and nearly killed him, but you know what? That wasn't enough. I still think of ways I'd like to hurt him."

I couldn't think of anything to say, and finally I said, "I'm sorry, Trey."

Trey turned to me, and I saw something in him that I had never seen before. "If I see that dude again, I *will* kill him."

He turned away without another word and left. I watched him go, and then I started toward home, but when I got there, I was still thinking about the fight. I was having some kind of reaction and my hands were shaking. I went up the stairs easily without thinking anything about it.

It was early, and I took a shower and looked at the top of my head, which hurt. I wondered about the poor kid I had battered. I read for a while, but I couldn't forget about Trey and how the violence had exploded out of him. When I went to bed, I replayed the scene again and again, still not quite believing that I had been part of it. I had never done anything violent in my life, but I saw now that I could. "Do I want to be like this?"

When I went to sleep, I was still seeing the bloody face of the young man I had battered—and I didn't like it.

CHAPTER
FOURTEEN

Einstein was right—all time is relative. As someone pointed out, sixty seconds in a dentist's chair can seem like a month, while sixty years with the one you love can seem like nothing.

For the past seven months, time had seemed to be on hold. As I stood in my bedroom holding the slacks in my hands, I thought back over the months that had slid by, and in one sense it seemed like an eternity. But in another, it seemed like only yesterday that I first went to meet with Trey at the fitness center.

I thought of the hopelessness when the weight just simply would *not* come off. When I had *plateaued*, as Trey put it, and no matter how little I ate or how much I worked out, the stubborn bathroom scales refused to go down even an ounce. But I also remembered how shocked I was when I had in one week lost enough weight that I could not believe what those same scales were saying.

All of the days and weeks and even months were now joined in a seamless memory, and as I slipped my left foot and then my right foot into the slacks, I realized that this was one of those moments in life that you never forget. Everyone can remember where they were the day the World Trade Center and Pentagon were attacked, and I knew that in that same way I would always remember pulling up the size thirty-six slacks that I had kept as a test. I pulled the waistband together and, without holding my stomach in, snapped them. I pulled the zipper up and then stood there numbly. I had never really believed that I would be able to get into a size thirty-six waist. It was sort of a forlorn hope that goes into that little box that everyone keeps called "impossible dreams."

But the slacks fit perfectly! I walked into the bathroom and looked at myself in the full-length mirror, and it was as if I were seeing a stranger. I hadn't put on my shirt, and my mind went back to what I had been most of my life, spilling out of my clothes with the largest belt that I could find cutting me in two, pale, pasty-looking with mousy-colored hair and eyes hidden behind thick glasses.

But what I saw now was entirely different. I leaned forward and studied my face. Now that all the fat was melted away, the V-shaped structure of my face that I had never even dreamed of was evident, from a broad forehead down to a chin that was prominent but determined. I had a deep tan, something I had never had before because I was too ashamed of what I looked like—a beached whale. California was the place for a tan, no doubt about that, but I had gotten help from the tanning salon.

The hair, which had been a nondescript brown, was now, according to the master work of Jacque the hairdresser, a tawny color. Not blonde and not brown but somewhere in between. It was crisp and curly and much longer than I had ever worn it. The eyes were a warm brown—nothing like the blue eyes I'd had all my life. They gave me a direct look, instead of the watery blue that I was accustomed to.

I studied my neck—not thick like an offensive lineman's, but strong, and the chest beneath it swelled out, with the pects pushing against the T-shirt. The waistline was trim, and the abs were clearly defined. The arms and shoulders were lean but corded with muscle.

I stared at myself in the mirror, and it was like staring at a stranger. At six feet, I was an even one hundred and eighty-nine pounds, which Trey said was just right for me—that if I gained any more I would lose a little reaction time and speed.

But I still *felt* fat, especially when I closed my eyes. It was as if this man who could have stepped off the pages of *GQ* disappeared, and in his place I was still Ollie Benson, obese and pale and carrying enough inhibitions for an army. I opened my eyes then and said aloud, *"That's* who you are, Davis—that guy in the mirror. Forget about Ollie Benson." But I knew I would never be able to forget Ollie Benson. A lifetime of living as I had lived with the limitations that I had borne can't be wiped away.

I went to the closet, got out a grey houndstooth sports shirt with a button-down roll collar, and slipped into it. I studied myself in the mirror, thinking of how much money and effort went into the world of fashion—and how worthless it was. The instant a human being's heart stops beating, it couldn't matter less what necktie you have on or what dress label you have. It's all over.

I picked up my billfold, put it in my pocket, and the thought crossed my mind that I had more cash in it now than I would have had in a year of hard work repairing videos. The television was on—an interview with the latest celebrity and his burning flame of the moment. The two of them would swear eternal loyalty and love—and within a few months, each of them would have been replaced by another eternal love. I had spent a great deal of time over the past months going to plays, watching the new movies, reading the gossip columns. I knew now not only about the stars but about the directors and the critics, and I could talk froth with the best of them.

As I left my apartment and walked down the stairs, the thought crossed my mind, *There's no way that anyone could ever recognize me except through fingerprints.* I had kept in touch with Eli but had used a drop so that the letters he received were postmarked from different cities. I had not revealed anything about my new life, and as far as Eli knew, Ollie Benson had simply moved away and was keeping in touch.

I went out on the street and glanced up at the hard blue sky. Spring, which comes early here, in March, was already upon us. I got into the car and drove across town. Los Angeles is a Disneyland in many respects. It's not the real world. Make-believe, pretend, images are all very important here. Of course, there are ordinary people here too—by the thousands. But even they, I think, are affected by the artificiality of Hollywood more here than in other places. I'd come to believe that New York and California were all a man needed to control America. If he controlled those two places, the heart of the image-making factory that tells us how we are to think and feel about things, he wouldn't have to worry about all the states in between. People got up in the morning throughout the country and tuned in on either New York or California to find out how to feel. Most of the smiling, sleekly groomed media are born—or maybe assembled—in these places, or find their way there. I couldn't think of anything more depressing than having Peter Jennings tell me how I ought to feel.

But by the time I got to the Porsche dealership, I put all of this out of my mind. When I'd parked the Town Car and gone inside, I was greeted by a tall man, immaculately dressed. He had a sincere expression and greeted me with an artificial warmth that froze any good feeling I might have felt toward him. "Yes, sir, may I help you?"

"I want a Porsche."

"Which one, sir?"

"The best one you have. If you were going to buy a Porsche to impress people, which one would you buy?"

My question caught him off guard. He was evidently accustomed to more sophisticated approaches and actually began to stammer.

"Cut to the chase," I snapped. "I want the most expensive, impressive Porsche you have. We both know that people don't buy a Porsche to go from point A to point B. They buy them to make a statement about how important they are. Most of them don't know that more good people drive Fords and Chevrolets and Dodges than drive Porsches."

The salesman simply stared at me, unable to respond. I laughed and said, "Sorry to be so blunt, but I'm in a hurry. Bring me the best you've got at the ranch . . ."

∽

As I drove the Porsche back toward the apartment, I couldn't help thinking how shocked the salesman had been to be confronted with truth. He had become convinced that the important people in this world could be identified by the cars they drove, but it was easy enough to see how he had come to this conclusion.

It was early then, and I decided to get something to eat. The restaurant I stopped at was exclusive, and I had eaten there often enough to be recognized by the maître d'. He smiled warmly. "Ah, Mr. Burke. Good to see you, sir."

"Thank you, George."

"Come this way, sir. I have a very good table for you."

I'd run across a most unusual verse in the Bible. I had been reading the Bible some, especially the Old Testament, the past few months—more out of curiosity than anything else, perhaps spurred by the street preacher Trey and I had defended, or by the time I'd spent with Eli. I was amazed at how many things I recognized in it. I felt like the young student reading Shakespeare for the first time who had been shocked to discover how many quotations were in it.

As I sat down and George smiled and informed me that a server would be there quickly, the quotation leaped into my mind: "Money is the answer for everything."

The server came, a short Mediterranean type, gave me what he considered his winning smile, and then took my order.

When I had first read that line about money answering all things, I had felt something almost like an electric shock. My first thought was, *Everyone's been reading the Bible all wrong*. Most people believed that the Bible taught that money was an evil of some kind. I vaguely remember a sermon I had heard when my mom took me to church—something about a rich man who came to Jesus Christ, and Christ told him to sell everything he had. And I remember clearly that when Jesus' followers asked him why he'd said that, he said, "It's hard for a rich man to get to heaven."

But how did that match up with "Money is the answer for everything"? As I sat watching the customers eat, I was still puzzled. I had gone back to that verse again and again, and finally I decided that it was absolutely true. If you translated it into modern English, it would be something like, "Money will buy anything."

I decided, as I waited for my order, that if you put the emphasis on *thing*, that's true enough. Bill Gates can buy any *thing* he wants, any car, any house. He could even buy his way into power in any country. Money buys *things*.

It was even going to buy me revenge, and revenge isn't exactly a thing. I realized that if I didn't have plenty of money, my master plan to cut the ground from under the feet of Dane and Marlene would never work. Money was good for that.

Yet I wondered: What about something that's not a thing? Love, for instance, is not a thing, and no matter if I've got a hundred million dollars, it can't buy me love from a person. The thought disturbed me, and I pushed it out of my mind, glad when the food was set before me.

I'd ordered fish and steamed vegetables. By now I had reached the point where I was simply maintaining, as Trey was. I didn't have to starve myself or work eight hours in the gym. My body had reached the point now where as long as I maintained it, I would pretty well remain the same. I had worked out the things I liked to do, such as swimming, tennis, and running—not on an indoor track but outside. These things had become a pleasure to me. As far as the food, I would even eat a Little Debbie now and then just to show myself I could do it.

As I ate, I became aware that a woman sitting across the room from me was very much interested. It was not that she looked at me so much. There just seems to be some mystical attraction between men and women. I had read that the male butterfly is aware of the female in a way that scientists had not yet been able to understand. They would come from miles to find this female. I had discovered that the human species is not a great deal different. As I had dropped my excess weight and slowly begun improving my appearance, women that would never have given me a look before suddenly seemed to be everywhere—in the theater, on the streets, on the beach. They were just simply there in a way they never had been before. It puzzled me, and I wondered exactly how it worked. But in all likelihood, there is no logical explanation. Money answers all things—and money had transformed me into nectar that had brought the butterflies from wherever they come from to wherever I happened to be.

She was in her late twenties, I guessed—tall with rich, auburn hair and a perfect complexion. Her face was a cross between a fashion model's and a porn queen's, both reserved and sensuous.

She was wearing a navy silk sheath dress with a low neckline and short sleeves, and it ended just above her knees. It hugged her figure perfectly, yet still left a little bit to the imagination. A jacket of the same material, with white opal buttons along the front and at the wrists, hung on the back of her chair, and her exquisite shoes were blue leather with three-inch heels. The dress and the rings on her fingers made two statements that should have been mutually exclusive: "Hands off!" and "Come to me!" Right now the "come to me" was not obvious, but it was there. Only once did she look at me, and when my eyes met hers, she did not look flustered but studied me in a way that I couldn't quite understand. I still knew very little about women, but during the last few months I had gone out several times, mostly with women like this. I had no idea how to pick them up, but I discovered that if you have enough money and if you're good-looking, there's no wrong way.

I finished my meal, got up, and had to pass her table. I stopped beside her and said, "The food's good here, isn't it?"

It wouldn't have mattered what I said. I might have said in Swahili, "There are chinch bugs in the cucumber patch," and I would have gotten the same reaction. She was obviously waiting for me to speak, and she looked up and smiled and said, "Yes, it is."

That was all she said—"Yes, it is"—but I knew that she had opened the door. It was easy for me to say, "Do you eat here often?" And from that moment on she and I were bosom buddies, so to speak.

At her invitation I sat down and had a cup of coffee while she had her dessert. We left the restaurant together and went to a place where there was dancing. She drank and was surprised and intrigued when I drank only Diet Coke.

As we danced, she made her offer to me just in the way she touched me, and something in her eyes sent out a signal. She leaned against me deliberately, and I was stirred by the raw sexuality. All the time I was thinking, *There's not much difference between this and butterflies. The male butterfly doesn't ask the female butterfly what she thinks about anything. He's not interested in that.* It was pure animal magnetism—that's what this woman was offering. There was no pretense that we were soulmates or had values in common. This was simply a thing of the flesh.

The evening for me was an exercise in a skill that I needed to hone. I had missed out on years of learning how women think and how they operate, and now I was taking a crash course on how to play the game. I took her home, and she turned to me and asked me in for a drink, and when I said that I was sorry but I had an appointment, she stared at me in disbelief. I knew that I had bruised her ego. When I turned and left, I noticed that she was staring at me as if I were an alien from another planet.

So I went home, thought about how easy it would have been to have stayed the night with her, but for some reason that was not what I was after—although I certainly felt the urges that come to a lonely man when a beautiful woman offers herself. As I brushed my teeth and went to bed and read for a time, the thought kept coming to me, *What is it you want? She was right there for you.*

It was then that I realized that no woman would satisfy me. The only thing that would satisfy me was to see Marlene and Dane suffer. The thought disturbed me, and I lay awake for a long time that night trying not to think of what I had spent every spare moment and every effort to achieve. On that night I dreamed about Eli and his cat and how simple life had been at one time—but was no more.

∽

The next morning I left Los Angeles. I dressed and did what little packing I had to do. I had bought enough clothes to make the impression I needed to make. I had said good-bye to Carmen, my diction teacher, and to Caitlin, my dance instructor, some time earlier. I had given each of them a bonus, and both had seemed sorry to say good-bye.

I left the apartment for the last time, locked the door, dropped the key off, and left without a backward look.

I drove to the fitness center and waited until Trey was finished trying to get a woman to do curls and not succeeding. When he saw me, he said, "Hey, dude, what's happening?"

"I'm leaving town, Trey. I wanted to stop by and thank you."

Trey's smile vanished. "Leavin' for good, aren't you?"

"I expect so."

"I'll miss you, man."

"I'll miss you too. Here, I wanted you to have this. A little extra in there."

I handed him the envelope, and he took it without looking at it and studied me carefully. "I don't know what's going on inside that head of yours, man, but I'll be here. If you ever want to tell me what this is all about, give me a call."

I knew that the Bible verse—"Money is the answer for everything"—didn't work here. Money had hired Trey to help me get in shape, but there was another level to our relationship, and I knew it wasn't something that had to do with the money I was giving him. I felt a warmth for him, and the only other person for whom I'd felt this way was Eli. I hovered on the brink of telling him everything, but it didn't seem the time or the place.

"I'll keep in touch," I promised him.

"You take care, man."

I left the fitness center with a feeling of losing something. I didn't know how to handle it, so I put it out of my mind, got into the Porsche, and drove away.

As I left Los Angeles, impulsively I pulled over and reached into the briefcase on the seat next to me. I pulled out the picture of Marlene and Dane and stared at it for a long time. As always, it stirred up something in me that burned briefly and then settled down to a dull glow of hatred.

"I could just show up and say, 'Heeere's Ollie!' like Jack Nicholson in *The Shining*," I said out loud. Everything they had would belong to me legally. And if they resisted, I could get it back through the courts. Even if I didn't put them in jail for trying to kill me, I could take all they had. And if I knew them, that would be like death to them.

But it wasn't enough. I stared at their faces, aware that I had gotten hard inside, like flint.

Unbidden, another image came to me. It was the time Trey and I had encountered the street preacher, and his words cut into my mind almost like a small explosion. *But if you do not forgive men their sins, your Father will not forgive your sins.*

I was shocked at how clear those words sounded, and I could see every line on that man's face.

But I'd grown accustomed to shoving things under the bed. I put it out of my mind, started the Porsche, and left to find Dane and Marlene.

CHAPTER
FIFTEEN

The sign was discreet. It simply said, *Blue Springs, Population 14,000.* I slowed down and made a tour of the town. It was to be, after all, my battleground, and I needed to know the territory. From my research, I'd found that Dane and Marlene had moved here and bought a home shortly after they married.

As I cruised slowly, I noticed that someone had passed a law against poverty. All of the houses looked either new or respectably old. Of course, many of them had a Spanish flavor, but others were ultramodern, like large, shiny cylinders and immaculate squares. I saw the Moorish influence of the old South, which looked strangely incongruous in a beach town.

All of them, however, had the look of Money, spelled with a capital *M*. The yards were all manicured and the flowers so well trained that they looked artificial. It was the beginning of spring, and the gardeners were out getting ready for the season. A great many of them, I noticed, were Hispanic. Some of them would smile, their teeth white against their dark skin, as they saluted me. I'm sure they were saluting the Porsche, however, and not Davis Burke.

For a while I cruised around, trying to find the slums, but there didn't seem to be any. Finally I pulled into a full-service gas station, an endangered species in America. It was as spotless and shiny as an operating room, and the attendant who came up was wearing a pair of light blue slacks and a white, immaculate shirt. He looked like an all-American boy—tanned and handsome, with a stylish haircut.

"Fill it up, sir?"

"Yes. That would be good."

"Check the oil?"

"Shouldn't need it. It's brand new."

"I can see that." I popped the gas cover, and he inserted the hose and stood there studying me without appearing to.

"Nice town you got here."

"Yes, sir, it is. First time in Blue Springs?"

I climbed out and leaned against the side of the car. "First time."

"It's a nice place to live."

"Where are the slums?"

My question startled him, and he turned around to stare at me, his blue eyes careful. "Slums?"

"Yeah, you know, the place where you can get mugged after dark. Where the poor folks live."

"We don't have anything like that here in Blue Springs."

"Probably the only town in America that doesn't. How do you manage it?"

My question troubled him. He couldn't meet my gaze and shifted his feet, putting his attention on the nozzle. Finally he looked around and grinned. "I guess we just cater to people with money."

"Pretty hard to get people with money to do the chores. Who washes the dishes in the restaurants?"

"Oh, we've got folks to do that." He studied me guardedly and then grinned slyly. "Closest thing we've got to slums is over there on the east side of town." He nodded with his head and added, "Mostly slants and tamales. Not like Detroit."

"How's that?"

"Well, they have to keep their houses nice, even the poorest of them, and the police here don't put up with any trouble from them."

I was fascinated. It seemed like something out of the *Twilight Zone*, a town where everybody was well-dressed, no crime, plenty of money. I nudged at the kid a little with the sharp end of my stick. "What if I want to get into trouble?"

He studied me for a time without speaking. Finally the pump cut off, and he lifted the nozzle and replaced it on the gas column. He closed the gas cap on the Porsche, then faced me squarely. "What kind of trouble?"

"Any kind. Maybe gambling or bad women."

My questions troubled him. I could see that he'd never encountered anyone who questioned the sanctity of Blue Springs. "That'll be twenty-two fifty," he said.

I pulled out my billfold, handed him a twenty and a five, and said, "Keep the difference."

He still wasn't satisfied. I had shaken his day. "If you want stuff like that, better go out to San Pedro. Take County Road 28. Only fourteen miles. Plenty of trouble there, any kind you want."

"Well, it's nice to have the riffraff all isolated." I got back into the car, started it, and pulled out. As I headed toward what I thought would be the center of town, I glanced into the rearview mirror and saw that he was still standing there, facing me squarely, staring. I probably made his day.

The business section wasn't overrun with tattoo parlors and hockshops. Evidently the riffraff were kept out of the business areas as well.

I was studying the town so closely that I was startled when a light blinked in my mirror—a blue light, which always means trouble. I pulled over at once and sat and waited, watching the policeman get out. He was a tall, lanky man with a tan, which was probably standard equipment in Blue Springs. When he came and stood over me, I saw he had eyes the color of spit. I had never seen anyone with eyes that color.

"May I see your license, sir?"

I reached into my billfold, took out my license, and handed it to him. He studied it for a long time and said, "You ran through a light back there."

"I'm sorry, officer. I didn't see it." He had a look of efficiency about him, but there was cruelty in his look as well. He was the kind, I thought, who would have made a good guard at Buchenwald, although he didn't look German but Swedish. When I didn't say anything else, he said, "You're from Los Angeles?"

"Temporarily."

He handed me the license back and nodded. "Are you visiting someone here?"

"Don't know a soul. I'm thinking about moving here, though. Just headed downtown to tour around and see if I like it."

He was torn between two desires. One was to give me a ticket and prove that he was more powerful than I was by virtue of the gun he carried on his hip and his right to give tickets. The other was to give deference to the Porsche and my clothes and my money.

"Well, Mr. Burke, I hope you like it here. The town is right up there."

"Thanks, officer."

I waited until he went back to the car, then pulled away. He didn't get in, and when I looked back I saw that he was studying me as the kid had done at the gas station. The more I thought about it, the more I thought it would make a good *Twilight Zone* plot. Stranger comes into a town, and everybody acts peculiar toward him. Everybody in town is rich and prosperous. There are no poor people.

But there was something sinister about that to me. I knew that this was big-time money here in Blue Springs. I had put out a few feelers In Los Angeles and knew that it was a prosperous place. Not just middle-class prosperity, but jet set, movie star, NBA-type prosperity.

I drove the length of the main street, which wasn't long but was spotless. The people I saw were all well-dressed and purposeful. They seemed happy. When I pulled up beside the First National Bank, I sat there for a moment, trying to make a plan.

I had been making plans for a year. It had been simple enough to figure out how to hurt Marlene and Dane as much as I could. But now that I was here on the scene and ready to execute, my strategic planning seemed a little grandiose. Tactically, I still had to make the thing work. My plan was based on money, and the bank was where they kept the money, so I got out of the Porsche, noticed that there were no parking meters, and walked inside.

Banks have a peculiar atmosphere; they're more like mausoleums. The floor and pillars were made of pink marble. The lights were all recessed so that there was sort of a glow over the entire area. Four desks were scattered in the main area, with three women and one man sitting at them looking important. I walked over to the first one and waited until the woman looked up.

"May I help you, sir?"

"I think you might. I'd like to see the president."

Something flickered in her eyes. She evidently was paid to keep out the riffraff, and she looked me over closely. I was wearing Cassini slacks, a Borgini shirt, Johnston and Murphy shoes, and Gargoyle shades. Anyone with threads like that can't be all bad.

She finally decided in my favor. I think it was the Gargoyles that decided the issue. "May I ask your business?"

"Yes."

She waited and flushed as she saw I wasn't going to say anything else. "Do you intend to open an account?"

"That's a possibility." I smiled. "I'm thinking of moving to Blue Springs, and I'll have to do some pretty heavy financing, so I thought I'd like to meet the president."

"If you'll have a seat, I'll see if Mr. Leighton is available."

She walked away, and I watched as she did. She was wearing a dress that was official and sexy at the same time. I don't know how that can be, but she was well aware that I was watching her—although she didn't look back to see.

I sat and looked at some of the magazines, all of them boring, of course. Magazines about finance are always boring, at least to me. I'd have preferred one about computers or a *People* maybe, but no such luck.

When the woman came back, it was as if the iceberg had melted. She gave me a big smile and said, "Mr. Leighton will see you now, sir."

"Thank you very much."

I walked across the room. The sign was plain enough that even a fool couldn't miss it. It simply said *President*.

I walked through the door, and the man sitting behind the desk stood up. "I'm Robert Leighton," he said.

"Davis Burke."

He had a firm handshake—he had undoubtedly read all the books on how important it was to have a firm handshake when meeting prospective victims, facing them squarely and making eye contact. He motioned to a seat, and when I sat down, he said, "First visit to Blue Springs?"

"First visit. I'm thinking of moving here, though."

"You'll like it." Leighton began to give me the list of reasons I would like Blue Springs, and as he did, I studied him. He had fair hair which he was losing. He had the requisite tan, and I suspected that it came out of a bottle. His mouth was small and pursed, and he had mild blue eyes. In all likelihood, the mildness was merely appearance. You don't become president of a bank through mildness.

As a matter of fact, I had arrived at an opinion about how power works in corporate America—or in a town like Blue Springs. There was a medieval flavor to it. At the top was the king, who could cut off anybody's head without asking permission. Beneath him were from three or four to half a dozen barons, all of whom had to go through more routine to cut off someone's head but could still do it. Beneath them were the knights—still royalty, sort of, but really gofers for the barons—who were gofers for the king. Draw a heavy line beneath that and write *serf* below it, because that's what everybody else is no matter what they do. The power was always consolidated at the top of the pyramid. I had been doing my homework on power structures, and I was wondering if Robert Leighton was the top of the diagram.

Pretty soon he got to the heart of the matter, asking in a most innocuous way what sort of business I was in. The question really could have been put bluntly: How much money do you have? But Leighton was too sophisticated for that.

I said, "I've got several ventures going, and I don't like Los Angeles."

"Who does?" Leighton smiled. "That's why all of us who do business there live in Blue Springs. Would you be moving here, do you think?"

"I think I will. I'm looking around. I'll make a token deposit today just to get started. Say five hundred thousand, just for lunch money."

Leighton grinned, managing to look like a shark even with his small, pursed mouth. "Pretty expensive lunch, Mr. Burke."

"It'll do for what I need now until I get settled down. Good to be back in the country."

"You're Australian, I take it?"

"You have a quick ear."

"Well, not really, but I see all the Australian movies."

"I have several interests in Australia still, but I can handle them from here as well as anywhere."

"Well, we're at your service, of course. That's why we're here—to serve."

I'll bet you are! You're here to rake everybody for what they've got. But it was too soon to discover whether Leighton was a king or only a baron.

"Maybe you could recommend a realtor."

"Yes, of course. Wilkerson's your man. Jeb Stuart Wilkerson."

"Must be a Southerner."

"As a matter of fact, he's from Pennsylvania. One of his ancestors rode with Stuart, though, in the Civil War, so he was stuck with the name. We just call him Jeb usually."

"Well, if you'll let one of your ladies out there write me up, I'll be on my way."

"I'll call Jeb and tell him you're coming." Leighton rose as I did and said, "Why don't you join my wife and me at the country club this evening. Everyone will be there."

I knew that by "everyone" he meant everyone who counted. I was pretty sure the king would be there as well as the other barons and a few of the knights. "That would be very nice."

"Make it seven o'clock. Come along. I'll have one of our people write you up to get you started."

I went through the form of persuading Miss Smith to take my money, and if she was impressed by a five-hundred-thousand-dollar deposit, she didn't show it. It might have been a hundred dollars. She gave me a small checkbook containing half a dozen checks, smiled at me as she had been taught to do, and I left the bank.

I went to check into the hotel and found that it was first-class. As I unpacked my clothes, I wondered about the dinner. It would be interesting. Most of all, of course, I wondered whether Dane and Marlene would be there. The thought of meeting them gave me a funny feeling. My game of charades might go up in smoke if either one of them recognized me, but after all, Ollie Benson was buried, and the man they would meet was another creation.

∽

I changed my outfit carefully, wanting to make just the right impression. I picked a cashmere turtleneck of a light mushroom color, a pair of light wool, patterned trousers, and a bone-colored, window-paned sport coat. I put it on and stood gazing at myself in the mirror—and, as always, had the weird feeling that I was looking at a stranger. The trim waistline, broad shoulders, and wedge-shaped face wasn't me, but it was what I had hoped for. I went downstairs and across the lobby, nodding to the clerk, then got into the Porsche and drove to the country club. I had already staked it out earlier. Now I studied the cars. Lots of BMWs, but surprisingly few Cadillacs.

Inside, I was greeted by a tall woman in a simple black dress which probably cost enough to feed an African village for six months. "Yes, sir?" she asked.

"I'm looking for Mr. Leighton's party."

"Yes. They've already arrived. Come in. I'll take you to them."

I followed her out of the foyer, down a hall, and into a large dining area. The round tables were scattered, and she led me to one where three couples were sitting. One of them was Robert Leighton, and he waved a hand at a chair and said, "Davis, you're here." He got to his feet. "Glad you could make it. Let me introduce you. This is my wife, Allison." He motioned to a sturdy redhead beside him. "This is Jeb Wilkerson and his wife, Barbara." Wilkerson was a well-built man in his fifties. His wife was a petite woman with a spectacular figure, blonde hair, and green eyes. "And this is Leo Fant and his wife, Estelle." Fant was a small man, compact, well-built, with direct gray eyes and a mouth like a steel trap. His wife Estelle was a tall woman, with brown eyes, brown hair, and speculation in her expression. I nodded to all of them and sat down.

Leighton said, "Davis is thinking about moving here."

"What's your business, Davis?" Fant asked directly.

I don't know why, but as soon as he spoke, I knew that this was the king. Leighton and Wilkerson were his barons, but the power lay in Fant. He was the physically smallest, least impressive man at the table, but he emanated some sort of aura, and his gaze penetrated down through the flesh to the bone.

"Investments, mostly. I'm just a poor Aussie trying to make a living." I smiled.

Estelle Fant said, "I just love Australia. I've been there twice. What part are you from?"

I named a village so far inland that no one would be likely to know it, and I was right. Then I said, "Of course, I lived in Sydney for the past few years."

"I understand you are looking for a place to live," Jeb said.

"Oh, now, Jeb," his wife Barbara said. "Don't talk business at the table."

"It's all right, Mrs. Wilkerson. I am looking for a place. If it's all right, I'd like to meet with you tomorrow. Perhaps you can show me a few places."

"Be glad to," Wilkerson said at once.

The server came then, a well-endowed brunette who took our order and then left. As soon as she had gone, Estelle Fant said, "I suppose your wife will be joining you."

She wasn't particularly sophisticated; it was the same as asking, "Are you married?" But obviously there were games going on with this group.

"I'm not married," I said. "Never had that good fortune."

"I suppose men marry later in life in Australia," Fant suggested. He was toying with his water glass, and I noticed that his hands were strong and brown. He looked like a welterweight prizefighter in the peak of condition.

"I suppose about the same as here overall."

For the next thirty minutes the three couples tried their best to find out how much money I had and what I intended to do with it here in Blue Springs. I had not been born in their circles, but I had learned to protect myself and was able to field their questions.

The meal came, and by the time we were halfway through, a few couples were dancing to a four-piece band making soft music. They were playing the songs of the forties, which I liked a lot. Finally we were drinking coffee, and a woman came up and spoke to Barbara Wilkerson. "Barbara, don't forget tennis tomorrow at ten."

"I won't forget," Barbara said. She turned and said, "Let me introduce the newest addition to Blue Springs. This is Davis Burke. Davis, Maggie Osterman."

I got to my foot and smiled. "I'm glad to know you, Mrs. Osterman."

"Just Maggie." She studied me and said, "I think it would be nice if you would ask me to dance."

I smiled and said, "Would you care to dance, Maggie?"

"Why, I believe I would."

Maggie Osterman was no more than medium height but seemed taller because of her erect posture. She had hair as black as the darkest thing in nature and widely spaced, bluish eyes. Her mouth was wide, well-shaped, and splashed with color, and she was wearing a peach-colored dress that advertised her figure. We moved out onto the dance floor. She turned to me and I put my arm around her, and then she leaned against me and said, "Did any of them tell you my nickname?"

"No. What is it?"

"They call me the Black Widow. Not to my face, of course."

"Why do they call you that?"

"Because I've had two husbands, both of them well off. They both died."

"Of natural causes, I take it."

Maggie laughed. "You do come right out with it, don't you? Yes, of natural causes. You're a good dancer, better than most men."

"Well, I got my start in life as a professional dancer."

"Really! How interesting!"

"Not true, of course. You dance better than I do."

We moved around the floor, and I was very much aware that most people in the room were watching us, especially the three couples at the table that we had just left. "You started at the top," Maggie said, "having dinner with the unholy trinity."

The name surprised me. "Unholy trinity?"

"That's my name for them. The women all hate me, of course." Her eyes glinted. "The men find me interesting."

"I can see why." She had a subtle aroma. Her perfume was like none I had ever known. It almost had the effect of incense. Her skin was perfect, and the way she put herself against me as we moved around the floor left no doubt as to her intentions. She was a sexual being if I ever saw one.

"Which one of the three ladies back there at the table have marked you?" she asked.

"Marked me?"

"Oh, we're all of us here looking for excitement."

I couldn't help but grin at her. "Why don't you just come out and say what you mean, Maggie?"

"They're hypocrites, of course, but I'm not. You can do what you please with Allison and Barbara, but Leo Fant's a different story. I really think he would shoot Estelle and her partner if he caught them."

"I'll keep that in mind."

As we danced, I kept waiting for her to mention Dane and Marlene, but she didn't.

We went back to the table. She nodded and said, "I'll be seeing you, Davis." She turned around and walked away without another word and I sat down.

"She's pretty blatant, isn't she?" Allison Leighton said.

"Very attractive woman," I said noncommittally.

Leo Fant said little in the conversation, but when they gave up trying to find out how much money I had, he said, "Where are Marlene and Dane tonight?"

"They went out on their boat, I think," Jeb Wilkerson said.

"Have you talked to them about the Williams thing?"

"Not yet, but I think they'll be interested."

I wanted to ask more but didn't think it was wise. I spent the rest of the evening pleasantly enough, and once when I danced with Barbara Wilkerson, she mentioned Marlene, and I said, "Marlene? Who is that?"

"Oh, you haven't met them. Marlene and Dane Fetterman are very nice people. They're into computers, I understand."

"They live here year-round?"

"Oh, they travel a lot, but, yes, this is their home. She had a rather tragic first marriage. Her husband was killed. She and Dane haven't been married long. You'll like them. They're very attractive people."

"I'll look forward to it. I like attractive people."

CHAPTER
SIXTEEN

After a week at Blue Springs, I knew how a goldfish in a big bowl felt, with people staring in at him. I had picked up that Marlene and Dane would not be back for at least a week, and I had spent the time studying the terrain as a soldier would study a battlefield. Most of my time was spent at the country club, where they had a first-class fitness center and an Olympic swimming pool. It still was amazing to me that I could maintain the hard body that Trey had helped me to build simply by going three times a week.

I made it a point to integrate myself into the society of the town, and one of the most amusing things was how many daughters there were who had parents anxious to marry them off. One of these was Shirley Fant, the daughter of Leo and Estelle. I met Shirley early in the week at the tennis court. I was playing with Jack O'Brian, the tennis pro, and was aware that the young woman was waiting over on the sidelines. Jack was about five ten and made out of steel springs; he never seemed to grow tired. When we finished our set, Jack came to the net and winked. "You'll be stealing my thunder, Mr. Burke."

"Not likely."

O'Brian glanced over and said, "Hello, Miss Fant. Ready for a set?"

The young woman nodded, and I could barely hear her reply. "I guess so, Jack."

O'Brian waved a hand toward me. "Why don't you knock a few around with the newest member of our club? Have you two met?"

"I don't think so," she said. She was of average height and had a good figure. Her face was round, and she too had a tan. Her most attractive feature was her eyes, large and well-shaped. For one coming from such a wealthy family, she had a rather hesitant air. I had learned much about Leo Fant who was, indeed, the king of the castle, but it surprised me that his daughter had such a lack of assurance.

"Shirley, this is Davis Burke. Mr. Burke, let me introduce you to Shirley Fant."

"I am happy to know you, Shirley. I've met your parents."

"Yes, they mentioned you." She didn't say what they had said about me, and I didn't ask. I waited for her to make the first move, and when she didn't, I said, "Care to hit a few?"

"All right." O'Brian left, and the girl went to the other end of the courts. She was wearing white shorts and a white shirt. As soon as we began to play, I saw that she was very good indeed, and I let her win the first set, but it didn't take much on my part.

She didn't speak except to say, "Good shot" or "I should have had that one."

We played the game out, and then I said, "That's enough for me. Let's go get something to drink."

"All right."

Inside, she ordered a Diet Coke and I had the same. It was hard to make conversation with her, and I realized that she was even more introverted than I had thought.

While we were drinking our Cokes, her father came over and smiled at her. He had that look that fathers have for daughters they really care for. It made me think better of him. "You've met Davis, I see."

"Yes, we've been having a game, Dad."

"Did you win?"

"He let me win."

She turned and smiled at me, and although she was no beauty queen I saw that there was an attractiveness to her that went more than skin deep.

"A gentleman always lets a lady win," I said.

Fant smiled at me then, the first smile I had gotten from him that looked real. "Are you about to get settled in?"

"Still looking for a place."

"Jeb hasn't found you anything yet?"

"I guess it's hard to help someone who doesn't know what he wants."

Shirley said, "Have you seen the Norris house?"

"No, not yet. Is it a nice one?"

Shirley looked surprised. "It's Chad Norris's house. You know, the movie star."

Chad Norris had indeed been a famous movie star. He had died only three years earlier but had dominated the screen. "I didn't know he had a house here."

"Yes, he stayed here a lot when he wasn't making pictures. Everybody knew him."

"That house might not be Davis's cup of tea," Leo said doubt-fully. "Chad spent far too much money on it."

I saw a chance to move myself into a higher realm in the eyes of Fant and eventually of Marlene and Dane. "I think I'd like to look at it. Maybe some of his glamour will rub off on me."

Shirley laughed. She had a nice laugh, and I found myself liking her. "He wasn't really romantic off the screen."

"He wasn't? Did you know him well?"

"Yes. He used to make homemade ice cream, and he'd have all the kids in. He did it because he was a friend of Dad's."

"Well, I'll take a look at the house."

"I don't think you'll want to sink that much into it," Fant said cautiously.

"It doesn't cost anything to look, does it?" I said cheerfully. "Shirley, another game?"

"All right, but don't let me win this time. I play with Jack a lot. I've never beaten him, but I will some day."

"Take care of my girl, Davis," Leo said. He gave me a peculiar look and then said, "Maybe you'd like to come over for dinner some night to our place."

"I'd like that, Leo."

As we went back out, I had one of those occasional flashes of intuition. There was something almost plaintive about Shirley Fant, and I realized that her father was very protective. I could tell in the way he spoke to her, in the way he had touched her hair. A very fond father indeed. She was probably twenty-five years old and not married. That meant that the Fants were looking around for a son-in-law. As we began the set, I thought, *Nobody's really good enough for their daughter. Leo is so rich that whoever she marries will have to have money. She's not really beautiful, and she never really knows whether a man's courting her because she's Shirley or because of Fant's big bucks.* I found myself feeling sorry for the poor little rich girl.

∽

I don't usually get involved in the day-to-day sales," Jeb Stuart Wilkerson said as we drove toward the Norris place. "I'm really into developing. Just started this local office to keep my hand in." He turned to look at me and said, "You heard about Chad Norris's house, did you?"

"Shirley Fant mentioned it. Thought I might like it."

"Well, she may be right. It's a pretty big bite. Bad business to mention that the price on a house is high, but Chad put everything he had into it. You know, for a movie star, he was a nice guy. I think most of them are horse's rears, but he never changed even after he got famous."

"You knew him when he was younger?"

"Oh, sure. He bought a smaller place here when he was just starting his career, then when he moved up he built the house of his dreams. Maybe I'd better warn you. It's not everybody's cup of tea."

I turned and grinned at him. "I don't see how you made a success as a salesman. First you tell me the place costs too much, and now you tell me I won't like it."

"I always tell the truth about real estate." Jeb winked at me. "Except when I have to lie, of course."

"Of course."

"You met Shirley, then," he said. "I'm surprised she hasn't gotten married by now. Of course, her folks are pretty hard to please."

"She's an attractive young woman."

"Yes, she is. Fine girl. Leo and Estelle have all their hopes in her. They wanted boys, but they didn't get any, so the fellow who gets Shirley will get a pretty good deal."

"Leo Fant really that rich?"

"The richest man in Blue Springs. He doesn't always show it, but he's into really big-time developments in Los Angeles and some in New York too." We had reached the edge of town, and Jeb said, "There's the house back over there." He turned into a driveway, and I studied the house as we approached. I don't know what I'd been expecting, but whatever it was this wasn't it. It seemed like a combination of modern and Old South, if you can imagine such a thing. There were columns in front and a wide veranda, but there were also modern touches that took it out of that style. "Unusual house," I said. "How much ground goes with it?"

"Only five acres, but it takes a full-time yardman to keep it up."

For the next thirty minutes Jeb walked me through the house. It wasn't as large as I had expected, and I commented on that. "Well, Norris could have had as big a house as he wanted, but he designed this one himself. He came from Mississippi. I think he tried to give it the Mississippi look and mixed it up a little bit with modern stuff."

The house had everything a rich man's house should have, but only four bedrooms, a study, a game room with a billiard table, and a fitness center and kitchen with all the newest appliances. Everything was spic and span and in place.

"There's a pool outside, of course," Jeb said.

"This house would need a lot of taking care of."

"Aside from somebody for the yard, it takes a pretty good maid. Of course Norris wasn't here much." He hesitated, then said, "There's a nice house out in the back. A family lives there now. The woman takes care of the inside of the house. The husband's an invalid. The woman's done a good job. She came after Chad died and keeps the place up."

"How much is it?"

"Four million nine hundred thousand."

I knew that Jeb was watching my face, trying to read my expression, and I tried to let nothing show. "Well, I might be interested, but I'll never buy a house until I can try it on to make sure it fits me. What about I lease it for six months?"

"Sure, that would be fine." I knew from the quickness of his reply that the house had not been an easy place to sell. "Five thousand a month sound okay for a six-month's lease?"

"That's fine, Jeb. If it's okay with you," I said, "we'll go to your office and I'll sign the papers and give you a check. I'd like to move in today. I don't like hotels."

"That's great. You'll take care of the maintenance. The family who keeps the house is named Doren."

We went back to town and I signed a lease. I went by the hotel and checked out, then drove back out to the house. I knew that, by nightfall, everyone would know that the rich, handsome young bachelor had leased the Chad Norris house with an option to buy. Just what I wanted!

It didn't take long for me to move my clothes into the bedroom, and I was amused to see that there was a mirror on the ceiling above the bed. "Playful fellow, Chad Norris," I murmured. Then I left to go meet the Dorens.

The smaller house was discreetly hidden behind some trees and seemed almost disconnected from the main house. Yet it was only a hundred feet or so from the back door. The house itself was modest enough, a white frame house with a hip roof—typical ranch style. I knocked on the door, and after a few moments it opened and a woman stood there. "Yes, what is it?"

"My name's Davis Burke. Are you Mrs. Doren?"

"Yes, I'm Joelle Doren."

"I just leased the house, and I thought we might talk about your continuing on to take care of it."

She looked relieved. "Why, yes. Shall I come to the house with you?"

"Maybe that would be better. You can show me around."

"I'll be just a minute." She closed the door. I heard voices and then she came outside. "I have a daughter, and my husband is an invalid."

"Mr. Wilkerson told me about your husband. Was he injured?"

"It's Lou Gehrig's disease."

I gave her a quick glance. She answered calmly enough, and I saw that she intended to add no more. "I'm sorry," I said. She didn't answer. She guided me through the house, showing me everything. "I don't know whether you cook," I said, "but I'd be glad to pay extra if you'd fix a meal once in a while."

"I'd be glad to do that," she said quickly. "Would you like dinner tonight?"

"Yes, as a matter of fact. I'm tired of eating out."

"What kind of food do you like?"

"Tex-Mex would be fine."

She smiled then. She was an attractive woman. She had tawny hair cut just above her shoulders and gray-green eyes. She was full-bodied, strong-looking, and I guessed her to be in her late twenties. She was tall, at least five eight, and carried herself well. "I like Mexican cooking myself. I grew up in Guatemala."

"Guatemala? What were you doing there?"

"My parents were missionaries."

"Interesting. Are they still there?"

"No, they died there. Killed by guerrillas."

There didn't seem to be anything to say to that, so I said, "I hope I won't be too much trouble."

She smiled, and I noticed a cleft in her chin. "That's what you pay me for, Mr. Burke. What time would you like to eat?"

"Oh, about six, I guess."

"It'll be ready for you."

∾

I took a nap, and when I got up I walked through the house, seeing what I could sense about the famous movie star. He had left many of his own things, Jeb had told me, and some of the pictures he had painted himself. He was pretty good too.

I went outside and stood for a while looking down at the aqua water of the swimming pool. Continuing around the house, I saw a child sitting beside a bicycle which was lying on its side. I said, "Hi there."

"Hello." She had dark hair and eyes, not at all like her mother, but she had the same cleft in her chin that her mother had.

"I'm Mr. Burke. I'm going to live in this house."

"Mom told me. I'm Rachel."

"Well, Rachel, that your bicycle?"

"The dumb old thing is broke."

"Bicycles do that. Maybe I can fix it."

She looked up at me and studied me carefully. "I wish you could."

The chain had simply slipped off the sprocket. I got the small tool kit out of the Porsche, and when I'd fixed the chain, I spun the wheel and said, "There. Let me see you cut some wheelies."

"I can do that."

She got on the bicycle and indeed was very good. I applauded her and said, "You're a fine bicycle rider."

"Thank you."

I heard a voice then and saw Mrs. Doren, who had come out the back door. "Dinner's ready."

"Is there enough for this young lady?"

"I think so."

"How about joining me, Rachel? I hate to eat alone."

"All right."

We went into the house, and Mrs. Doren had set the table in the breakfast room. "I didn't use the big dining room because it's so formal," she said.

"Mr. Burke fixed my bicycle, Mom."

"Well, that's good." She turned and smiled at me. "Thank you so much. She's been after me to fix it, but I couldn't."

"No trouble."

I sat down, and as she set a plate for Rachel, I said, "I wish you'd eat with us too. As I was telling Rachel, I hate to eat alone."

She hesitated, and for a moment I thought she would refuse. Then she said, "All right."

The meal was outstanding. Cheese enchiladas, tacos, guacamole salad, chips, and a cheese dip that was the best I'd ever had.

"You need to open your own restaurant," I said. "You could call it Mama Joelle's Mexican Restaurant."

"Maybe I'll do that some day."

"You're a fine cook. Don't you think so, Rachel?"

"Mom can cook anything."

She got up, and I said, "I'll help with the dishes, Mrs. Doren."

"Oh, you don't have to do that, and you can call me Joelle."

"And you can call me Davis."

"No, I think that wouldn't be good." She spoke with a firmness that was like a door slamming.

"All right," I said. "If you won't call me by my first name, I won't call you by yours."

"You can call me by my first name," Rachel said, "and I'll call you Davis."

"No, you won't," Joelle protested.

"How about Mr. Davis?" I suggested. "That's a good compromise."

"Do you like to play with Barbie dolls?" Rachel said.

"Nothing I like better."

Mrs. Doren laughed. "You never played with a Barbie doll in your life."

"No, but I'm going to like it. I can tell. Why don't you go get Barbie and Ken and bring them over."

Rachel beamed and left at once. I insisted on helping rinse the dishes and putting them into the dishwasher, and then Rachel came back with a boxful of Barbie dolls, sixteen of them. I had to learn all their names and which ones were going with whom. I had thought there were only Ken and Barbie, but it seems that there are little sisters and big brother and all sorts of difficult things to remember.

Finally Mrs. Doren came and said, "It's time to go home now, Rachel."

"But I don't want to. Mr. Davis and I aren't finished."

"Yes, you are. Take your dolls and go home."

"Come again tomorrow," I said. "I'll try to remember their names, Rachel."

"You promise?"

"I promise." I watched as the child carried the dolls off and then turned to face Mrs. Doren. "I really wish you'd call me Davis, and I wish you'd let me call you Joelle."

She hesitated then gave me a smile. She had a world-class smile, but I suspected that people rarely saw it. "I suppose that will be all right, except when there are people around."

"We'll become fellow hypocrites. Mr. Burke and Mrs. Doren when people are around and Davis and Joelle when they aren't."

"I've got to go. I've got to feed my husband."

I went into the living area, plopped into a recliner, and watched the news. I thought, *That's the longest I've gone in a long time without thinking about how to get even with Marlene and Dane.* I spent the night reading a book, and when I went to bed that night, I slept without a dream—which made me feel very good indeed. My dreams had been unpleasant for the past year, and I would be just as happy not to have them anymore.

CHAPTER SEVENTEEN

The best thing Chad Norris did when he built his house was install the swimming pool. It was Olympic size, of course, and as I plowed through the water full speed ahead, I felt a faint memory of my fat days. I had been able to float well enough, but gave out too soon when it came to actual swimming strokes. Now I had done twenty laps with a crawl and was finishing off with the butterfly stroke. If there's anything that takes it out of a human being, it's the butterfly. I have always contended that the best athletes in the Olympics were those who could win the butterfly event.

By the time I'd finished five laps, I was gasping for breath and barely had strength enough to haul myself up over the edge of the pool. I rolled over onto my back and lay there, my heart going *whomp! whomp!* and closed my eyes against the brightness of the April sun. Unexpectedly, a line I had read once came out of my subconscious, powerfully, almost like a banner with large black letters against a white background. It was from *The Diary of Anne Frank*. I had read it at least five years before and thought I had forgotten it, but now it came sharp and clear: *How wonderful it is that nobody needs to wait a single moment before starting to improve the world.*

The words resounded inside my head, then started to fade, dissolving into faint echoes. The words troubled me. There was a poor girl facing a deadly future against the monsters of the Gestapo, and yet something in her produced words like this. If

I were to put my own thoughts into a single sentence, it would be, "I'm going to destroy two human beings in the most painful way I can."

I felt small and insignificant and dirty. I got up quickly and slipped into my robe and started toward the house. As I did, Rachel came by with her bicycle, yelling, "Hi!"

I yelled, "Hi, back at you. What's going on, Rachel?"

"I got a new Barbie doll, Mr. Davis. Come and see it."

"Well, let me go get some clothes on, and I'll be right over." I moved quickly into the house, glad to get away from my thoughts. I dressed quickly, putting on a pair of jeans, a T-shirt, and a pair of sneakers, and went out the back door.

When I got to the Doren's cottage, Joelle was hanging out sheets on a line strung between two palm trees. That struck me as odd, and I said, "Hi. Is your dryer broken down?"

"No, it's working fine." She turned, and the breeze blew her tawny hair over her forehead. She brushed it away and said, "I like the smell of sheets that have been dried in the sun."

"That sounds nice."

"I'll be glad to do yours for you if you'd like."

"Too much trouble," I said.

"Stop and smell the roses." She turned, fastened the last sheet, and said, "Rachel just flew by here and said that she'd twisted your arm into playing with her dolls again. You don't have to do that, Mr. Burke."

"I'm going to go batty if you don't stop calling me Mr. Burke. Just Davis is fine, as we agreed on."

"All right. That's a nice name. Who were you named after?"

"Jefferson Davis, president of the Confederacy."

She gave me an odd look. "Why would an Australian care that much about our Civil War?"

How stupid of me! Quickly I lied: "My father was a history buff. He loved to read about wars, and your Civil War was one of his favorites."

"Better not say that around here. We've got a lot of transplanted Yankees."

"The South is gonna rise again." I grinned. "Save your Confederate money. I'm going in to play dolls now. If anybody calls, tell them I'm busy with a very important client."

I went inside the cottage and found Rachel on the living room floor. She had gotten all of her dolls out and piped up at once, "Sit down, Mr. Davis." She waited until I sat down and then said, "Do you remember their names?"

"I've got a very short memory. You'd better go over them again."

I sat there as she went over the dolls' names. I remembered that, over the years, there had been all sorts of problems with Barbie dolls. Some feminists had said that the shapely dolls with their long legs and pointy bosoms were giving young girls the wrong ideas about what they themselves would develop into. I didn't see any harm in it myself, and it gave them something to do.

Music was playing from somewhere back in the house. I recognized "In the Mood" by Glenn Miller, and then "Sentimental Journey" by Tommy Dorsey. They really knew how to write them back in those days. But I soon forgot the music, caught up with the drama that Rachel set before me with the dolls.

She not only had named them all—she had created a whole world for each one. One of them, for instance, was Barbie's little cousin named Susan. Susan had a complete life of her own and was very much in love with an adolescent boy doll named Kevin. She went on and on, naming each one and giving their background, until she said, "This is Henry. He's very bad."

"What did he do that's so bad? He looks all right to me." It was a presentable-looking doll, a boy form of Barbie with sandy hair and a muscular figure.

"He's been going with another girl and lying to Susan about it, and that's not all. His father, Larry, is having an affair with one of the neighbor ladies. Her name is Harriett."

"You've been watching soap operas."

"Yes. When Mama's not around, Daddy and I watch *The Young and the Restless*."

"I'll bet if your mama finds out, you'll get it."

"It's Daddy's secret." She looked up at me, alarmed. "Please don't tell, Mr. Davis."

"I won't. Why don't we just make these dolls all good? That way there won't be any problems."

"No, that's not the way things are. There are good people and bad people."

I was intrigued at how her mind worked. We sat there for almost an hour, with Joelle peeking in on us from time to time. I tried my best to learn the dolls, although they all looked alike to me. Finally I began to get stiff. Joelle came in and said, "You're going to tire Mr. Davis out, Rachel."

"No, I'm not."

"Yes, you are. That's enough for now." She turned to me and said, "Would you have time to meet my husband?"

"Of course." I got to my feet and winked at Rachel. "Remember, we've got our secret, Rachel."

"I remember. I won't tell if you won't."

Joelle took this in, and when we walked out in the hall, she said, "I won't ask what secrets you have."

"Nothing serious. I haven't been around children much. I'm amazed at how her mind works."

"She sees too much television, but there's so little for her to do here. Come along. Frank's in bed."

I followed her down the hall, and we turned into a bedroom. There were two large windows, both of them open, letting in the fresh air and the bright sunlight. The man who was sitting upright against pillows gave me a shock. I knew that Frank Doren had Lou Gehrig's disease, but I didn't realize it was in such an advanced stage. I could tell he had been a handsome man once, but now his cheeks were slack and his eyes sunken back into his head. But those eyes were alert enough as he greeted me.

"This is our employer, Frank—Davis Burke. Davis, this is my husband, Frank."

"I'm glad to know you," he said. "Have a seat."

I sat down beside him, shocked at the shrinkage of his muscles. I knew little enough about Lou Gehrig's disease—amyotrophic lateral sclerosis—except that the great baseball player had died from it and his name had been applied to it. Frank looked almost like a skeleton, his bones making sharp points at his shoulders. He was wearing a pair of pajamas with the sleeves cut off, and a sheet covered his legs. It was gathered around his waist, and I could almost count his ribs even through the pajamas. I've never been good around sick people, and despite my efforts I knew that some of my reaction must have showed.

"I'll leave you two alone," Joelle said. "You want anything, Frank?"

"No, nothing." He waited until she left the room and said, "I've heard how you've been a friend to Rachel. I appreciate that."

He had a deep voice, in startling contrast to his frail body, and I quickly said, "She's a fine girl. I know you're very proud of her."

"I think she's going to look like her mother. That's good. But she's got some of me in her too—in her mind, anyway."

I couldn't think of anything else to say, so I talked about Rachel and her dolls and the little worlds she had created.

"The imaginative side of her comes from Joelle, but she got some logic, I think, from me. I used to be a pretty good teacher."

"What did you teach?"

"History. Of course that's over now. I still love history. Do you read much history yourself?"

"Not as much as I should. Maybe you can recommend some books."

We talked about history for a while, and all the time I was still, more or less, in a state of shock. I could tell he was a tall man, and then he said something about playing tennis and football.

He smiled and said, "You don't have to be embarrassed about my condition. I'm not."

"It must be tough," I said. Then I shook my head and frowned. "That sounds stupid. But anything I can think of saying, Mr. Doren, sounds stupid."

"Call me Frank, please. People want to say good things but don't know how. I understand that. I'm the same way when I meet someone with a problem. I don't think it's the words themselves that count. It's the attitude. You can sense when people really have a feeling for you, and I think you do."

"How did you handle it—when you first got sick, I mean?"

"Not very well. I blamed God, but I got over that. As a matter of fact, if I hadn't been stricken down like this, I don't know that I would ever have found the Lord. It was the helplessness at first that enraged me. When you're flat on your back, there's no way to look but up. So I began to think about God, began to put my house in order, so to speak. I knew I wouldn't be here long and I'd soon be standing before God to give account. So I began studying the Bible, and the more I read it, the more I became convinced that what's really important is not whether a man is well or sick, but whether his soul is clean before God. So I set out to try to please God."

"Never heard it put like that."

"It's a hopeless task," Frank said quietly. "I tried everything I can think of. I was in better shape then. But the harder I tried, the worse I felt. Then finally I read enough of the New Testament to know that two things were pretty clear. Jesus died for our sins. That's one thing. The other is that nobody can win God's favor by doing good things."

"No? I've always thought you could."

"Impossible. That was my trouble too. But then I said, 'God, I just can't do anything to help myself. I give up.'" He smiled, and he had a good smile still. "And it was as if God said to me, 'Good. That's what I've been waiting for. Now I can help you.'"

"What happened?"

"I called on the Lord. He forgave me of all my sins. So now, if I die tonight, I'll be in the presence of the Lord."

"But what about—"

When I broke off, he said, "About my sickness? God can heal me if he chooses. If he doesn't, I'll know that he's made the wise choice. I don't worry about that anymore, Davis. The one thing I did worry about was leaving my family, not being able to care for them. But now that's settled."

I thought he meant that he had a big insurance policy, something like that. Obviously they didn't have much now. I said, "I don't understand what you mean, Frank."

"God's given me a promise. Whatever happens to me, my wife and daughter will be taken care of. If that were a man's promise, I'd doubt it, but God can't lie. So, Joelle and Rachel, somehow, are going to be cared for."

He talked awhile about his assurance. I couldn't believe that anyone in such poor shape could have such faith. Then he said, "How about you, Davis? Do you know the Lord?"

I swallowed hard and shook my head. "No, I don't."

"I hope you'll find him," Frank said quietly. Then he said, without any particular emphasis, "You never know when the bottom will fall out of your life."

Those words hit me like a lightning bolt. That was exactly what had happened. The bottom *had* fallen out of my life. I had been struck—maybe not as hard as Frank Doren had, but I had definitely had my entire life uprooted. I knew I couldn't let him see my sudden turmoil, so I quickly said, "I guess I'd better go, but if there's anything I can do for you, Frank, you just let me know."

"All right, I will. Do you play chess?"

"Sure I do."

"Maybe we can have a game now and then."

"I don't know, Frank, I'm pretty good."

"So am I," he said. He lifted his hand with an effort, and I took it. He had no power at all, and I held it very gently. "I appreciate your coming by," he said, "and all you've done for my family."

"I'll be back for that chess game. Probably tomorrow."

"I'll look forward to it."

I left the room pretty well shaken up. As I walked down the hall, I saw that pictures of the family lined it in a family gallery. I stopped and stared at one. It was a picture taken at the ocean. Joelle and Frank were coming out of the ocean after a swim. They were dripping wet and laughing, and the photography was excellent. I stared at the figure of the strong man holding his wife's hand. His muscles were firm. He was broad-shouldered, with strength obvious in every inch of him, and I thought about the man lying a few feet away on the bed. I was still staring at it when Joelle's voice said, "That was taken on our honeymoon." I turned quickly; she was looking at me in a peculiar way. "He was so handsome."

I said, "Listen, if you need money for medical care, anything like that—"

But she shook her head quickly and broke in. "Nothing like that, Davis. Just spend some time with him. It would mean a lot to both of us."

"I'll do that," I said, and I knew that I had taken on a special obligation.

∞

Well, I don't think you two have met the latest addition to Blue Springs society. Dane, this is Davis Burke. Davis, let me introduce you to Dane and Marlene Fetterman."

I had come to the party at the country club more to kill time than anything else. I'd had my back to the room and was talking to Jeb Wilkerson when I'd seen his eyes light up. I knew someone was approaching, but as I turned and saw Marlene and Dane not eight feet away, coming right at me, and heard Jeb's words, it took every bit of restraint I had to keep from showing anything. I made myself smile, nodded, and said, "I'm happy to meet you."

Dane put his hand out and I shook it. He gave me a hard grip, which I matched, and he said, "I'm glad to know you, Davis."

Marlene was wearing a black linen dress with a square neckline and short sleeves and a hemline that ended just above her ankles. It was free from any decoration other than a large diamond-and-ruby necklace that hung around her neck. She smiled brilliantly, saying, "So this is the mystery man." She put out her own hand and I took it, and when I felt the firmness of it, for some reason it brought back memories of the times we had made love. She held it a moment longer than necessary, and then I pulled my own away.

"Mystery man? I don't think there's a lot of mystery about me."

"Oh, yes, there is," Marlene said. "You don't know what it's like in a little place like this."

"That's right." Dane grinned. "We hadn't been back for half a day before we got the story of the handsome, wealthy young bachelor from Australia. There must be half a dozen parents around here who have eligible daughters that are all panting to get their bid in."

"Oh, come on, Dane," Jeb said. "It's not that bad."

"I'm afraid it is," Marlene said. The music was playing, and she said, "Come along, Davis, dance with me. I'll worm my way into your affections so that you'll tell me about yourself."

I glanced at Dane, who shrugged and said, "Watch out for her. She'll do what she says."

We went out onto the dance floor, and she came to me with the assurance she always had. She hadn't changed, but then she didn't have any need to. If anything, she looked better. She had a light tan, and the auburn lights in her brown hair were reflected by the lights overhead. She still had the same sensuous mouth and direct green eyes and exuded a sexual force that was almost physical.

"Come now. I'll have it all. Don't be shy. Mama Marlene will never tell."

"Not a lot to tell."

"I love that Australian accent. That's all I really know about you, that you're loaded and that you came from Australia."

"I'm from Australia all right, but as for being loaded, you know how things like that get blown up."

"Now don't be modest. Just tell me one thing. Have you got a wife hidden somewhere in the background?"

"No wife."

"Are you gay?"

The question hit me forcibly. She had asked it as if she would ask, "Are you a Republican?"

"No, I'm not."

"But no wife. That's unusual. Why not? Don't you like women?"

"I like some of them." I was glad in a way that she was talking, for it gave me time to pull myself together. I couldn't help but think of the life we'd had together as I answered her questions, or rather fended them off. She was good at asking them, but she was also coming on to me. I don't know why that shocked me, but it did. She had tried to murder me so that she could have Dane, and already she was obviously seeking out an affair with another man.

Finally I said, "I'm just a poor Aussie trying to make a go of it in this world."

"I'll bet." She smiled cynically.

"I heard how you lost your first husband. That must have been hard."

She didn't miss a beat, but her smile disappeared. "Oh, yes," she said, allowing just the proper tone of regret to creep into her voice, "it was very hard, but when things like that happen, we must move on."

"That's a good way to think of it. Well, according to what I read, you don't have to worry about making a living."

"Oh, I manage to scrape by."

I laughed then, and it was almost genuine. "With all the millions you got from your husband's estate, I imagine you scrape by pretty well."

The music ended, and we walked back to where the wives were standing. Fant appeared and said, "Come on, we're having a little meeting."

"A meeting? What about?"

"They'll never tell you that," Marlene said. "When Leo calls a meeting, all the men jump up like frogs."

"Nothing like that, Marlene. Just a little bit of business." He looked at me and nodded, and I turned and said, "Thanks for the dance."

"You're welcome."

I followed Fant out of the big room and down the hall into a smaller room with a large table in it. Robert Leighton, the banker, was there along with Jeb Wilkerson and Dane Fetterman. They all looked at me and smiled, and it was Dane who said, "Welcome to the club, Davis."

Fant turned to me. "I've got a little proposition here that we could all do well at. It occurs to me you might be interested."

"What kind of proposition?"

"Sit down. We'll talk about it. Dane, will you fix drinks?"

I saw something flicker in Dane's eyes, and I knew it was anger. I knew him that well, at least. I sat down, and Dane proceeded to fix drinks for everyone. "Just Perrier for me," I said.

"You a teetotaler?" Fant demanded.

"When I'm doing business I am. I'm just a dull Aussie. I have to watch myself among you big city chums."

"I think you got the right idea there, Davis," Jeb laughed as he took his drink.

Robert Leighton shook his head. "Leo," he said, "before you let this out, you may want to think about it."

Fant turned to stare at him. "I have thought about it, Robert." There was such finality in his words that Leighton's mouth shut and he shrugged and said no more. Fant turned to me. "I don't know much about your business, but that's your right. What we have here is a little real-estate deal."

I listened as Fant outlined the deal, which involved putting a group of condos at a spot on the coast. He made it sound very fine until something clicked in my mind. When I had been with the Sierra Club, I had heard about this particular site—Marlin Cove. It was a valuable piece of ground, for the coast was being lost rapidly. Then the details swam to the surface. Marlin Cove was the nesting site for an endangered species of bird, one of only two such sites left in the country. I hadn't been involved with this myself, but, of course, I was aware of it. As Fant continued to speak, I saw the whole program in a flash. He ended by saying, "So, we get this property, Marlin Cove. It's a beautiful site, and the condos will make a bundle."

"I understand there are some laws against development on that particular site," I said and saw the surprise flare in Fant's eyes.

"You heard about it?"

"You're not the first, Leo, to think about putting something there, but the laws are pretty stringent."

Fant took out a cigar, clipped the end off, and lit it without speaking. When he got it going, he said in a tight voice, "I think I can guarantee that we can get the laws bent a little bit."

"What kind of money are we talking about?"

"Not a whole lot for the land. We've decided to put in five million apiece, but if you'd come in, we could cut it to four."

"I guarantee you we'll double our money," Robert Leighton said. "I've looked into this thing from every angle, Davis."

"That's right." Jeb nodded. "It can't miss."

I studied Fant, for after all this was his deal. The rest were the barons, but he was the king. "I might be interested. I'll go out and look at the site."

"I'll be glad to go with you," Fant said.

"Good. The rest of you want to go?"

"I'd like to see it," Dane said. He had said nothing at all during the discussion, but he had been drinking rather steadily.

Fant shook his head slightly. "Some other time, Dane. I need to spend some time with Davis alone." He grinned, but it did not reach his eyes. "We've got to know each other pretty well to get into a thing like this."

"That's right," I said noncommittally. "And I assume you want none of this to get out."

"That's right," Fant said flatly.

"I'm ready to go whenever you have time."

"Tomorrow, then," Fant said. I noticed he didn't ask but gave it as an order.

At that instant, I made up my mind: Whatever else I did, I was going to poke a stick through Fant's wheel. They would never get that property!

Anne Frank's words flashed through my mind again: *How wonderful it is that nobody need wait a single moment before starting to improve the world.* Well, I could improve the world in one way—by seeing to it that King Leo Fant did not get his way at Marlin Cove.

∞

The Black Widow was at the party, and somehow she arranged it so that I would take her home. It was late when we pulled up in front of her house, and she turned to me and put her hands on the back of my neck. "Come on in," she said.

"It's pretty late."

"Who cares?"

"All right. Just for a while."

We went inside. It was a rich woman's house and fairly impressive, but I was not thinking about houses. We sat down, and she drank some more. I stuck with Perrier.

"Are you some kind of a Puritan? You don't drink?"

"I'm a bad drinker," I said. "Totally irresponsible."

Her voice was slurred, and she leaned toward me, pressing herself against my arm. "So am I," she said. "Take advantage of me."

"I never take advantage of a woman. Superman and I keep the world safe for democracy and protect helpless women."

She found that amusing, and I was able to fend her off. Her intentions were obvious, but finally she said, "I don't know what kind of deal Leo Fant was offering, but be careful, Davis."

"Why? Is he so dangerous?"

"He's never been caught, but some of the people who've been with him have been hurt. I was surprised you were asked in. I won't ask you about the deal. I know you won't talk." She took another drink. "It'll make a bundle, I'd guess. Those men don't lose money."

"Well, Dane Fetterman doesn't need any more money, if what I read in the papers is true."

Maggie laughed. "Dane? He doesn't have any money."

I stared at her. "When Marlene's husband died—what's his name? Ollie something?—he left a bundle. Right?"

"He didn't leave it to Dane. She got it all."

"But it's his now as much as hers."

"You think that? You're more naive than I thought. She's got the money, not Dane."

I got a little more out of her, but sensed that I couldn't push her too far for information without arousing her suspicion. I made my getaway, and as I drove home, I thought, *So Dane's really Marlene's gofer now. She says go for it, and he does. I thought something was peculiar about him.* Even though Fant let Dane into the deal because of the money, it was Marlene's money, not Dane's. Somehow that pleased me. It would be easier now, I thought. I tried to work up some sympathy for Dane but couldn't.

Marlene's the Black Widow in Blue Springs, not Maggie Osterman, I thought, and I realized that I'd have to reorganize my plan a little bit. But that was all right. I had time.

CHAPTER
EIGHTEEN

I had read, of course, of people being obsessed, but I never really understood it until after my first glimpse of Dane and Marlene. I managed to carry out my role pretty well, I think, even though, since the moment I first looked at them, I'd been able to think of nothing else. It's as if their images were painted on the inside of my eyelids, so that even when I closed my eyes, I still saw them.

In the week following that first encounter, I saw them twice, once at the club and once at the fitness center. I tried to occupy myself with reading, exploring the country, or walking up and down the beach, but no matter where I went, no matter whether I was awake or asleep, I could not get away from them. I even went so far as to rent a Taurus and follow them for three days, but they didn't do anything suspicious. I don't know what I was expecting. I did find out through talking with the manager at the club that Marlene always worked out three times a week, twice in the afternoons and on Tuesday evening from seven to nine.

Obsession was not totally new to me—I was obsessed by computers for much of my adult life, but even then I was able to turn my attention to a few other things. Now that seemed to be impossible. Trying to break that pattern, I had Joelle fix dinner for me twice, but it was no fun eating alone. She put the food on the table, then left and came back afterward to clean up.

On Monday afternoon, I swam for an hour, then dressed and went to knock on Joelle's door. It was three o'clock. When she came to the door, I said, "Do you need anything from the store?"

She paused and said, "No, but there's one thing that you could do for me, if you wouldn't mind. I need to pick Rachel up from school. Would you mind staying here with Frank?"

"Not a bit," I said quickly. "I promised him a chess game, and I should have been here before."

"He'd like that very much," she said, and I could hear the gratitude in her voice. "Would you mind if I took a little time to go do some shopping?"

"Stay as long as you want," I said. "I'll enjoy the game."

"Go right on in," she said. "Oh, he'll probably ask you to help him into his wheelchair. Would you mind?"

"Not at all."

"I can do it if it bothers you. I know some people are a bit finicky about sick people."

"I can handle it. You go right on."

"All right. I'll be back in an hour or so."

"Take your time."

I went directly to Frank's room. I found him sitting up in bed with a book on some sort of rack that held it up at an angle at eye level.

"Hello, Frank. I came to wipe your eye at chess."

A gladness came into his eyes. "We'll just see about that."

"Let me help you into the chair," I said, not giving him a chance to refuse. I picked up the book rack and put it on the table. Frank was wearing pajamas, and I moved the wheelchair over, picked him up, and set him in it. I doubt that he weighed much over a hundred and twenty-five pounds. It was like picking up a child.

"You do that so easily. It's hard on Joelle. I help her all I can."

"You're lucky to have somebody as strong as she is. Where's the game?"

"Let's go into the breakfast room. The set's over there on that chest."

I picked up the chess box and board and pushed him through the house. When we got to the breakfast room, I moved one of the chairs out of the way and pushed him up close. He put his arms up on the table. I sat down opposite him and opened the box. As soon as I saw the chessmen, I laughed. They were all dressed in uniforms of the Confederacy. "I never saw chessmen like this."

"It's for us good old Southern boys. All Confederate figures."

I picked one and held it up. "I guess this is the king. It looks suspiciously like Robert E. Lee."

"That's Marse Robert." He showed me the rest of the set, which was beautifully done, and then we set up the board. I was a better-than-average chess player. As a matter of fact, I think I could have gone into competition. But Frank beat me so quickly that I sat there staring at the board.

"I think you're a ringer," I said. "Nobody ever beat me that quick before."

"I told you I was good."

"Well, let's try it again," I said grimly. "I have a bad side to my character. I hate to lose."

The next game was still going on when Joelle and Rachel came in. Rachel ran over and put her arms around her dad. He kissed the top of her head and said, "You can't have Mr. Davis play with you and your dolls. I'm busy beating him at chess."

"You won one game already," I said.

"I've won this one too."

"No, you haven't."

He reached out and moved his queen. How hard it was for him even to do that—such a simple thing as moving a chessman!

"Checkmate!" he said, grinning with satisfaction.

I stared at the board and then laughed. "You cheated."

"How did I cheat?"

"I don't know, but you did."

"I'll give you a chance to get even."

"No, Daddy, I want Mr. Davis to play with me."

"You had him yesterday. It's my turn today. Scoot on off, sweetheart."

"Come along, Rachel," Joelle said firmly. "Maybe Mr. Davis will come back another time and play."

"As soon as I whip your dad's tail in chess, we'll have a session with Barbie and her friends," I promised.

I turned back and Frank was smiling at me. "You have a way with children."

"No, I really don't, Frank. I've never been around kids. Rachel's the first child I ever played with."

"Well, you've won her heart."

"Hitler could win her heart if he'd play with her Barbie dolls." I grinned. "Now, let's see about this game, and I'm watching you this time."

The next game lasted half an hour, and I won, but I think it was because Frank was getting tired. He finally said, "I think I'd like to go back to bed now."

"Sure," I said quickly. I got up, put the men back in the box, folded the board, and then pushed him back to his room. After I put him in the bed, he said, "Would you mind setting up that tape recorder for me and putting it where I can turn it on?"

I put the book rack back on the bed, and he told me how to adjust it so that the surface was flat instead of tilted. I put the cassette recorder on it, and he said, "Give me one of the tapes out of that set over there—number fifteen."

I took tape number fifteen out of the case, closed the cover, and then went back and put it in the machine. "What is this, Frank?"

"The Bible on tape. It's read by Alexander Scourby. He has a great voice. It's easier for me to listen to him read than it is to keep turning the pages. Have you ever heard him read?"

"I heard him read some poetry, I think, but never the Bible."

"Start the machine. I think I've got it set where I left off."

Scourby's magnificent voice broke the silence: "Second Samuel chapter eleven. 'In the spring, at the time when kings go off to war, David sent Joab out with the king's men and the whole Israelite army. They destroyed the Ammonites and besieged Rabbah. But David remained in Jerusalem.

"'One evening David got up from his bed and walked around on the roof of the palace. From the roof he saw a woman bathing. The woman was very beautiful, and David sent someone to find out about her. The man said, "Isn't this Bathsheba, the daughter of Eliam and the wife of Uriah the Hittite?" Then David sent messengers to get her. She came to him, and he slept with her. (She had purified herself from her uncleanness.) Then she went back home. The woman conceived and sent word to David, saying, "I am pregnant."'"

Frank turned the tape off and said, "Do you know the rest of that story, Davis?"

"No. That was David who did that?"

"David the king. He took the woman and committed adultery with her. The rest of the story tells how that David tried to get Uriah to come home from the battle where he was fighting. Uriah came home, but he refused to lie with his wife. He said that his fellow soldiers weren't with their wives, and he was no better than they."

"That put David in a spot, I guess. What did he do?"

"He murdered Uriah."

"Murdered him! King David? I didn't know that."

"He didn't do the deed himself. He had his commanding officer Joab do it. He told him to place Uriah in the part of the battle where he'd be sure to get killed, and Joab did it, so Uriah died in battle."

"What about the woman?"

"David married her."

"That was pretty rough. I didn't know a Bible character would do a thing like that."

Frank looked at me. "Strange you don't know this story. It's very common. They even made a movie out of it."

"Well, what about David and the woman?"

"It's very dramatic. Bathsheba bore David a son, but God—this is in chapter twelve—sent a prophet called Nathan, and he told David a beautiful story, a parable, about a man who had only one little lamb. But a rich man who had many lambs came and took it away from him. The story enraged David, and he said that the man who had done this thing should die, and Nathan said, 'You are the man.'"

I stared at Frank and shook my head. "That must have been pretty dangerous, for a prophet to talk to a king like that."

"With most kings it would have been deadly, but David was a man after God's own heart. He had done two very wrong things, but he knew that he was guilty, and he said, 'I have sinned against the Lord.'"

"So he got off."

"No, he didn't. Nathan told him, 'You are not going to die, but the son born to you will die.' And he told David that God would bring calamity on him from his own family."

It was very quiet in the room. I could even hear the mantel clock ticking over on the chest of drawers beside the wall. "And did he have trouble?" I asked.

"He had nothing but trouble for the rest of his life. One of his sons murdered another of his sons, and then Absalom, David's favorite son, conspired and raised a rebellion to kill David and take his crown. He paid for his pleasure with all of the things he treasured most." Frank shook his head and said, "The Bible says, 'A man reaps what he sows.' David lost everything for just a brief moment of pleasure."

I couldn't think of a thing to say. The thing that I had planned was every bit as vicious as David's crime. I didn't have to speak, though, because at that moment Joelle came back with Rachel. Rachel said, "Come on, Mr. Davis, you've been in here long enough."

"Well, I guess that's my master's voice, Frank. I'll come back again, and I'll practice up on my chess."

"Thanks for the game." Frank hesitated and said, "If you ever want to borrow any of these tapes, feel free."

"I may get a set," I said. Rachel grabbed my hand and dragged me out to the living room, where she had the dolls set up. I plunked myself down with my legs crossed like a tailor and for the next fifteen minutes mostly watched Rachel's face. She was a beautiful child, and I had become very fond of her. After a while I noticed that she had stopped playing with the dolls. She was just holding her favorite and looking down.

"What's the matter, Rachel?" She looked up, and I was shocked to see tears in her eyes. "Don't you feel well?"

"I'm afraid."

I moved over and put my arm around her, and she reached out and clung to me. "I'm afraid my daddy's going to die and leave Mama and me alone."

I couldn't think of a single thing to say for, of course, this was exactly what would happen. I sat holding her, and she seemed like a small bird with fragile bones. It was the first time that I'd ever really held a child in my life, and I felt something change in me—something turned over, is the best way I can describe it. I wanted to help her, to solve her problem, but I knew I couldn't.

Then Joelle was there saying, "Come along, Rachel, it's time for you to go in and see your daddy. He'll read to you a little bit maybe."

"All right, Mama." She got up and I rose with her. When she left the room, Joelle said, "I'm sorry, but you know how children are."

"I really don't. I don't think she's like other children."

"She's holding up well, but she's so smart." Joelle shook her head, and in that silent moment, I saw that she was tall and shapely in a way that would affect any man. The light ran over the curve of her shoulders, deepening her breast, and her face mirrored her feelings, as I was sure it always did.

"I don't see how you handle it all, Joelle," I said.

"I didn't handle it well at first. When Frank first got sick and I found out how bad it was, I went to pieces. But you know, Frank helped me."

"How was that?"

"He's the bravest man I know, Davis. You saw the picture of him. He was so strong and athletic and full of life, and all that has been stripped from him. A lot of people would have given up and hated God, but his illness brought him closer to God. He gave his heart to Christ, and I've watched him since then." Tears came into her eyes. "He had faith in Jesus in spite of losing everything, and I knew I had to have a God like that myself. I know I'm going to lose him—" She hesitated, then took out a handkerchief and wiped the tears away. "But Christians never say good-bye, you know."

That struck me hard. I said, "I'll do the best I can to come back and be some company for him."

"Thanks for coming, Davis."

I left the house. Everything about this family shook me up. The vulnerability of Rachel, the sad plight of a strong man struck down, and now a woman who was sticking by him regardless of how hard it was. I glanced up and saw clouds drifting across the sky, and a flight of birds cried out as they passed close overhead. I was strong and had a brand-new body, and yet I didn't have the peace that Frank and Joelle Doren 'had. I was missing something, and it made me restless. I tried to blot it out of my mind and decided that I couldn't afford to think about things like that.

CHAPTER NINETEEN

I had become accustomed to three worlds. One was in the house I'd leased, where I felt completely out-of-place. It wasn't my house, and I got no thrill out of living in a movie star's home; it was no better to me than the Marriott. The other world was out back at the Doren's home. For the next week, I didn't miss a day of playing chess with Frank Doren and Barbie dolls with Rachel. I had also been there two evenings, and while I played with Rachel, Joelle put Frank to bed. Later, after she had put Rachel to bed, she and I drank coffee and talked, sitting at the kitchen table. Mostly Joelle did the talking. I'd had to invent a background for myself, but I stayed away from those lies as much as I possibly could. I didn't like to be dishonest with her, which surprised me, since I'd been dishonest with practically everyone else since I'd decided to get revenge on Dane and Marlene.

The other world was the world of Marlene and Dane Fetterman. That included my new "friends," whom I was helping to stamp out a beautiful site and fill it up with ugly condominiums. I had met only once with the whole group, and according to Leo Fant things were progressing. He wouldn't name names, but I knew that he and the others were talking to members of the state legislature. It would be necessary to get some state laws changed before they could make the grab. As for Dane, he came to the meeting and said nothing, but drank steadily the whole time. After the meeting, Jeb said, "I can understand why Dane's drinking so much."

"Why's that? It looks to me like he's got everything," I said, to spur him into revealing more.

"Well, nobody understood it at first, but I found out that he doesn't have control of any of the fortune that Marlene inherited."

"But I heard he made a bundle marketing Ollie's movie-making program."

"He did—and lost it all playing the stock market."

"He's broke?"

"Pretty much. Sure, he gets some royalties yet, but he's got expensive tastes. He doesn't have enough money to do anything he wants, and that eats him alive. He's playing with fire, though—running around with different women, taking them out on that yacht of his—or of hers, I should say. I think Leo made a mistake asking him into this. You can't trust drunks."

"If he doesn't have any money, I can't see why either."

"Leo believes that Dane can influence his wife to put up the money. I'm not sure about that. It seems to me like she keeps him on a pretty strict budget."

I hadn't changed my mind about torpedoing the deal. I was picking up all the names I could, and if I had to, I would hire a private detective to find out which legislators were being bought off.

When Tuesday night came, I went down to the fitness center. I dressed, and when I got up to the indoor track, as I had suspected, Marlene was already there. I did my stretching exercises and then started jogging slowly. She had worked up to a faster speed, and when she caught up to me, she said with some surprise, "Why, hello."

"Hi, Marlene." I trotted along beside her, picking up my pace. "You mind if I join you? I hate to run alone."

"No problem."

We moved around the track, and she was in great shape. We talked about unimportant things for a while, and then we upped the pace to the point that it was hard to talk. I kept up with her, and when we slowed down, she said, "That's about enough for me. Do you do anything besides jog?"

"I do about thirty minutes on weights."

"Come on. We'll do them together."

We went into the weight room, and I went through the routine with her. As I was doing curls, she reached out and touched my biceps. "You're in great shape, Davis. You always been into weights?"

"All my life," I lied cheerfully. "I think it's important for a man to keep his figure."

"More important for a woman," she said.

"Well, you've done that," I winked, lewdly I hoped. She laughed and we continued to talk about keeping in shape.

When I'd completed my workout, I said, "Well, that's about enough for me."

"Me too. I guess I'll shower."

"Nice having company, Marlene."

"Yes, it was."

I went down to the shower room as quick as I could, showered, dressed, and went out to the Porsche. I lifted the hood and leaned over the engine, waiting for Marlene to come out. It took her much longer. When she did, I didn't say anything. She saw me and came over.

"What's wrong? Car trouble?"

"Blasted thing won't start. The more you pay for something, the more worthless it is."

"You want me to give you a ride home?"

"If you don't mind. I'll have the garage tow this thing in later. I don't want to fool with it now."

We got into her Mercedes, talking about cars. She stopped in front of my house, and I asked, "Have you ever been inside this place?"

"No, I never have."

"I wish you'd come in and look it over. I just leased it with an option to buy. I'm no expert on houses, but someone told me you did some decorating once."

"I'd like to see the place."

We walked up to the front door. I unlocked it and let her in. As I gave her the tour through the house, I had a weird feeling—sort of *déjà vu*—thinking that one of the first things we'd ever done together was to look at my house, and that I had fallen in love with her while she was decorating it.

I said, "Why don't we have a drink and you can tell me the bad news—that they want too much for it."

"Let's."

We went into the recreation room, which had a bar. I motioned her to a table, and she said she'd have a Scotch on the rocks. I fixed her one, then fixed one for myself—only I used tea instead of Scotch. I took the drinks to the table and said, "I always have doubles. That all right?"

"Sure."

I sat down and said, "Well, tell me about the house."

As she talked about the house, I managed to get another double down her, while I drank tea. She didn't handle alcohol well—I knew that already—and soon her speech began to slur.

By the time she was all talked out about the house, I'd gotten a third drink into her hands, and as she sipped it, I said, "It must have been hard losing your husband. I read about it in the papers. What was he like?" I asked, as carelessly as I could.

"Oh, Ollie was fine. Dull as dishwater, of course."

"Couldn't have been all that dull if a sharp woman like you married him."

She gave me an odd look and then laughed slightly. "Let's talk about something else. It was hard losing Ollie."

It took all the acting ability I had to smile and say, "But you've got a good life now. I like your husband. A woman needs a man to take care of her, especially a rich one." She smiled at that, and I knew exactly what she was thinking. I added, "You know, if you hadn't married Dane, I might have come courting you along with the rest of the herd."

"You'd marry for money?" she said.

"No, I don't think I would. Not now. Maybe before I had any. You know, Marlene, if you get a certain amount of money, more money is meaningless."

This interested her, and she said, "What do you do then?"

"I live."

"Why haven't you married?"

We were sitting on the couch, and I reached over and let my hand fall on her shoulder. "I'm waiting until I have one of those Hollywood movie miracles. You know, where a guy sees a woman and it's almost as if he gets struck down by lightning. He falls in love. He can't think, can't behave. Kind of like the flu."

She was amused by this. "No, you're lying. I can tell when a man's lying. Tell me the truth."

How funny—I was lying with every breath, and she had no idea. I said, "I want a woman as strong as I am. I need somebody to hold the rope."

"Hold the rope. What does that mean?"

"You haven't heard that story? There was a man who fell into a shaft of some kind, and it was so small that only a boy could get through. So they were going to lower this boy on a rope to save the man, but the boy was afraid to go down. They kept after him, and finally he said, 'If you get my dad to hold the rope, I'll go.' So they got his dad, and when his dad held the rope, the boy went down." I sipped more of my tea. "I want a woman I can trust to hold the rope."

Marlene was staring at me, but her eyes weren't quite focused. She wasn't drunk, but her reaction time had slowed, and her thinking was plodding. She said, "That's interesting. I've never heard a man talk about a woman like that."

"I believe in equal rights. I'd want someone who would trust me to hold the rope if she bottomed out."

"I don't think that kind of relationship exists between men and women."

"Sure it does. I've seen it three times in my life. If it can happen once, it can happen again."

She was quiet for a while, and I said, "What do you think about this deal Leo Fant is suggesting? I'm thinking about going in on it. I guess Dane must like it, if he's thinking of putting that much of his money into it."

She laughed and held her glass up. "Give me another drink."

I got the drink and handed it to her. I had another glass of tea. She sipped it and said, "Dane doesn't have any money to put into anything."

"But I thought you got all of Ollie Benson's estate."

"That's right. *I* got it, not Dane."

I knew by this time that she was over the line with her drinking. She had to form the words carefully as she said, "Dane's been after me to put his name on everything, but I won't."

"That must be hard on Dane," I said.

"He's got everything he wants. He's got that stupid boat and his women to go on it, cars, clothes ... But I know men too well, so I'm keeping my hands on the money." She straightened up and stared at me. "Are you getting me drunk?"

I laughed and said, "I thought you were getting *me* drunk." She thought this was terribly funny, and she got up and started to get another drink, but she staggered. I jumped up and caught her as she nearly fell. She put her arms around me, and I kissed her, as she wanted me to. I had known her kisses before, but she had improved—or, even more likely, she had never given me the real thing before. She clung to me, and although I hadn't had much practice I gave it my best shot. Finally she drew back and said in a slurred voice, "I need to get away from you. When I'm drinking, I do foolish things."

"I'm no danger. Just a good old Aussie."

She shook her head, but she didn't step back. "I don't trust men."

"Better you don't. I don't trust women."

"Why not?"

"Well, to tell the truth, quite a few have tried to put me in their pockets after I made money. I never know now if a woman likes me or my money."

Marlene stared at me and blinked her eyes and then had to lick her lips before she could speak. "I've got the same problem."

"I don't mean to hurt your feelings, Marlene. You're about the most desirable woman I've ever met, but I have to be careful."

Marlene stared at me and tried to think. "You think I'm after your money?"

"I don't know. I hope not."

"But—but I've got plenty of money."

"I know you do, but when people have a lot of money, they want more." I knew I had pushed the envelope, so I kissed her and said, "Come on. I've got to drive you home. I'm not quite as drunk as you are. I wouldn't want anything to happen to you."

I got her out to the car. When I started it, she said, "How will you get back?"

"I'll walk. I've been known to do it before."

I took her to her home, but as I approached, I said, "Maybe I'd better get out a block away from the house."

"Why would you do that?"

"So Dane won't see us."

"He's not there. He's cheating on me, but he doesn't think I know it. He's on his boat with a cocktail waitress named Debbie."

"How do you know that?"

"Private detective."

I pulled up in front of the house, and she said, "Come on in. Dane won't be home until morning." She leaned over and pulled my head down, and her caress left no doubt about her meaning.

I let her hold onto me for a long time, then I drew back. "I meant what I said, Marlene. I've got to be careful and so do you. I've got money, but maybe I want more. You have to be careful about guys like me."

She stared at me as if I were some sort of strange specimen. "I've never met a man who talked like you. Come on in and we'll talk about it."

"No. If I did, we'd make love, and I'm not into playing games, Marlene." I had practiced this speech carefully, and I knew exactly where I wanted to go with it. "I've done enough of that. I haven't seen much of the real thing between men and women, but I've seen enough to know what can happen. Maybe I'll never find a woman that I'll trust to hold the rope, but that's what I've got to have."

I got out, opened the door, and helped her out. She was looking at me with an odd expression. "If I were you," I said, "I wouldn't drink around guys like me. Not everybody is as noble as I am."

She laughed and said, "Maybe you *are* noble. I never met a noble man. It's a new experience."

I kissed her on the cheek. "Good night, Marlene."

I made my exit, and I knew I'd timed it just right. She was stunned, which was exactly what I wanted. As I walked down the street toward my house, I was thinking, *She likes the challenge. She'll try me again. Maybe I ought to think about going into movies. I didn't know I was such a great actor.*

Walking through the darkness, I was startled by something that swooped past me, near my left side. I caught a glimpse of an owl falling on something, and I heard a frantic thumping, then a high-pitched, frightened squeal. There was just enough light for me to see the owl rise, carrying a rabbit in his talons, and the rabbit squealed as he died.

CHAPTER
TWENTY

The house that Marlene and Dane had bought was ostentatious even for them. It was modern—which to me meant ugly. Everything was sharp angles and slick surfaces with paintings on the wall that neither I nor anyone else could understand. I was a little surprised that Marlene would decorate a house in that way; I knew she had good taste. But who knows what money will do to a person? I think they simply found the most expensive place they could, trying to throw money away with both hands.

I was working on my tan, lying down on one of those cot affairs that sits up or lies down as you prefer, and talking to Shirley Fant and her young man Ted Blakely.

Shirley was wearing a rather modest bathing suit, as such things go, and looked very pretty. Every time she looked over at Blakely, she lit up like up an incandescent bulb.

Blakely was a tall, rangy fellow who looked as if he would have made a good forward on a first-class basketball team. He wasn't handsome. He looked, more or less, like a young Abe Lincoln, and he could not keep his eyes off Shirley.

"If you two don't watch out, as the song says, people will think you're in love."

"I've always loved that song," Blakely said. "Maybe I'll break out singing it, like they do in musicals. It always tickled me how they could burst into song and no one paid much attention, as if people did that all the time."

Shirley took his hand and looked at him in a manner I could only call adoringly. I don't think I had ever looked at anybody adoringly, but she had it down.

"You're probably wondering about us, aren't you, Davis?"

"I don't think anybody has to wonder much. When's the wedding?"

Shirley gave me an odd look and shook her head. "There's not likely to be a wedding unless something happens."

"Why not?"

"I'm not rich enough for Leo." Blakely shrugged.

"I don't think anyone would be," Shirley said, and there was a petulant expression on her face. "We just don't know what to do, Davis."

"Well, you can always go to one of those know-it-all women who write columns. They always know how to solve everybody's problems, except their own, probably. But I know what to tell you to do."

They both looked at me with surprise. It was Blakely who said, "What should we do?"

"Do the right thing."

Shirley laughed. "Well, that's certainly nondirective counseling."

"It's the best advice in the world. Do the right thing, and you can't go wrong." I saw that they were disappointed, and I said, "Look, it's your life. Don't let anybody else live it for you."

At that moment Maggie Osterman came up. She was wearing a bikini, which was a mistake. She was one of those women who looked better in her clothes than out of them, and she plumped down beside me. Almost at once Shirley and Ted got up and walked away. Blakely grinned back over his shoulder and said, "I'll be sure to take your advice, Davis."

Even before they were beyond hearing distance, Maggie said, "Well, Father O'Malley, you have blessed the young people."

"A man is poor indeed if he can't be a blessing to those he encounters."

"All right. What about me? Give me some counseling."

"My own philosophy is: Never eat at a café named Mom's and never play cards with a man named Doc," I said. "That's about the extent of my wisdom. I do feel sorry for those young folks, though."

"Young folks! They're as old as you are."

"Well, they *seem* young."

The sound of an argument, loud and vociferous, floated across the pool. We both looked across to see Dane and Marlene walking along under an umbrella, their faces twisted with anger.

"That's not going to last long."

"What's not going to last long?"

"Dane and Marlene. She'll get rid of him. He'd do the same to her if he had the money and she didn't." She moved closer, leaned against me, and whispered, "Come on. This place is dullsville. Let's go party."

I got up, saying, "I've got to get my exercise in." I plunged into the pool quickly and thrashed back and forth until I saw that she had left. Then I got out and continued sunning. I went to sleep there in the sun, and when I woke up, Marlene was standing over me. "You've been sleeping for two hours out here. You're going to be cooked."

I blinked, got up, stretched, and yawned. When I looked down to see if I'd burned, I still could not believe that this body, arched and firm with muscles and slender in the middle, was mine. I hoped I wasn't becoming one of those muscle guys who stand around posing and looking at themselves and trying to get others to admire them too.

"Go get dressed and come inside," she said.

"Where's Dane?"

"Off with some bimbo, I suppose. Go get dressed."

I went into the pool house, showered, got dressed, and went back toward the clubhouse. I thought about leaving, but Marlene saw me and said, "Come keep me company."

We went into one of the ugly rooms that had at least a decent stereo. It was playing Ravel's *Bolero*, a piece I have always liked. It made me want to stick a rose between my teeth and dance around the room, but I managed to resist the impulse. Marlene had been drinking, and she insisted that I drink with her. Drunks always insist on that. I parked myself beside a big, ugly potted plant, and when she gave me the glass of Scotch on the rocks, I held it in my right hand. I waited until she was tilting her glass, and in one swift motion dumped it into the plant, then lifted the glass to my lips. She lowered her own. I shook my head and said, "That's good Scotch."

"Nothing but the best around here." She was wearing a pale green dress cut low and high. There was no denying that she was one feminine piece of work—one of those women who could make picking her teeth look sexy. She said, "Get us some more drinks, will you, Davis?"

"Sure." I got two more drinks, handed her hers, and sat waiting for the chance to dump mine. She twirled the ice around with her forefinger, then looked up and said, "What about this deal that Leo Fant's putting together?"

She'd apparently been so drunk the other night that she'd forgotten I'd asked her the same question. "Do you know anything about it?"

"I know it'll be only semilegal if Leo has anything to do about it. He's smart, though. He's managed to keep his own skirts clean. Some of his friends have gone to jail or gone broke."

"I think you'd be smart to stay out of it, Marlene."

"Dane's been telling me it would make us a fortune."

"You've got a fortune."

"That's what I say, but you know Dane."

"Not very well."

She gave me an odd look and lifted her drink. I got rid of mine, and when she lowered the glass, her voice was slurred. "I know Dane better than anybody." I waited for her to say more, but her mind was still on the deal with Fant. "You're telling me to stay out of it?"

"I'm not telling you," I said. "I'm just suggesting it could be too risky."

"But you're in it."

"Not all the way."

She continued to pump me for all she was worth. I got up to get her another drink, which she had asked for, but when I handed it to her, I didn't sit down. I walked around the room, looking at the pictures on the wall. Some were photographs, and I was surprised to see one of my old self, the fat Ollie, with Marlene. It had been taken on our honeymoon, and, of course, I was dressed in expensive clothes that had been tailored to hide my paunch as much as possible. It wasn't successful, of course, and I stood there staring at it. It was like looking at someone else. That man was gone. Ollie was no more. Rest in peace, Ollie Benson.

"That was taken on my honeymoon with Ollie." She had come up behind me.

"He must have been a genius to invent that movie-making software."

"He was brilliant. No question about that."

"What was he like besides being brilliant with computers?" I took a chance and added, "You didn't marry him for his looks, I take it. Why, he must have weighed three hundred pounds."

Marlene shook her head and looked down in the glass that was almost empty. She glanced up and said, "He was a slob. But at least he was honest."

"That's always good." Something prompted me to keep poking at her, to figure out what she really thought—although

I already knew the answer. "Didn't you care for him at all, Marlene?"

"No, not really." She drained the glass and then turned to face me. "Are you shocked?"

I glanced back at the picture, and memory suddenly flooded me of how happy I'd been when she had agreed to marry me, and on the honeymoon when I, who had no experience with sex at all, had been introduced to it by this woman who didn't love me.

"He looks sad," I said.

"I don't want to talk about that." She put the glass down on a round glass table, then she reached up and put her arms around me, fastening them in back. She put her head down on my chest and stood for a moment. Her voice was blurred as she said, "What's wrong with me, Davis? I've got all the money I can ever spend, but life's no fun."

I put my hands on her shoulders lightly. She was pressed against me, and, as always, I was stirred by this woman. I couldn't help it. She had a power I couldn't deny. "Doesn't that tell you something, Marlene?"

"Tell me what?"

"Tell you that money isn't the answer. Look at Marilyn Monroe. She had what almost every woman in America wants—love, fame, fortune—but she couldn't accept life on those terms. She killed herself."

She looked up at me, and her face was close to mine. Her lips looked soft and vulnerable, and there was a smoldering in her eyes. "I drink because I'm afraid—and I don't know what I'm afraid of." She pulled my head down then and kissed me. Her lips were soft and yielding, and she pulled them back and whispered, "Come to bed with me, Davis."

"Marlene, sex isn't the answer any more than money is."

"It is for a little while. Come on."

Looking back, I honestly don't know what I would have done. I had gotten stronger physically through exercise and weight training, but I was still weak as far as this woman was concerned. I felt myself drawn to her—and it would be so easy! The thought came to me at that moment, *She's my wife. There wouldn't be anything wrong with going to bed with her.* But even with that thought came the memory of how she had laughed at me when she had told me I was nothing but a slob and that she was going to kill me.

I'm pretty sure I would have wiggled out of her invitation, but I'll never know—because at that moment a shout caused both of us to turn quickly. Dane had come in, his face flushed with drink and his eyes bright with anger. He was shouting something unintelligibly, and he started straight for us. He had been drinking, but he was still fast. He threw a karate chop at me, and I blocked it automatically, caught his arm, and shifted to a come-along. I had his fingers so that I could easily break one of them, and the pain, I knew, was excruciating. He sank to his knees.

"Grab him where it hurts and he'll follow you anywhere," Trey had told me, and had demonstrated it most painfully.

Holding Dane's fingers, I said, "Look, Dane, there's nothing wrong here. Nothing's happened."

He cursed and cried out and tried to get loose. I applied enough pressure that he cried out in pain. "I'm going to turn you loose, Dane. Don't try to make anything out of this. Marlene was just feeling a little sad. That's all."

I released his hand but kept my eyes on him. He was good at karate, good enough to shatter your throat with the edge of his hand.

But he had been convinced by the speed of my movement, and by the strength I'd shown. He rose to his feet, red-faced, cursing and shouting, but at Marlene. It was as if I had ceased to exist.

I went outside, got into the Porsche, and drove away. As I did, I began to give myself one of those little inner examinations that I suppose we all do. It was almost like an interrogation.

"Well," I said to myself, "they're both miserable, and you got to hurt Dane. Are you happy?"

"No," I answered myself, "I'm not."

"Well, you should be."

"I know I should be. That's what I've been living for all this time. That's why I've gone through all this business of changing myself."

"Then just enjoy it."

But I found I couldn't. As a matter of fact, as I drove toward home, I discovered I was rather sickened by the whole affair.

∞

The big house was lonesome, quiet as a tomb, and no matter how much music I played on the fancy stereo it didn't help. Finally I went back to the Doren house. When I knocked on the door and it opened, I said, "Hello, Joelle. I thought I'd play chess with Frank."

"You can try, but it might be better if you just talk to him."

Something in her voice grabbed me. As I stepped inside, I turned to face her. "What's wrong?"

"He's been worse, Davis. A lot worse." There was a tremor of fear in her voice, unusual for Joelle. She was the strongest woman I had ever seen, in the best sense of that word.

I said, "Maybe you're right. I'll just go talk to him."

I followed her back to Frank's bedroom, but when we looked in, she shook her head and put her finger to her lips. "He's sleeping," she said. She closed the door and led me back to the living room. She asked, "Would you like something to drink—coffee or a Coke?"

"No, thanks. You're worried about him."

"Of course. I'm always worried about him."

"I mean something more than just the usual burden you have to carry."

"He's dying a little bit every day."

I saw clearly then that what Joelle had to endure was much worse than if her husband had been killed instantly in an automobile accident, or died some other quick death. As little as I knew about death, I knew that although her grief would have been sharp, it would not have been like this. Day by day, I had watched her keeping her head high, going about her duties, being a mother and a wife to the best of her ability, but I had not realized the terrible burden that lay upon her. It made my own problems seem inane.

"Joelle, I've asked you this before, but let's talk again."

"About what?"

"I don't know how to say this without sounding like an idiot, but I'd like to help you financially." I saw something change in her eyes, and she started to speak, but I interrupted her. "No, listen to me. Let me hire special nurses. Just someone to help you with the physical demands that you face every day. Don't worry about the amount—I spend more money on a watch than it would cost to buy some home care for Frank. I've never told you how much I like him, but I do. He's got more guts than any man I've ever seen. Let me do this for him—and for you."

"Davis, he needs me, not a stranger. It would be cruel to him."

Her hands were trembling, and I knew that she was on the verge of breaking down. I put my hands on her shoulders, and she leaned against me. I could feel the tremors going through her body as she struggled to contain them. I let her lean there without saying anything, but despite the fact that I had been totally earnest and sincere in wanting to help Frank and to make life easier for her, holding her was a sensation strong enough to almost make me forget about those concerns.

I was suddenly aware of old hungers arising within me. She felt both soft and firm leaning against me, and I had the almost irresistible desire to pull her closer and kiss her as a man kisses a woman. And I was a little shocked to discover that it wasn't a matter of sex—at least not all of it. She was an attractive woman and I was a normal man, but there was something else in it too. A desire to help her, to protect her from the blows that life was raining down on her. She was weeping over her husband, and I was struggling with a longing that I didn't want her to know.

She drew back, and I saw that her face was stiff. "I–I shouldn't be around you, Davis."

I was surprised. "Why not?"

"Because I—" She turned away from me. "I can't say why, but please leave right now."

"All right. If you need me for anything, please come, will you?"

"Thank you, Davis."

She did not turn around, and she was standing as stiffly as a soldier at attention. *Does she feel the same thing I do?* I wondered. But that couldn't be. She was a good woman, and her love was all for the man who lay in the bedroom, dying.

I left the house and went home, although it wasn't really a home—just a house. I stumbled around trying to read or listen to music, and finally I went out and got into the Porsche. I left the city limits of Blue Springs and drove the highways at highly illegal speeds. I tried to think through my plot to bring Dane and Marlene down, but in the light of Joelle's problems, that seemed sinful. There was no other way I could put it. It was wrong, and I knew it.

∽

Frank Doren continued to grow worse, and Joelle continued to refuse my help. I mentioned it once more, and she cut me off as sharply as if she had used a knife. I went for another meeting with Leo Fant and his two barons. They were all excited by their progress, although they avoided giving details. I had gone out to look over the land with Leo himself. I had been stunned by the beauty of it, but all Leo could do was point out what excellent views there would be from the condominiums' balconies.

While we were there, I watched some variety of mouse that I assumed was native to the area. He was a cute little fellow, rather bold. He sat up not ten feet away as Leo was talking, held his paws together, and he looked like a pious little monk praying. His black eyes were shiny and glowed with light, and I thought, *You don't know how close you are, old buddy, to being put out of a home.*

It was time to move ahead with my plans or forget it, so I drove to Los Angeles and looked up private detectives in the Yellow Pages. I wound up in the office of one called Max Drummond. He had a suite of offices in an old section of the city, and he didn't spend a lot on decor. He saw me looking around and said, "I can give you the names of some good investigators that spend a lot of money on carpets and furniture and pictures on the walls."

I laughed. "I guess not."

"What can I do for you?"

"I want some wiretapping done. Probably illegal."

"Not always. Tell me about it."

"A group of men are planning to influence the legislature to change some laws so they can proceed with a business deal."

"That happens all the time. That's what they call politics." He was a short man with highly intelligent gray eyes that never wavered. He listened as I explained that the land was protected, but that it would take the passage of only one bill to change that.

Drummond looked out the window and was silent for a time. Then he looked back and said, "Are you a tree hugger?"

"I guess so. I like most trees better than I like some people."

"Me too," he said. "Tell me exactly what you want."

"I know that this group is talking to state senators and representatives. I know they're putting money out to get the votes. I want proof of it."

"I can do that."

"Legally?"

"That's a matter of opinion," Drummond said with a straight face. He mentioned his fees, and I said, "Hire whatever help you need. It's very important to me."

"All right. If you're ready to spend money, I can get you quicker action."

"Get it," I said. I stood and held out my hand. He rose with me and said, "We'll do what we can to put a crimp in these suckers."

∽

I went by the fitness center and found Trey in his office, staring at the wall. He jumped up when I came in, and I saw the welcome in his eyes and felt it in his grip. "You look like you're losing it," he said. "You'd better come in, and I'll get you back in shape."

"No, let's go out to eat, and I'll get you out of shape."

"Man, that sounds like a winner."

We left at once. Just to shock him, I ordered the most fattening meal I could think of, and he laughed and said, "You ain't gonna maintain long."

"I don't think calories count as long as your mother doesn't see you eat them."

"One excuse is as good as another." We talked for a while, and finally Trey, who had been watching me rather strangely, said, "What's the matter with you, man?"

"What do you mean?"

"You look awful."

"I weigh the same as I did the last time you saw me."

"That's not what I'm talking about. It's something in your head. You're miserable—I can see it in your eyes. You're not smiling."

I felt uncomfortable. Trey was too sharp for me. I wanted to tell him the whole story, but it wasn't time for that. Maybe someday. For now, I settled for telling him a bit about my new life in Blue Springs and about the people I'd met there.

We finished the meal, and I told him I'd be coming back soon, got in the car, and drove back home. I parked the Porsche, went inside, and checked messages. The first one was Joelle's voice, and I knew instantly that something was wrong. "Frank's in intensive care. I wish you'd come."

CHAPTER
TWENTY-ONE

The calendar on the wall featured two children making their way across a bridge. Over them an angel hovered, protecting them from harm. I had been looking at that calendar for two weeks now, ever since Frank had been put into intensive care. I had thought once of marking off the days, but that seemed a bit presumptuous. The angel looked a little like my third-grade teacher, with a straight nose and classic features. At the age of nine I had fallen in love with her, but now she was probably a grandmother.

Rachel was sitting on my lap reading to me from a Bible storybook. I had sent Joelle home, begging her to get some rest. Ever since Frank had been hospitalized, she had insisted on staying at the hospital even though she could only see him once every four hours. Rachel was reading the story of Noah, and she had already asked me about twenty questions that I couldn't answer. Now she turned around, twisted her head so that she could look me in the face, and asked, "Were there snakes on the ark, Mr. Davis?"

"I think so."

"Good snakes or bad snakes?"

"Both kinds." Rachel had a way of considering things in a way that was somewhat disconcerting. When there was any doubt at all in her mind, she would grow absolutely still and look at me. I felt as if I were weighed in the balances and found wanting. "Why would God want bad snakes?"

I considered saying "To bite bad people," but that didn't seem theologically sound. "I don't know, honey. I've wondered why God made mosquitoes too. I suppose they had some purpose, but I just don't know what it was."

"Maybe they were all good when they got on the ark and they got bad after."

I smiled. "I think that's probably the way of it."

She continued reading, and I realized that I was practically illiterate where the Bible was concerned. I had read it through once when I was sixteen years old, just so I could say that I had read it through, but most of it had not lodged firmly in my head. I stared down at the picture of the ark and thought, *The ark couldn't look like that. The Bible says how wide it was and how long it was and how tall it was, but that picture looks like an old sailing ship with a curved front. The ark wouldn't have needed a curved front. It wasn't sailing anywhere. It was just floating. I think it looked like an oversized cracker box with a smaller one on top.*

"How did they get enough food on the ark to feed all those animals, Mr. Davis?"

"They had special compartments. They kept the feed in those."

"But tigers eat meat, and if they put meat in a special compartment, it would spoil if it wasn't refrigerated. But Noah didn't have refrigerators, did he?"

I laughed. "You can ask more questions than any woman I ever knew." I squeezed her and said, "You'll have to ask your mom these questions. I just don't know enough about the Bible."

"Well, you ought to," Rachel said, nodding firmly. She began to read again, and I thought, *You're probably right about that.*

I looked up at the clock and said, "Okay, we can go see your dad now."

Rachel got off my lap and put the book down, turning a page so that she could find her place. We went down the hall to the

ICU door, where we had to press a button, and the disembodied voice asked, "Who would you like to see?"

"Frank Doren."

"All right. Come in." We walked inside and passed the nurse's station. I knew all of them by this time. The large one named Jennifer smiled. "Hello, Mr. Burke, how are you today?"

"I'm fine."

"And how are you, Rachel?"

"Very nice, thank you."

We walked over to Frank's room; the door was open. As always Frank was lying perfectly still. It always gave me a chill to see all the tubes that kept him alive. I picked up Rachel and placed her on the bed. She leaned over and put her hand on his cheek and said, "Hi, Daddy. We came to see you." Frank's eyes were half opened, and his lips moved very slowly. "Hello . . . honey."

"Mr. Davis and I have been reading about the ark. He doesn't know much about the Bible."

"I'm afraid she's right, Frank. You and Joelle will have to be her Bible teachers."

Frank smiled briefly and managed to nod. "That's good," he whispered in a voice so low I could hardly hear it. I stood there, as always, feeling helpless. There wasn't one single thing I could do to help this man that I had come to respect. I listened with half my attention while Rachel spoke of what she had done at school and what was happening to her at the house. I had no idea whether she knew that her dad was probably not going to get out of this room alive. I suspected that she was fearful of it. I remembered that she had told me once, before Frank was brought in, that she was afraid he was going to die. Now I kept waiting for her to talk about it again—but she never did. I decided I would ask Joelle if Rachel ever talked to her about losing her dad.

Finally the time was up. I lifted Rachel down, and she walked over to the door. I took Frank's hand and squeezed it. I felt the faint pressure of his own. He began to whisper, and I leaned closer. "Thanks for what you're doing for my family," he said.

"I don't want you to worry about them, Frank. I'll take care of them as best I can."

"Remember, I want you to find the Lord, Davis."

I could not answer that. As a matter of fact, I could not even meet his eyes. "I'll bring her back the next visiting hour."

"Trust in the Lord with all your heart," Frank whispered. His eyes closed, and I could feel his grip loosening. I moved away from the bed, and as we left the intensive care ward and went back down to the car, Rachel said, "What did Daddy say to you when we were leaving?"

"He told me to take good care of you and your mama until he's well." When we got to the car, I opened the door, and she got in. By the time I got in, she had fastened her safety belt. I fastened my own, then started the engine. "You want to go get some ice cream before we go home?"

"No, thank you."

"You can have any kind you want. Even blue moon or bubble gum."

"No, thank you, Mr. Davis."

I tried to think of something to offer her that would make her feel better, but when a child is losing her father, ice cream is a poor substitute.

∞

For the next five days Joelle, Rachel, and I followed our usual pattern. Joelle spent most of her time at the hospital. They had broken the rules for her, and now she was allowed to sit with Frank whenever she pleased. He was unconscious most of the time, and she never mentioned what they talked about when he woke up. I would take care of Rachel when she wasn't in school and take her by the hospital for her visits.

On Tuesday afternoon, we were in the backyard playing croquet. I had bought a set, and the game fascinated Rachel. I let her control the game, and she was so delighted when she made a good shot. She looked so much like Joelle, and I thought, as she was lining up one of the balls, *She's going to be as beautiful as her mother.* I watched as she whacked the ball, and it missed by a foot. "Oh, fuzz!" she complained.

"I think you ought to bring it back and try it again," I said.

"Isn't that against the rules?"

"It's a new rule. I just made it up."

She smiled and said, "All right, but when you miss, you get to try again too."

"Hello, what are you two doing?"

I looked around to see Marlene coming around the house. She was wearing white shorts and a lime-green top, and her hair was free on her shoulders.

"Just a little croquet," I said. "You want to play?"

"No, I'm no good at sports."

I said, "Have you met Rachel?"

"No, I haven't."

"Rachel, this is Mrs. Fetterman."

"How are you, Mrs. Fetterman?"

"I'm fine, Rachel. Are you winning the game?"

"He lets me win sometimes."

"Well, I'm glad to hear that Mr. Burke is a gentleman."

I stood and watched Marlene charm Rachel. She had the ability to do things like that, and after a time she said, "I haven't seen much of you lately, Davis."

"No. Rachel's dad is ill. He's in the hospital. I've been taking care of her while her mother stays with him."

"I did hear something about that." She turned to Rachel and said, "I hope your dad gets well."

"Thank you."

As we stood talking, Joelle's car pulled up. Marlene turned to watch her as she came carrying a sackful of groceries. "This is Mrs. Doren, my housekeeper. Mrs. Doren, this is Mrs. Fetterman."

The two women exchanged greetings, and without saying more Joelle said, "Come along, Rachel. You can help me fix supper."

"All right, Mom."

The two left, and Marlene watched them carefully as they did. "She's a good-looking woman, your housekeeper."

"Yes. She's got a tough row with her husband ill like that."

"What's wrong with him?"

"Lou Gehrig's disease."

She blinked her eyes. "That's a bad one."

"I don't think he's going to make it."

"Is he able to move or speak?"

"He's in poor shape, Marlene."

Her eyes went to the house where Joelle and Rachel had disappeared. "Are you sleeping with her?"

"No."

She studied me for a moment, and I thought she meant to press her question, but finally she said, "She must be a good woman."

"You remember once, Marlene, I told you that there are some real love stories? People who are faithful to each other, who can depend on each other no matter what? Well, you just saw one. Her husband was a fine-looking, strong man until he was struck down. When I first met him, he was nothing but a skeleton. He had to be pushed in a wheelchair. But Mrs. Doren never faltered. She still cares for him. I don't think he'll make it out of that hospital, but she never changes."

"You don't see much of that," Marlene said. She was staring at the house and then turned to look at me. "I can tell you admire her."

"She's got the kind of loyalty I'm looking for. What's the Marine motto? *Semper fidelis*."

My words seemed to mean more to Marlene than I had thought. She stared at me for a time and then said, "I want to see you more, Davis. I know you're busy, but come when you can."

"All right."

She turned without saying good-bye and left. I couldn't tell what she was thinking. What I had said about Joelle and Frank had hit home with her. I doubt that she had ever known a couple like them. She had probably decided there weren't any good love stories. I went back inside and took a nap. But as I lay trying to sleep, I could think of nothing but Joelle and her absolute loyalty to her husband.

∞

Over the next two weeks, Marlene and I went out twice, and both times, in one way or another, she tried to seduce me. I knew she didn't understand me—she even got angry once and said, "What's the matter? Aren't you a man?"

I had simply told her that I wasn't looking for cheap sex. That was something she had never encountered in her life, I don't think. She couldn't believe it. But she didn't run me off either. She kept trying.

Meanwhile, Frank had continued to go downhill. Very rarely now was he even conscious.

On a Thursday afternoon, the twenty-second of June, I got a call from Fant. "I need to talk to you, Davis," he said. "Leighton and Jeb will be coming to my house tonight. I want you there too. We've got to get moving on this thing."

"All right. I'll be there."

I thought about Fant and his band of merry men most of the day, and that night he greeted me rather abruptly and led me into his study. Jeb and Robert were already there.

"Hello, Davis," Jeb said. "What do you think about the house?"

"I'm still thinking about it."

"Maybe I can get the price down a little bit."

"I'll let you know," I said. I was watching Fant, who was obviously rather short-tempered tonight. I had heard that Shirley had informally announced her engagement to the young man I had met at the swimming pool. I had also heard that Fant wasn't taking it well, but that was his problem. My heart was with Shirley.

Fant lit a cigar and blew smoke. "We've got to get moving on this thing," he said again. "It's time to start putting the money up."

"Looks like we'll have to cut Dane out," Jeb said. "He hasn't gotten his wife to pony up any money. Besides, I found out she's one of those tree-hugger Sierra Club types."

Fant frowned. "Why didn't you tell me that sooner? She could kill this whole deal if she talked."

"Oh, Dane never told her what the money was for. But it wouldn't be good if she found out."

Fant turned to me. "What about you, Burke. Can we count you in?"

I sat back, narrowing my eyes. "I'll have to think about it and get back to you." Inside, I was thinking, *Sure, I'll get back to you, but not in the way you expect, Mr. Fant.*

After the meeting I drove home, and the first thing I did was head around the back—but the lights were out at Joelle's house. I figured she had taken Rachel to the hospital with her. There was no school the next day, so she would probably keep her there with her.

I walked the floor and tried to watch a television program, but I couldn't. I went to bed, but I hadn't yet gone to sleep when the phone rang. I picked it up. "Hello."

"This is Joelle."

Instantly I knew what it was. "Is he gone, Joelle?"

"Yes. He died ten minutes ago." Her voice was strong and steady, but there were tears in it, and I suspected that they were running down her face.

"I'm sorry," I said. "I wish it could be different."

There was a moment's silence, and then Joelle said, "He was the best man I ever knew, Davis." There was a silence, and she said, "One of the last things he said was, 'Tell Davis I'll be waiting for him.'"

Her words hit me with an almost physical force. I'd thought more about God and death and my soul in the last few days than I ever had in my life. And I knew why: I'd been watching a man who knew he was going, very soon, to meet God. Frank had gone out physically beaten, but his spirit had been victorious. I knew I didn't have that in me.

I said, "I'll come down right away."

"All right. I think that would be good, especially for Rachel, and . . ." She hesitated, then said, "I need you too."

∞

The funeral wasn't like the ones I was accustomed to. It was held in the church that Joelle and Frank belonged to. The auditorium was packed, and the songs were not mournful and slow, but happy and full of joy. I sat with Joelle, at her insistence, with Rachel between us, and I knew that everybody in town was aware of that. I even saw Marlene in the congregation, staring at us, although Dane wasn't with her.

Throughout the funeral, Rachel held my hand, and once I took my handkerchief and gave it to her to wipe the tears from her cheeks. I can't really remember what the preacher said. I was thinking about Frank Doren and how he loved God and died without a single complaint.

There was a ceremony at the graveside. After everyone had come by and shaken hands and whispered something to Joelle and Rachel, I went with her back to the house. When we got there, I said, "I guess you probably need to be alone for a time, but I'll be right over there in my place." I saw that the strain had gotten to her; she was wearing down. I said quickly, "Joelle, I want you to stay in this house with Rachel. If you need me, I'll be there."

She looked at me, and I saw the strength in her. "All right, Davis," she said quietly. "I don't know what we'd have done without you."

I walked away quickly, and I heard Rachel say, "He's not going away, is he, Mom?"

"No," Joelle said. "He's not going away, sweetheart."

CHAPTER
TWENTY-TWO

Sometimes a man bends over to pick up something that fell out of his hand, and when he gets up—the whole world has changed. Yes, I'd lost hundreds of pounds of weight and changed my accent, but now the death of Frank Doren had done something to me that I sensed might be the most profound change of all. Maybe it was the fact that he never gave up, even when everything went wrong. In light of the way Frank lived, I couldn't shake off the thought that I was a sorry bit of humanity for not believing in God.

Two weeks had gone by since the funeral, and things had been quiet. Joelle had almost nothing to say. I never saw her crying, but I could tell from the strain around her eyes that she did when she was alone at night. I spent a lot of time trying to think up words that would help her, but that was useless. Words failed. They break down and sound trite no matter which words you use. A whole dictionary full of words, and I couldn't think of a single word to say to her!

All that time, I found myself growing more and more edgy. I had never been ill-tempered, but I was getting that way fast. Just this morning I was trying to find the bottle opener in the kitchen and I couldn't find it. I went around jerking drawers open and slamming them, and finally I said out loud, "You stupid idiot! Why don't you put the bottle opener back in the same place each time, then you'll know where it is!"

Nothing was working out as I had expected. When I was at Eli's cabin, spending weeks planning the thing, it had all sounded very smooth. But I had left something out. Somewhere along the line, I had lost something, and I didn't know what to call it. I remembered a line from William Faulkner's speech when he won the Nobel Prize. He said that we have to get back to the old verities—like *truth* and *honor*. But I had lost honor somewhere along the way. It was as if rodents had come in the night and carried it away bit by bit, so that I never even knew I was losing it. But when I thought about Frank Doren and his fate, I knew that he had a ton of it, while I had none. Even my desire for revenge was a bitter taste in my mouth.

I think the one thing that kept me going during those two weeks was the time I spent with Rachel. Every day I did something with her. We would play with her dolls, or I would take her to the zoo. I took her fishing once, and when I'm an old man and bring out my memories from the past as a man brings photographs out of an old scrapbook, one of them will be of Rachel Doren catching her first fish, holding it up, her eyes sparkling, joy pulsating through her features. I'll always have that. I remembered Eli saying once, "Make yourself some good memories, boy. You'll have to live on them when you get old."

∞

I drove up to L.A. to visit Max Drummond on a Tuesday morning. I wanted to get away and think, so the drive aired me out. It was July now, and hot, but I put the top down on the Porsche and let the wind blow through my hair. I kept mostly to the speed limit, aware of the power under my foot.

When I got to Max's office, he had a client with him. When I finally got in, Max motioned to a chair and said, "You want a drink?"

"No thanks. Just came in to see how things are going."

"Like they say, as well as can be expected. I'm getting some conversations, but a lot of it's not anything that'll put anybody in jail. Your friends are buddying up, talking about taking these senators out on the yacht. Stuff like that." He poured himself a drink, downed it, then grinned at me. "You know what my definition of a criminal is?"

"No. What is it?"

"A criminal is a guy who can't get enough money together to form a corporation."

I had to laugh at that. "You're a cynic, Drummond."

"It goes with the territory. I don't know any private detectives who aren't. Aren't you?"

"I didn't use to be."

"Neither did I, back when I was six years old."

"What made you so cynical when you were six?"

"I went in on a lemonade stand with my best friend. We worked hard, saved our money, and then he swiped it all and bought himself a bicycle. He was bigger than I was, so he could beat me up when I tried to argue with him about it. Since then I haven't been too trustful."

"Sounds like my story, only I was a little older than six."

"Look. What do you really want to do with these guys? It makes a difference, Mr. Burke."

I thought for a moment and found that I didn't have any answer. I had been so angry with them for wanting to ruin something beautiful that I had wanted to see them all in jail. But somehow, without my knowing it, I had changed. "They're not truly evil, I suppose, Max. I guess I'd be satisfied just to stop them from this land steal."

"Well, that makes my job easier. Those guys are big money. It's hard to put twenty million bucks behind bars, but I can do something with this. Give me a little more time."

"All right. Call me when you get something."

∞

I left his office and thought about going by to see Trey, but I really didn't feel up to it. Instead, I drove back to the house, parked the car, and went inside. I checked messages and found that I had four. I listened to them—all from Marlene. The first was almost incoherent. She was crying so hard I couldn't understand it. On the second, she was calmer and I could understand what she was saying—"Please, you've got to come over here, Davis, and help me"—but it sounded as if she had been drinking. On the next two, she was drunker still but sounded desperately frightened.

I raced out of the house, jumped into the Porsche, and drove over to her place. I didn't see Dane's car. I rang the doorbell about ten times, and finally it opened. She had the chain on, and she shut the door again to let me in.

As soon as I stepped inside and took a look at her, I didn't have to ask what was wrong. "You've got to go to a doctor, Marlene." Her face was swollen, her lips especially. She had taken a hard punch in the mouth, and her left eye was swollen almost shut. "Dane?" I said.

She came to me, her hands fluttering, and I put my arm around her and took her into the living room. I sat her down. She had been drinking so much she had trouble speaking. "He—he's going to kill me," she muttered, and she hung onto me as if I were an anchor.

"Why did he do this to you?"

"He wants money. He wants me to sign half of everything over to him. He's tried it before, but he's never done anything like this."

"You can't put up with this, Marlene. I'll go have a talk with him."

"No, don't leave me!"

"It'll be all right. You can get a restraining order. You can have him arrested for this."

"No, he'd kill me if I did that."

"Dane's not going to kill anybody."

She was sobbing, but she caught her breath, and I could feel her trembling. "Yes, he would. You don't know him, Davis. He's cruel. He'd kill me in a minute."

I tried to calm her, but she insisted on drinking more, and two drinks later she was falling apart. She began to plead with me. "Let's run away. I've got the money to go anywhere. We'll get away from him."

"You can't run away from things, Marlene," I said. "You've got to face up to them."

And as I held her, the most amazing and shocking thing happened. I had hated her from the moment I had caught her in bed with Dane, and I'd spent a year getting ready to destroy her—but now that I had my arm around her and she was sobbing, I found myself feeling sorry for her. It was almost like an electric shock. I thought, *I must be the world's biggest sucker. She'd do it to me again if she had the chance.*

Still, I couldn't help it. She was hurt. She was lost. And I pitied her. "Come on," I said. "I'll help you into bed. Then I'll go talk to Dane."

I took her into the bedroom, turned the covers back, and put her in. I pulled her shoes off and covered her up. She was nearly unconscious, but she held onto me and said, "He's out on the boat, but take a gun with you. He's got one."

"I will."

"Then come back after you've talked to him. I can't be alone, Davis."

As I drove down to the docks where his boat was anchored, I thought about what she had said about Dane having a gun. I put that aside. He wouldn't risk shooting me—at least I didn't think so. Then I wondered what to say to him. He had taken everything away from me, and I had hated him for so long it had become second nature. Why wasn't I willing to let the two of them battle it out and destroy each other? Still, I went. Good old Ollie Benson raises his head again. Can't keep him buried. The total Boy Scout!

∞

The sea was quiet and the tide was out. I walked out on the dock. Dane's boat was anchored and the lights were on. It was dark, and there was no moon that night. The few stars seemed faint and far away. I was ready to step onto the boat when a voice brought me up short. "Who's there? Who are you?"

"It's me, Dane, Davis Burke."

Silence, then Dane appeared. "What do you want?" His voice was thick, and I knew he had been drinking.

"Just to talk to you."

Again a silence, then he said, "Sure. Come on aboard." I stepped on board, and he said, "She send you?"

"Not exactly. I talked to her. She's pretty badly roughed up, Dane."

He stared at me. I couldn't make out his features in the darkness. He turned away and said, "Come on inside."

I followed him along the deck, and we turned into the doors that led to the big stateroom—the usual expensive cabin that such boats had. I didn't pay much attention to it. I was watching Dane carefully, and I didn't miss the bulge in his pocket.

"What are you drinking?"

"I don't need anything, Dane."

"Well, I do." He poured whiskey into a glass, sloshing it. He didn't bother with ice. He took a big jolt of it and turned and stared at me. His eyes were red-rimmed, and his lips were drawn back from his teeth in a grimace as the liquor hit him. He had lost that sleek Madison Avenue look, and he had lost weight too, I could tell. Dane Fetterman's life had gone down in flames. I knew him well enough to know that he had expected, once I was out of the way and he had Marlene, that he'd control everything. But he had badly misjudged Marlene. She was just as tough and ruthless as he was.

"She's not hurt," Dane said defiantly.

"She took a couple pretty good shots."

"She's lucky she got off that easy." Dane's voice seemed to drift. He stood in the middle of the floor holding the glass in one hand and studying it. "You getting it on with her, Davis Burke?" he demanded.

"No, I'm not."

"Make me believe that."

"I can't make you believe anything, but it's true."

"Don't give me that. She's been chasing you."

"Well, if so, she hasn't been catching me."

Dane blinked slowly. He leaned forward, studying my face. "Maybe you're smarter than most guys. Marlene can get anybody, but maybe you're different."

"Dane, she could have you locked up for this."

"Sure she could, but she knows what would happen when I got out." He was still studying me and said, "You know that Osterman woman? She's been after you too, hasn't she?"

"I think she's after any man."

"That's right. The Black Widow, they call her." He laughed hard, then shook his head and closed his eyes for a moment, swaying. "Marlene's the black widow. Not that Osterman woman."

It seemed much more sinister, hearing him say it, than when I'd thought the same thing just a few weeks before. And as I stood listening to him rant and rave about Marlene, I wondered why I had come. He was a dangerous man, and I felt naked before him. All he had to do was reach into his pocket and pull that gun out, and I'd be out of everybody's way. It would be easy enough to tie something heavy to my ankle and dump me out in the deep water. The idea made me nervous, and I wanted to get away. "I'll be going now, Dane, but be careful."

"Sure, I'll be careful," he said. "You tell her to be careful too."

He had the best of the argument with that gun in his pocket, so I turned and left the boat. I went straight back to Marlene's house, and when I went inside I found her in a drunken slumber. I didn't even try to wake her, but there was a notepad beside her bed, and I wrote a note: *I talked to Dane and told him to stay away from you, but it would be better if you got away from this place.* I signed it and put it where she couldn't miss it. I went home, made myself an omelet, and then sat up watching *Gone with the Wind.*

That shows you how bad off I was, watching a soupy thing like that! I couldn't sleep, and I was only half watching the screen. But finally, when I got to the last half of the movie, when Scarlett got so rotten mean, even hiring starving convicts in the county to work her plantation, I couldn't help but identify with her. There was Rhett trying to straighten her out, and Scarlett, beautiful as ever, but as mean as a snake.

I switched it off and went to bed. The scene that stuck in my mind, as always, was when Scarlett raised her hand and said, "I'll never go hungry again!"

Well, I was nearly always hungry, but I was finding out in a hurry that there was more to life than just not being hungry.

∞

The next day I took Rachel out for a motorboat ride. I rented the boat and, since I didn't know much about them, I had to have a little instruction, but it was fairly simple. As we pulled out, I caught a glimpse of Dane's yacht still sitting there, no sign of life. I knew Marlene would call me again, but I didn't know what I would tell her. She and Dane had woven a nice web, and both of them were caught in it now.

It was a great day. The sky was blue with white clouds drifting across it. It was hot, and I made sure Rachel wore sunscreen. We just puttered around the shore, and when a group of dolphins caught up with us, I was as excited as she was. They came arching themselves out of the water, staying close to the boat, going in front of us. I told Rachel that sometimes, when people fell out of boats, the dolphins saved their lives by pushing them into shore. I had no idea whether that old story was true, but she liked it.

I'd brought some lunch out, and we stuffed ourselves. She had insisted on bringing some of her dolls, so we let Barbie go swimming in the surf.

Finally, late in the afternoon, we headed in. She sat beside me, and I let her steer the boat.

Back home, we found Joelle cooking supper. She said, "You'll have to stay. I can't afford to pay a babysitter, but I can feed you."

She was wearing a pair of pale blue shorts and a white T-shirt. Her eyes were clearer than they had been, and I could tell that she had passed through some stage of acceptance. We both played Barbie dolls with Rachel, which pleased her immensely. I watched Fox News while Joelle tried to get Rachel to bed, but Rachel came in and said, "I want you to put me to bed, Mr. Davis."

"Right." I picked her up and carried her to her room. The covers were folded back on the bed. I held her high and let her drop. She squealed with delight. "Do it again!"

"No. Don't want to get you too excited." I bent over and she held me and said, "Mom always prays with me. Will you say my prayer for me?"

I couldn't do it. I couldn't even fake it, but I didn't have to because Joelle was right there. She put her arm on my shoulder, leaned forward, and put her hand on top of Rachel's head. She prayed a simple prayer, then kissed her. "You sleep tight now."

I kissed her on the cheek and said, "It was a good day, wasn't it?"

"Yes. Let's do it again tomorrow."

I laughed and said, "We'll have to see about that."

We went into the kitchen. I sat at the table, and Joelle put out two more of the brownies she had made and poured coffee. She sat down across the table from me and we talked, mostly about Rachel. I admired her calmness. Finally I said, "How are you doing, Joelle?"

She found a smile, a small one, but said, "Fine." Reaching across the table, she put her hand over mine and squeezed it. "You've been a big help, especially with Rachel, but with me too."

I was very much aware of the warmth of her hand on mine. She was a woman like none I had ever met. "I wish I had your faith."

"You can have it, Davis."

"I don't know. I'm pretty far gone."

"All of us are pretty far gone. Can I read you something in the Scriptures, Davis? I don't want to embarrass you, but it's very real to me."

"Sure." She left the kitchen and came back with a Bible in her hand. "This is Frank's Bible. It looks terrible, doesn't it?"

She held it out to me. It was well-worn leather with frayed edges. I opened it and let the pages riffle through my fingers, pausing now and then. He had written in the margins and underlined things. I stopped and read one notation, dated only six months earlier:

God has given me a promise not that I'll be healed but that I will receive his best.

I read it aloud and looked up. "I don't understand it."

"Well, Frank has God's best now. Best for him, not for me or Rachel—but best for him." She took the Bible, opened it, and said, "The clearest verses in the Bible about getting right with God are in Romans, chapter ten, verse nine. It says, 'If you confess with your mouth, "Jesus is Lord," and believe in your heart that God raised him from the dead, you will be saved.'" She looked up and said, "That's all I did when I was saved. I believed in my heart that Jesus is the Son of God, and I asked God to save me, and he did it."

Something troubled me. I couldn't put my finger on it. "It sounds too easy," I said.

"It has to be easy—or impossible. For years I tried to do the impossible—I tried to be good enough to please God. But I could never escape from my sins. Even if I could have become perfect from that moment on, I would have had a past lifetime of bad thoughts, bad deeds, bad things, Davis."

Her words cut deep. This outstanding woman was lamenting her bad deeds and bad thoughts—but surely nothing she had ever said or thought or done was even close to my plan to destroy two human beings.

Joelle said, "In the thirteenth verse it repeats that thought: 'Everyone who calls on the name of the Lord will be saved.'" She closed the Bible and said, "Frank asked me to give you his Bible."

She held it out and I took it, protesting, "You should keep it. You and Rachel need it."

"He asked me to give it to you. Remember what he said just before he died—'Tell Davis I'll be waiting for him.'"

I stood up, nervous, feeling some kind of a weight pressing on me. "I guess I'd better get home," I said lamely.

Joelle walked to the door with me. When we got there, she grasped my arm and I turned around. "You know how to get saved, Davis, but nobody can do it for you. And I'm praying that you'll find Jesus as I did, and as Frank did."

I couldn't even say good night. I turned and walked through the darkness to the house. Overhead the skies were dark and blank and there were no moon and no stars.

CHAPTER
TWENTY-THREE

One of the secrets of losing weight—at least for me—is to give yourself a treat now and then. Of course, you have to pay for it somewhere along the line. If you eat a Snickers bar at three o'clock, that means that supper will have to be something about as tasty as carrot sticks and wheat germ.

But just the idea that I could have a Snickers bar if I want it had been a help to me. I don't think this would be popular doctrine among the people who invent diets, but it worked for me.

I slept late on Thursday, and I woke up thinking about Belgian waffles. They had always been a favorite of mine, and I had three waffle irons in my apartment back in Memphis so I could turn them out on a production-line schedule. I had only one waffle iron now, and the idea of eating six seemed rather obscene to me.

I made the recipe from scratch, poured it into the waffle iron, and sat down to drink my orange juice. While I waited, I opened Frank's Bible and began to read—not the text, but the notes he had written throughout the Bible. One note said, "I don't think I'm ever going to get a handle on myself. It's hopeless." Further down that page, he had underlined a verse that said, "But you are a shield around me, O LORD; you bestow glory on me and lift up my head." Beside it Frank had written with a very fine pen, "With God's shield in front of me, the Devil can't hurt me."

I studied that until the waffle was ready, then took it out and put it on a plate. It was golden brown, and I cut it into tiny fragments. I had some genuine maple syrup straight from Vermont, and I took a small morsel on my fork, swished it around in the syrup, and then put it in my mouth. I didn't chew it but just let it lie there, disseminating its flavor. The tongue is the great taster, so I moved the bit of Vermont syrup–soaked Belgian delight around, letting the taste buds have a treat. Finally I chewed it, trying to keep it in my mouth as long as possible.

That was the trick. Always before, when I had eaten like a terrible glutton, I had crammed things into my mouth. I couldn't get them in there fast enough, chewing with my cheeks stuffed out like a chipmunk. It wasn't the taste as much as the satisfaction of being absolutely stuffed that I was looking for.

But over the past year, I had learned to enjoy the taste and texture of food. It took me longer, by far, to eat that one waffle than it had taken me to cram down six before, and I enjoyed it a lot more.

I finished the last bite, drank some coffee, and knew that I would have to have a lean lunch, probably an apple with a slice of low-fat cheese. But that was all right. I was still savoring the experience of that Belgian waffle.

The doorbell rang, which was unusual. I got up and went through the house. When I opened it, I found Max Drummond. "Hello, Max. Don't tell me you were just passing through the neighborhood and decided to stop by."

Max grinned. There was an electric excitement on his face, and I knew he had something good.

"Come on in. I can see you've got news."

Max stepped inside, and I led him into the kitchen. I poured two cups of coffee and asked, "Do you take sugar or cream?"

"Only wimps and sissies do that. I take it straight black and as hot as I can get it."

"You're a wise man, Max Drummond." We sat down and sipped our coffee. I could tell he was savoring his triumphant moment here as I had savored the Belgian waffle. I finally grinned at him and said, "I can sit here as long as you can, Max, but you may as well tell me."

"All right." He leaned forward, and his eyes were actually glittering. "We've got 'em, Davis! You can nail their hides to the barn door!"

"What have you got?"

He reached into his pocket and pulled out a very small tape recorder. He felt in his other pocket and pulled out three tapes. "I brought you just samples, but it's enough to tell what we've got. This first one is short."

I watched as Max put the tape in, closed the gate, and punched the play button. There was a moment's silence, and then I heard Fant's voice.

"Well, Senator, I think we're about to get down to an agreement on this thing."

Another voice answered, and Max said, "That's Senator Ray Fuller, a big gun in the Senate. If you want to hear a man hang himself, just listen."

I listened—and heard Ray Fuller, esteemed state senator, bargain for a larger bribe exactly as a used-car salesman would argue about a price. I stared at the small machine, astonished, astounded, and sickened. This was the man that the people of California had elected to look out for their best interests! He was no more than a cheap, slimy crook, no better than the dope addict who rolled drunks in an alley!

I listened to ten minutes of the tape, then said, "That's all I need to hear."

"Oh, come on, Davis, I worked hard for these," Max protested. But when he saw my face, he stopped the tape, reversed it, and then said, "I've got pretty much the same thing on Leighton and Wilkerson."

"What does it mean, Max? I don't know the law that well."

"You've got 'em cold, but you'll hurt 'em worse if you let 'em go through with the deal so that they actually pay the money. Of course we'd have to catch 'em in the act."

"Isn't this good enough?"

"They'd wiggle out of it in court."

"But can I use this to stop the project?"

"Oh, definitely." Max grinned. "As a matter of fact, I wish you'd let me handle it. If I confront any of 'em with these tapes, they'd know that if I were a blackmailer, they'd have to pay me off big. And all I'd have to do is give these tapes to the state attorney general, and these legislators would all be kicked out of their jobs. They'd never hold office again. I know you said you didn't want to send your guys to jail, but if you're thinking about changing your mind, now's the time. It's your call, Davis."

I couldn't answer. When I had hired him, I had wanted to put all three of these men in jail. I knew now that it wouldn't be just the three men. It would be their families.

"You're sure, Max?"

"You bet! You've got them. All you have to do is pull the trigger and they'll all go down."

Max looked satisfied—but I wasn't. It was exactly what I'd set out to do, but the more I thought of it, the more I didn't like it. "Let me think about it, Max."

"Think about it? I tell you, you've got them in your sights. It's what you wanted."

"I just want to think it over."

He stared at me, then said, "You're still not going to hit them, are you?"

"I don't think so—at least not as hard as I'd first thought. But I want you to invoice yourself a big bonus for this, Max. You've done a great job. I couldn't have handled it better myself."

"It's been a pleasure, Davis." He drank the last of his coffee and got up. I walked to the door with him, and he said, "What about these senators?"

"Send them a copy of the tapes."

"And say what?"

"Don't say anything. Put your name on them, not mine. I don't feel much like taking revenge on folks today, Max."

"They're pretty low rent, all of them."

"So am I, Max."

He stared at me and shook his head. "I don't know what you mean. You're not like these guys."

"Put in their place, I'd be just like them." I reached out, and he took my hand. "Send me a whopping bill, Max. You've earned it."

I went back into the kitchen, poured myself another cup of coffee, and sat down. I should have been feeling a surge of triumph, but I didn't. It all seemed so grubby and petty and mean. I thought about Leo, Jeb, and Robert—and realized that they were no worse than I was. They might have tried to steal some land, but at least they weren't planning to destroy two human lives. I picked up Frank's Bible and thumbed through it. As I did, toward the back, I found a small piece of paper. I picked it up and read it. It was a note. I stared at it, unable to believe that I was getting a message from the dead. It said:

> Davis, when you read this I'll be gone. I'll be with the Lord and rejoicing. But God has given me a promise that you'll be saved. Read the sixteenth chapter of Acts. You and that jailer are a lot alike. Thanks for taking care of my family. It means a lot to me. More than you know. I'll see you soon, brother.

It was signed simply *Frank*.

My hand trembled as I turned through the Bible and found the book of Acts. I read the entire sixteenth chapter. It was a simple story about Paul and Silas being thrown in jail, but what really got to me was that they had first been beaten, then kept in the stocks. But at midnight, the Bible said, they sang praises to God.

That was Frank all over again. Here were two men in terrible shape, but they weren't down.

The rest of the story was pure drama. God sent an earthquake, the prisoners were all set free and could have escaped, and the jailer, who was going to kill himself because he would have had to pay their penalty, was stopped just in time. Paul shouted at him, "Don't harm yourself! We are all here."

So that jailer came in and fell down. He must have been pretty shook up, for he asked just one thing: "What must I do to be saved?"

That question hit me hard. That was what I needed to know. What must *I* do to be saved?

And I read Paul's answer: "Believe in the Lord Jesus, and you will be saved."

I stared at that verse for at least ten minutes. Then I got up, closed the Bible, and began to pace the floor. I felt that the walls were closing in on me, so, as I'd done before, I went out, got into the car, and began to drive. I drove and drove, and the question and the answer kept pounding at my mind. *What must I do to be saved? Believe in the Lord Jesus, and you will be saved.*

I drove so long that when I looked up and saw a road sign, I realized that I wasn't far from Eli's place. I thought of how my life had changed, and how he had saved me from almost certain death. I drove until I came to the very spot on the road where I had been thrown off, pulled the Porsche over, and got out of the car. I stared down the cliff. I couldn't see Eli's house, but I knew where it was. As I stood there, I began to tremble. I didn't hear any voice, but it was as if someone were saying to me, *What are you going to do, Ollie?*

I went back to the car, feeling stranger than I'd ever felt in my life. I shut the door, but instead of starting the engine, I leaned forward and placed my forehead against the steering wheel. And then I did something I hadn't done in a long, long time. I began to cry. I knew that this was my chance. I remembered the Scriptures that Frank had read, and the one that Joelle had read, and now the note from Frank. I was afraid. I wouldn't be able to face death as Frank had done, because I'd go straight to hell if I died, and I knew it.

I have no idea how long I stayed there, but at some point I grew absolutely, totally, completely desperate, and I cried out to God and begged him to save me in the name of Jesus.

Afterward, I sat for a long time, and gradually all the fear and the desperation drained out of me—as a matter of fact, *everything* drained out of me. I just sat there in the car, traffic whizzing by, and slowly realized that what I was feeling was the calm assurance that I would never be the same again. It was as if a burden had been lifted, and I grabbed the steering wheel, held it tightly, and said, "Lord, I don't know how to be the man you want me to be, but I've given you my life right here at this place, and I'll serve you the best I can. Just tell me what to do."

I started the car and headed back toward Blue Springs. All the way home I marveled at how different I felt. For over a year, I'd been planning how to get even with two people, and now that seemed so far away, so unimportant. All I could think of was getting back and telling Joelle what had happened.

∞

"Davis, it's so late. What's wrong?"
I'd had to knock loudly for a long time before Joelle came to the door. She was wearing a light robe, and her hair was loose, falling down her shoulders. "I've got something to tell you," I said.

"Come in."

I went inside, and when she turned to me, I handed her the note that had been in Frank's Bible. "Frank wrote that to me."

Joelle read it, and then she smiled. "That sounds like him."

"It made me sad at first, but I read that chapter about how to be saved and I remembered what you said. It scared me so much I got into the car and started to drive. I thought it would go away, but it didn't."

"What happened?"

"I parked the car, and then I began to call on God. I don't know how long I was there, but God did something to me, Joelle. I know it."

Joelle came to me. I lifted my arms and held her, and she looked up and whispered, "You've got Jesus in your heart now."

"Yes. That's it. And it's so different."

"I'm so glad, Davis. I'm so very glad!"

She took me into the kitchen. Over coffee, I told her the whole story again, in detail. Finally I got up. "I've got to go." She walked to the door with me and said, "Rachel will be glad to hear this."

"I'll see her tomorrow and tell her. I've got some things to straighten up, so I may be gone for a while, but I'll be back."

She didn't ask what I had to do. She just smiled and said, "I thank God for your salvation."

I went to bed and tried to sleep, but it was no use. There was too much going on in my mind.

CHAPTER
TWENTY-FOUR

I remember part of a poem I read long ago. I don't remember the name of the poet or the name of the poem, but it had a line in it that stayed with me. It simply said, "I awake each morning to the daily accident . . ."

That line jumped into my mind as I opened my eyes the next morning, but it was not like that at all—not in the least! I felt like I was waking up into a new world, and I was excited as I threw the cover back and stood to look out the window. The grass was greener and the sky was bluer, and miraculously, the sun had come up again. "You son of a gun, you did it again," I said, then laughed at myself for my foolishness.

I dressed quickly. I usually dressed neatly to fit the character of Davis Burke, but then I felt a freedom that was frightening, and I put on whatever came to hand. Looking in the mirror, I saw that I looked rather scruffy. "Neatness is dangerous," I said aloud. "Robinson Crusoe got too caught up with neatness and efficiency." When I realized that I was talking to myself, I came pretty close to something like a giggle.

I stood still for a minute, remembering in total detail what had happened out on the highway when I had bowed my head against the steering wheel of the Porsche. I knew that I had passed some sort of a milestone, and on impulse I went to the table by the bedside, picked up Frank's Bible, and opened it. I was excited about the idea of making all of this book mine, as I had once made computers mine. Now I was like a man turned loose in a huge store and told that he could have all that he could carry off. I had no idea where to start, so I simply thumbed through it until I came to a page that was well-worn and covered with notes. It was the book of Hebrews, and Frank had drawn a square around the first two verses of chapter 12. I read it aloud.

> Therefore, since we are surrounded by such a great cloud of witnesses, let us throw off everything that hinders and the sin that so easily entangles, and let us run with perseverance the race marked out for us. Let us fix our eyes on Jesus, the author and perfecter of our faith, who for the joy set before him endured the cross, scorning its shame, and sat down at the right hand of the throne of God.

The words brought an image to my mind. I saw myself and Joelle and others in a huge structure like a coliseum. We were moving and speaking and living, and all around us on every side there was a countless sea of faces, all watching us. I studied the verse again. Frank had underlined the words "fix our eyes on Jesus" and put a note beside it, saying, "This is what I need to do—and all of us."

There was a beautiful simplicity in those verses. I carried the Bible with me into the kitchen where I ate a bowl of cereal, all the time reading the Bible in the same chapter of Hebrews. I had just finished the cereal when the phone rang. I hoped it would be Joelle, but instead it was Marlene.

"Davis, is that you?"

"Yes."

"You've got to come over here right away."

"What's wrong?"

"I can't talk about it now, but I need you. Will you come right now?"

I didn't want to go, but there was distress and tension in her voice, and I knew I had no choice. "All right. I'll get over there as quick as I can."

"Thank you, Davis. I'll be waiting for you."

I left the house at once, and as I came out the front door, I paused for just a moment. I almost turned and went back to go see Joelle and Rachel. It was what I wanted to do, but I had told her last night that I had something to do, and now I made up my mind that I needed to get the business of Dane and Marlene straight.

When I got to Marlene's house, there were no cars in front. I got out of the Porsche and walked up to the front door. I rang the bell, and almost at once Marlene was there, wearing blue jeans and a shirt with small, blue-and-white checks on it. "Come in, Davis," she said. Her eyes were enormous, and she seemed to have trouble breathing.

"What's wrong?" I said, stepping inside. "Is it Dane?"

"Yes, it's Dane."

Dane had stepped out of a door leading to one of the rooms. He was staring at me with a strange intensity—and most noticeably he had an automatic in his hand. It was pointed at me, and there was no way he could miss at this distance.

"Dane, you've got to stop this! You've hurt her enough!"

Dane laughed, and I heard Marlene utter a choking laugh herself. "He's not going to harm *me*, Ollie."

For a moment I almost missed it, and then it came—*Ollie*. The world seemed to stand still, and I turned quickly and saw that Dane was grinning fixedly. "Yes, Ollie. I wouldn't have believed it, old boy. Whatever have you done to yourself?"

I couldn't think of a single word to say. I knew that everything was over. The gun in Dane's hand said that. They couldn't afford to let me live, for I could claim everything and divorce Marlene. The best she could hope for would be a reasonable settlement, and the worst, long jail terms. They'd had the world, at least Marlene had, and she wasn't the kind of woman to turn loose of it.

"Aren't you wondering how I found out you're my long, lost husband?" Marlene said.

"I guess I am."

"It was the note you left. You changed everything else about yourself except two things—your handwriting and your fingerprints."

"That was a bad mistake," Dane said, and he had stopped grinning now. "Obviously that wasn't you that we buried. Who was it?"

"It was a fellow I got to drive me. He robbed me, took my ring and everything I had, knocked me on the head, and shoved me over the cliff. Another guy found me and nursed me back to health."

Marlene stepped closer and stared into my face with a look of absolute disbelief. "I can't believe it. Standing right here looking at you, I wouldn't know you, Ollie. It wasn't just the weight. It was the voice and everything else about you." Then her face hardened. "But I can guess pretty well what brought it all on. You were out to get even with us, weren't you?"

"That was what I started out to do."

"Why didn't you just take a gun and shoot us?" Dane asked curiously. "That's what I would have done."

I knew there was no need explaining to these two, but the longer I talked, the longer I would live. "I started out with that idea. When I woke up, I was in terrible shape. It took me a long time to get well, and I lost a lot of weight. That's when I got the idea of changing my looks and finding you both."

"But you didn't shoot us," Marlene said. "Why not?"

There was an unreality about all of this. We were talking as though nothing had happened. Except for the gun in Dane's hand everything would have been very ordinary.

But the gun was there, and it didn't tremble in the least.

"I hated you so much that I didn't think that was bad enough punishment for what you'd done to me."

"Well, little Ollie filled up with hate. Hard to believe."

I saw death in their eyes, and I said quickly, "I could have killed you anytime, but something's happened to me. I've been finding out some things about myself."

"What sort of things?" Marlene asked curiously.

"For one thing, it doesn't do any good to hate people. You know that deal you were in of Fant's?"

"What about it?" Dane asked.

"I hired a private detective. He got tapes proving that those three have been bribing politicians."

"What were you planning to do with them, put them in jail?" Dane asked. "You couldn't put me in. I haven't made any deals."

"I just told the detective to give them the tapes and force them to leave that land alone. He told me I could put them in jail, but I wasn't interested. At heart, I'm as bad as they are."

"You always had too active a conscience, Ollie," Marlene said.

All the time we were talking I was desperately trying to measure the distance between myself and Dane. I knew I had developed very good reflexes, but he was taking no chances, for he stood seven or eight feet away and the gun was trained directly on me. All he had to do was pull the trigger and I'd be dead. He must have seen the impulse in my eyes because he said thickly, "Don't even try it, Ollie. Come on. Let's get this over with. Ollie, we're going to take you for a ride. Move down that hall."

I started down the hall, aware that Dane had stayed far enough behind me so that there was no chance at all. In the garage, Dane said, "Marlene, open the trunk." She opened the trunk of the BMW.

"Okay, in the trunk, Ollie," Dane said. I almost launched myself at him, but he lifted the gun and pointed it right at my head. "You can have it here if you want it. Nobody will hear the shot. I'll have plenty of time to clean your blood off the floor."

"You still hate me, Marlene?" I said.

She studied me as if I were a bug under a microscope. "You're an inconvenience, Ollie. We can't afford to let you live. It'll make a scandal when you disappear, but we'll get rid of your car, and everyone will think you decided to leave. Now get in that trunk."

Playing along might buy me another half hour or so of time. I got into the trunk and Marlene closed it. I lay there in the darkness. The air smelled like rubber and carpet, and I heard the two get into the car. The doors slammed, the engine started, and the car began to move. As it made the turn to start down the street, something closed in on me. I knew that this was death.

The BMW ran smoothly for a long time, and I knew that we were on city streets by the speed. Then the speed increased and the BMW moved very rapidly. Then it slowed again. All this time I was feeling around, trying to find the trunk release lever, but I didn't find it. Even if I got it open, if I jumped out at this speed, I'd probably break a leg. And even if I didn't, they'd see the trunk opening, stop the car, and there would be Dane with his gun.

I still kept hunting, thinking I might find something to use as a weapon, but I couldn't find a thing in the darkness. I gave up.

Knowing it was the end, I thought about Hemingway's short story "The Short Happy Life of Francis Macomber." The protagonist was a coward who finally got courageous, and then a few minutes later was shot dead by his wife—thus the *short* happy life. My story could be called "The Short Christian Life of Ollie Benson."

But strangely enough I was calm. The one thing that came into my mind and stayed there was, *I'm glad I asked Christ into my life last night. I'll see Frank a little sooner than either of us had expected.* I regretted that I wouldn't be around to tell Joelle that I loved her, which I would have if I lived. I realized that my love for Joelle had been the biggest thing in my life for some time, but I had been so blinded by hatred and bitterness that I couldn't see it. Now I saw plainly that I loved her as I hadn't known a man could love a woman.

It was hard for me to judge how far the car went, but after making a great many turns and hearing the branches scratch against the side, I knew we were in the woods. The car stopped, the engine died, and I had one chance. I got my legs under me and waited. As soon as the trunk opened, I shoved it open with one hand and launched myself out, trusting that Dane would be right there.

But even as I threw myself outward, I saw that he wasn't within reach. I hit the dirt and scrambled to my feet, and there was Dane standing ten feet away. "Good try, Ollie," he said. "But that was just what I was waiting for."

"Where is this hole in the ground you're talking about, Dane?" Marlene said nervously. She was pale and looked strange.

"To the left of that old fire tower." He pointed at a wooden tower, adding, "It's abandoned now. We have to take a path. Right down over there, Ollie. You move real slow." I started down the path that he indicated. Dane said, "Just purely accident I found this. I was out hunting one day and took that old path."

"What kind of a hole is it?"

"An old gold mine shaft, I think. They used to mine a lot in California. Sometimes they'd just dig straight down until they hit something. This one's shored up with timbers. I almost fell in the thing before I saw it."

Time was running out for me, and still I had no plan of escape. I had to duck under branches, for the woods were thick. Once I glanced back hoping to catch Dane off guard, but he simply shook his head and said, "No luck, Ollie. Keep on."

Finally I saw a dark square ahead. Brush had grown up around it, but it was exactly as Dane had said. We were, perhaps, twelve or fifteen feet from it, and my mind was beating like a bird in a box trying to find an idea. I glanced around me and saw something I hadn't seen since I was a boy visiting on a farm with a buddy of mine. We had been hunting in the woods, and he had shown me a ragged-looking round thing.

"That's a hornet's nest," he said.

"Let's take it home."

"Are you crazy?" he said, staring at me. "That thing is full of hornets. They'd sting you to pieces."

There, above me, was a hornet's nest almost covered by the branches. The trees were in full bloom now, and I saw a few hornets lazily visiting flowers. The nest was gray and ragged and looked like a paper decoration, but it was only three feet higher than my head. I stood directly under it and turned around to face Dane and Marlene. That hornet's nest wasn't much, but it was the only action I had.

"You don't have to do this," I said. I knew it was useless, but I was gauging how far I had to throw the hornet's nest to where Dane stood. "Believe it or not, I didn't have any intention of hurting either one of you—not at the last."

"Good try, Ollie. Exactly what I'd say in your place. But we just can't trust you. You see how it is."

Marlene said, "Give me the gun, Dane."

He turned and stared at her. "What for?" he demanded.

"I want to do it myself."

For a moment Dane stood staring at her, then he laughed. "The female is more deadly than the male. All right, sweetheart. I guess you've got first rights." He handed her the gun, and Marlene then moved away from Dane. She actually moved closer to me so that she was only five feet away.

My eyes went to Dane's face. Despite his big talk, he was tense. "Go on and do it then. He won't climb out of that old mine with a bullet in his heart."

The woods were quiet, but somewhere I heard a woodpecker as he hammered against a hollow tree. It made a rhythm that broke the silence of the glade.

"Go on," Dane said. "Kill him!"

Marlene turned and pointed the gun at him. She didn't say a word, but Dane yelled, "What are you doing?"

"I'm sorry, Dane, but it just hasn't worked out."

I think Dane and I saw at the same moment what the plan was. It didn't take a genius. She was going to kill us both, then she wouldn't have to worry about Dane's harming her. That one moment was all I had. She was lifting the gun and bracing it with her left hand as shooters do. Even as she did, I leaped into the air like a basketball player, and the shot rang out just as I caught the nest. One of the hornets hit the back of my hand, but the nest ripped loose. As I fell back to earth, I threw the nest directly at her. It wasn't all that heavy, and I was afraid it wouldn't travel true. But it did. I didn't take my eyes off of her, but I heard the gun fire again. As she turned to point the gun at me, the hornet's nest hit her right in the chest. She got off one shot, and I felt something rake my left side, but I had thrown myself to the right—if I hadn't, the shot would have taken me squarely in the chest. I hit the ground, rolled, and the gun was exploding. She got off three or four shots as I threw myself back behind one of the larger trees. It wasn't large enough actually to hide behind, but it was all there was.

Then I was up, running and dodging, the branches slapping me in the face. There was one more shot, and then I heard a piercing scream. I didn't stop—just kept dodging until there was only the sound of Marlene crying out in a queer muffled voice, and occasionally a piercing scream. I stopped running. I knew that the hornets must have gotten to her. I thought of going back to try to get the gun, but I was afraid. I was free now. Dane was probably dead, but Marlene still had the gun. I moved farther away—and then heard the sound of her voice crying in staccato bursts. There were no more shots. Quickly I moved through the woods in a large semicircle so that I came toward her from another angle. I eased up behind a tree. Peering out, I saw Dane lying still on the ground. Marlene, ten feet away, was rolling and beating at herself making bubbling noises. She no longer had the gun; she was using both hands to beat at the hornets that still swarmed around her.

I didn't even think about what I did next. I ran forward, grabbed her up, and threw her over my shoulder. The hornets were swarming, and I felt them hit my face and neck like redhot, burning needles. I brushed them off as best I could and ran fifty feet away.

Laying Marlene down, I fought the hornets off as best I could. There weren't many of them around us now; most of them, I could see, were still swarming around the spot where Marlene had gone down. My face and hands had been stung, and one of the wasps was crawling down my neck. I crushed him, then I picked Marlene up. As I moved through the woods, the remaining hornets seemed to give up.

When I found the car, I opened the rear door and tossed Marlene inside. Then I retraced my steps to the mine shaft. I waited behind a tree for a time until the swarm of hornets had mostly dispersed. I didn't know whether Dane was dead, but I couldn't leave him there. As I jogged toward him, wary of hornets, his eyes were open and blood was on his lips. He was trying to talk, but I ignored that, picked him up—and got another hit from a hornet on my left hand. I brushed it off and hustled back to the car. I dumped him into the back, next to Marlene. My right eye was closing from the stings, and I could imagine what Marlene felt like. She must have taken over a dozen stings. I started the car and managed to get it turned around. It bumped and jolted over the road, and it was all I could do to see out of my one good eye.

I got back to the highway and turned west—toward the ocean and Blue Springs and the hospital. I was driving over a hundred when I saw a flashing light behind me—a blue light. I pulled over at once, and when the cops approached, I could see well enough to know that they were surprised by what they saw. "This man's been shot," I said. "The woman's been stung by hornets, and so have I. Get us to the hospital."

They made me get out, and I got into the police car while the other cop got in the BMW. They put me in the backseat, and the cop, a tall, rangy-looking man, was staring at me. "You shoot him?"

"No."

"No?" He looked skeptical. "When we get you to the hospital, I've got a feeling you'll have to answer a few questions you might not want to answer."

He didn't have to tell me that I was in trouble. But I'd been there for so long it seemed like it was my natural habitat.

CHAPTER TWENTY-FIVE

A m I under arrest?"
"Not yet. If you'll answer a few questions, I may not arrest you."

"Can I have a lawyer?"

"Sure—but maybe we can do without that if you'll just tell me what's going on."

I hesitated. "All right."

"You waive your right to call a lawyer?"

"For now."

"So, you're not Davis Burke, as all of your identification shows. You're Oliver Benson, who's been dead for over a year. And you didn't shoot Dane Fetterman. Mrs. Fetterman, who is not Mrs. Fetterman, but your wife, Mrs. Benson, did it. Have I got all that right?"

The Blue Springs chief of police was a tall man with cream-colored skin and the unlikely name Deoris Flynn. I could barely see him out of my left eye which was opened only a slit. My right was completely closed. Flynn had movie-star good looks, and his uniform was molded on him as if he had been born in it.

"That's right, Chief." My lips hadn't been stung, but they had given me a shot for the pain, and I felt like I was floating on a cloud. We had been brought to the hospital instead of the police station, and both Dane and Marlene had been taken away at once. A medic had dressed the scratch on my side and dabbed something on my stings. The two officers who had brought me in were joined by Chief Flynn, who began firing questions at me.

"Where's the gun Fetterman was shot with?"

"It's back on the ground somewhere near the old mine."

Chief Flynn stared at me and then said, "Bowers, go back to the scene of the crime and find the gun."

"I don't know where that mine is," Bowers said. He was a short man, neat, with a pair of sleepy blue eyes. "How do I get there?"

"Give him directions?"

"It's just west of an abandoned fire tower."

"I know that one, Sheriff." Bowers nodded and left at once.

Flynn stared at me silently, and I didn't feel particularly like talking so I just sat there in the chair. Finally I said, "How's Marlene?"

"Not good. Turns out she's allergic to bee stings. One of those stings would have probably knocked her out. She was stung more than twenty times, I think."

"I need to see her."

"I want to hear your story, then we'll talk about seeing someone."

"Is Dane dead?"

"Not yet. He was pretty close. He was bled white when they got here, but I think they're pumping blood into him."

I tried to absorb all that, but I was pretty sick. Flynn, however, was demanding answers, and I knew that I was going to have to give him some.

"Ollie Benson died over a year ago. It was in all the papers."

"That wasn't me they buried. They identified the corpse's body only by a ring and a watch. Some guy knocked me in the head and stole my car, and he would have gotten away with it except he went over the side and was killed in the crash."

Flynn stared at me in disbelief. "So where have you been for the past year?"

"I was out of things for a long time. If you want to prove my story, take my fingerprints and send them through FBI."

"I'll do that," he said. "But for the moment, assuming you *are* Oliver Benson, what happened out there today, and how did Fetterman get shot? Here's how I see it: You disappeared for a year, then you came back ready to get revenge. You took 'em out in the woods and shot Fetterman and then somehow the hornet's nest got knocked off and stung your wife."

It was strange how quickly I came to a sudden conclusion. I had done nothing for a year but plan for the ruin of Marlene and Dane. Now I had them—all I had to do was tell Flynn the truth, and both of them would spend years in prison, assuming Dane lived. But now I found that I couldn't do it. Something inside me had changed. I had to improvise quickly, and I said, "When your man finds the gun, my prints won't be on it. It'll be my wife's prints."

"So she shot Dane."

For a moment I thought about telling the whole truth, but then I knew I couldn't. I hadn't been a Christian long, but I still knew it was a sin to tell a lie. But what if I told the truth? Both Dane and Marlene would be destroyed. Maybe a theologian would have thought of some way out of this, but I had only a split second.

"I think it was an accident. We were just doing some target practice. She was shooting at the hornet's nest. One of them stung her, and she fired the shot that hit Dane."

Flynn stared at me coldly. "That's the biggest cock-and-bull story I ever heard in my life! I'm going to get the truth out of you, Benson, or Burke, or whoever you are."

I shook my head stubbornly. "No more questions. Not right now. I want to see my wife."

"You're under arrest, but I suppose you can see her. From what I hear, she's not talking." He read me my rights, then turned to a tall, lanky officer who'd been taking all this in. "Don't let him get away from you, Billy." Flynn stalked out.

The officer nodded to me. "Come on. I'll take you to Mrs. Fetterman."

The pain medicine had dulled most of my senses. I walked right past Marlene's room; Billy had to grab me and say, "It's in this room here."

When we went inside, the room was fairly dark, and I had only part of one eye to see with. I did see a figure on a bed, and I walked over to it. Her face was swollen like mine, only worse. I would never have recognized her. Somewhere along the line I had lost whatever feeling I'd had for her as a woman, but I couldn't help but feel sorry for her. I stood for a long time only barely aware that Billy had moved and put his back against the wall. Finally I heard someone come in and turned to see a man with a stethoscope around his neck. "What are you doing here? She's not supposed to have visitors."

"He's her husband, Doctor, so he says."

"Her husband? Dane Fetterman is her husband."

"No, he's not," I said. I felt too sick to explain much, but I said, "Look, you'll get all of the juicy details later. I'm Ollie Benson. She thought I was dead, so she married Dane, but she's my wife. Now, tell me about her."

I couldn't see the doctor very clearly in the semidark room and with only one eye. He had a deep Southern accent. He sounded like a hillbilly, but he must have been a very well-educated one. "She's not good. Did you know she was allergic to stings?"

"No, she never told me."

"Well, one sting would have been bad enough, but she's got twenty-three of them. Her whole system has shut down."

"Will she live?"

The doctor stood quietly for a moment, then said, "She's got a very small chance, but I don't want you to build on it. Chances are she won't."

"Can I stay with her?"

"It can't do any good—but it can't do any harm either. We're doing all we can."

I could feel the eyes of the two men on me, and finally the doctor said, "If she has any family, I suggest you get them here."

After he left, I suddenly felt weak. "Can I have a chair, Billy?"

"Sure." I felt a chair pushed under me and collapsed into it. I could just see her swollen profile. I sat for a while trying to think, then I said, "Billy, will you call Joelle Doren and tell her what's happened?"

"Who's she?"

"She's my housekeeper. She needs to know this."

"What's her number?"

I gave him the number, and he pulled his cell phone out and dialed it. "Chief, the suspect wants to make a phone call to a woman named Joelle Doren. He says she's his housekeeper. Is it okay?" He listened and then said, "Right." He punched another number in and handed me the phone. It rang three times, and then I heard Joelle's voice.

"Hello?"

"This is me, Joelle."

"Davis, where are you?"

"I'm in the hospital."

"The hospital! What's wrong?"

"I can't tell you right now. Can you come?"

"Of course. I'll drop Rachel off at Eileen's, then I'll be there as soon as I can."

"Wait a minute. I've got to tell you something. It's too much to tell over the phone, but my real name is Ollie Benson, and I'm under arrest for attempted murder."

There was silence only for a moment, and then her voice came sounding full of faith. "I don't understand, but I'll be there as soon as I can get there."

"Thank you, Joelle."

I handed the phone back to Billy and said thanks.

He was silent as he took the phone and put it back on his belt. He went back to lean against the wall. I was barely conscious of him until he said, "Man, I've seen mixed-up lives before, but you take the cake!"

There was nothing I could say to that—it was the truth. I sat there in the darkness, thinking what a mess I had made of things.

∽

I felt a hand on my shoulder, and I looked up to see Joelle. I had expected to see disgust on her face, but there was none. "How do you feel?" she asked quietly.

I said, "Billy, can we have a chair for the lady?"

"Sure, but I'll have to stay here."

Joelle went over and looked into Marlene's face. She stayed for a long moment, then came back and sat, "Tell me, do you feel like talking about it?"

"I feel like I need to. Let me go back. Like I told you, I'm not who you think I am. I'm Ollie Benson. This all started over a year ago . . ."

I went through the whole story, step by step. Joelle didn't say a word. I was aware that Billy was also taking it in.

When I was done, I took a deep breath. I felt drained and said, "At first I wanted to just kill them, but then I decided that was too quick. So I dreamed up a scheme to do to them exactly what they did to me—take all their money and ruin their marriage. I set out to destroy them, and now I wish I had never thought of it."

"You had a hard time, Ollie. That's your name, Ollie? It'll be hard to get used to." At some point she had reached over and taken my hand in both of hers, and now I felt the warm pressure of them.

"Do you hate me, Joelle?"

"Of course not. You're a different man now from what you were a year ago."

We sat that way for a long time before the door opened, and I turned stiffly to see Chief Flynn come in. Billy had left the room after I finished my story, leaving another officer there, and now he came back in with Flynn. "Well, Benson, we checked your prints out through the FBI, and you're Oliver Benson, all right. We checked the prints out on the gun too. It had only Mrs.— what should I call her? Mrs. Fetterman? Marlene Fetterman's prints on it. I heard your story from Billy, and it sounds to me like you had plenty of motive for shooting Fetterman and your wife too. The best I can figure out, you took 'em out there to shoot 'em both and throw 'em in that hole, and something went wrong, and she got the gun. Maybe the part about the hornets hitting her and throwing her shot off was right."

"How is Dane?"

"He's gonna make it. He's still out so I haven't been able to get his story."

"Are you going to keep me in jail?"

"You're going before Judge Henley. I've already talked to him. You'll have to post a big bond and you can't leave town until we get this cleared up."

"Thanks, Chief."

He stared at me and shook his head. "I thought I'd seen everything, but I guess not. Do you realize that when the newspapers get hold of this, Blue Springs won't hold all the reporters!"

"Can't you keep it quiet, at least until it's cleared up?"

"We're doing our best, believe me."

I turned to Joelle and couldn't think of a thing to say. The pain began to come back, but I knew that eventually it would go away. I turned and looked at Marlene and she seemed to be barely breathing. "I think somebody ought to be here with her."

"I'll stay here until you take care of the legal things."

"Thanks, Joelle."

I left the room with Chief Flynn, and though he was silent, I knew he was studying me with a practiced eye. "We're off the record now. I've got a feeling you're not leveling with me. And I've also got the feeling that I'm not ever going to get the straight of all this."

"We all have our feelings, Chief."

"Sounds like something in a real bad movie to me."

"It sounds that way to me too."

We went to the courthouse, and the judge let me post bond. Afterward, Flynn said, "You'd better go home and go to bed. You look terrible."

"I can't do that until I find out how Marlene and Dane are. Will you take me back to the hospital?"

∞

We practically lived in that hospital for two days, Joelle and I, taking turns. I spread some money around and bought an extra room so that one of us could sleep in it while the other one was with Marlene.

Dane had made it, but he hadn't recovered consciousness yet. I knew that the police were just waiting for him to wake up so they could get his side of the story, and I didn't know how that would turn out.

Marlene didn't get any better, but she did recover consciousness twice. Once she couldn't even open her eyes, but when I talked to her, she must have recognized my voice, and she called my real name. I held her hand and said, "Can you hear me, Marlene?"

"Ollie?"

"Yes, it's Ollie."

"What's—what's wrong with me?"

"You were badly hurt. Stung by hornets."

"Where's Dane?"

"He's all right."

She began to talk then, but she was delirious and it made no sense.

She awoke again the next day, and this time both Joelle and I were in the room with her. We'd been sitting for a long time, silently, both talked out, and Joelle said, "Look, she's moving."

Both of us got up at once. My swelling had gone down now so at least I could see out of both eyes. I leaned forward and said, "Marlene?"

Her eyes opened slightly, but they were dull and dead-looking. "It's Ollie, Marlene. Can you hear me?"

Her answer was a thin, thready sound. "Yes, Ollie."

"I want you to listen to me, Marlene. You're not likely to live. I want you to call on God and ask him to forgive your sins. Jesus died for you, and he wants to forgive you. Will you do that?"

Her lips moved, but I couldn't understand her.

"I can't hear you, but just pray this prayer: 'God, be merciful to me, a sinner, in the name of Jesus.'"

Joelle had moved in close to me, and she leaned over and we listened intently. I guess my hearing was affected by all those wasp stings or by the medicine I'd taken. I couldn't make it out, but Joelle reached out and put her hand on Marlene's head. "That's right, Marlene. That's the right prayer." She turned to me and there was a light of joy in her eyes. "Did you hear it?"

"Not very well."

"She prayed that prayer."

I leaned forward then and said, "Are you all right, Marlene?"

"Ollie?"

"Yes, it's Ollie."

A tremor went over her body, and she tried to reach out for me. I caught her hand and said, "What is it, Marlene?"

I leaned forward, and her lips moved slightly. "Sorry . . . ," she whispered.

"It's all right. I forgive you. Are you trusting Jesus? I want you to so much."

We both watched, and she didn't speak again, but she nodded and then lay very still.

I knew she was gone, but the doctors did their best trying to bring her back. It was useless, of course, and I turned away, and Joelle was there with me. "We'll believe that she called on God. That's all it takes, one call."

I was feeling a great sadness. I knew that I had mismanaged everything. But Joelle must have known what I was feeling. "You did all you could, Ollie," she said. "Come on. Let's go home now."

CHAPTER
TWENTY-SIX

Chief Flynn had quite a few doubts about me, and I didn't blame him. But I knew I had to talk to Dane before the chief did, so I went to his room in the hospital and waited until the officer in the corridor went to get coffee.

I stepped inside the room and moved over to stand at Dane's bed. His face was colorless and his lips pale as chalk. He stared up from his bed, and fear leaped out of his eyes.

"Dane, I want you to listen to me. Don't say anything—just listen." I told him the whole story, and he didn't move or speak. Finally I said, "Dane, I want you to back up my story. It's feeble, but it's the only way we can get out of this thing."

He stared up at me from the bed and said, "Don't you hate me, Ollie? You could put me in jail forever."

"I've had enough of that kind of thing. I want to tell you one thing, Dane: Jesus Christ was my only hope, and he's your only hope too." Dane listened quietly while I spoke to him of the miracles God had done in my life.

Finally he whispered, "I don't get it, Ollie. After what we did to you, you must hate us both."

"I can't afford hate, Dane. It's too expensive."

"Am I going to jail?"

"Not if you do as I say." After all, I hadn't told Flynn about either of Dane's attempts to kill me, and other than the two of us, no one knew. I had no bitterness in me for this man, and I told him so. "I hope you take this as a wake-up call from God. You've got another chance."

Dane stared at me for a long moment, then said, "When I thought I was going to die, I–I knew my life had been all wrong. I was scared, Ollie!"

I sat down and said, "You don't have to be scared. Listen . . ."

For over thirty minutes I told him how God had changed my life. He listened hard, and when I finished, he said, "I don't understand it, Ollie, but I–I'd like to."

I squeezed his shoulder and said, "I'll be glad to talk about it. Give me a call."

"I will!"

I left the room with a strange feeling. The man I'd longed to kill was now the man I wanted to help. God does some strange things!

∞

Chief Flynn had been right about the newspaper reporters. The story leaked out that Oliver Benson was still alive, and the reporters swarmed into Blue Springs. I knew that I couldn't take all of that, so I made an arrangement to tell my story to half a dozen reporters. They fought among themselves until finally they were selected, and I met with them for one hour. I told them the story as simply as I could, changing the facts slightly. I left out the part about Marlene and Dane trying to kill me. I told the truth about how I had been hijacked and left for dead. I didn't give any details about Eli but simply left the impression that I was suffering from amnesia after being terribly beaten.

Of course, the difficult part came when they began popping questions at me about the shooting and Marlene's spectacular death.

I did the best I could with it, but by that time I'd been cleared of any wrongdoing because only Marlene's prints were on the gun. I hated to lie, but I stuck with the story I'd invented—that Marlene, during target practice, had hit the hornet's nest and, when swarmed by hornets, had squeezed the trigger, accidentally hitting Dane. It was a feeble story, and I think everyone saw through it, but I had made up my mind and I didn't change it.

∞

I stood in front of Leo Fant. He had called Robert Leighton and Jeb Wilkerson; now all three of them sat watching me, their curiosity obvious. Like everyone else, they'd heard by now that I was Ollie Benson, and Leo said, "I called us all together for one more meeting." He looked almost stunned as he said, "Well, Oliver, this makes a big difference. You've got money enough to do this deal by yourself."

"That's right, but we hope you'll let us stay in it with you," Jeb urged.

The three of them looked pleased. I had enough money, or would have when the legal things were straightened out, to buy them all.

I took the tape recorder out of my pocket. Drummond had made me one copy that had the voices of all three men. "I want you to hear this tape."

"What's on it?" Fant said immediately, his eyes suspicious.

"Just listen, Leo."

I played the tape all the way through. We heard all three of the men talking to prominent legislators. They were absolutely still as fear crept into their eyes, even Fant's.

"All three of you are dead," I said.

"Wait a minute," Leighton said. His voice was shaking. "You can't do this to us."

"Do what?" I asked.

Fant became the spokesman. "That won't stand up in court."

"There are differences of opinion about that, Leo, but I think you know that it will." I stared at them as they all three tried to talk at once. They saw their careers, their families, and everything they held dear going up in smoke.

Finally I said, "All three of you shut up. Here's what's going to happen. You're going to drop this project, immediately and forever. As long as you do that, nobody will ever get the tapes."

Fant laughed shortly. "We don't have a choice. You know that."

"Then I guess we ought to thank you," Jeb said nervously, "for not—"

"There's more," I said, and they all grew absolutely still. "You'll all make a contribution of one million dollars each to the Sierra Club. When I'm notified by the Sierra Club that you've made these contributions, you won't hear any more from me about these tapes."

"That's blackmail!" Leighton cried out.

"Shut up, Leighton!" Fant said. "He's doing us a favor. Don't you see that, you fool?" He turned to me quickly and said, "Anything else?"

"I'm sending a copy of these tapes to the legislators you talked to. Those men will come back to you. You can inform them that copies of the tapes are being kept in a safe place. If they ever make a move at this land again, they'll be front-page news. That's all."

I turned and left the room. It seemed as if a load had been lifted off me. At least I had done one right thing.

I hurried to the car, but I didn't drive back to the house. The reporters had staked it out. Instead I used my cell phone and called Joelle. She had been staying under another name at a hotel in the next town. "I'm coming over," I said.

"Hurry. I want to hear about it."

∽

Joelle had already picked Rachel up, and as soon as I came into the suite, Rachel came running toward me. I caught her up, and she said immediately, "Will you take me out on the boat?"

"I may. We'll see what your mom says. Give me a few minutes alone with her, and I'll see what I can do."

"All right." She ran at once out of the room, and Joelle, who had been standing and watching, said, "How did it go?"

"They were scared out of their minds. The land is safe."

I walked over to her and took her hand and held it. She was watching me in a strange way, and finally I said, "I've got to get away from all this, and I think you need to get away too."

"What are you going to do?"

"I don't know, but I can't do it in this place. Too many bad memories."

I had been making up a speech for days now, ever since things had started winding down, and now I made it. "Joelle, I don't know what's going to happen. I've got all this money, but it's not my money. It belongs to the Lord. I've got to use it in a way that pleases him. And I know there will be people after me, hoping to try to influence me to use it for the wrong things. I want to please God, but I can't do it alone."

"Can't you, Ollie?"

I couldn't finish my speech. I knew what I wanted to say— but what if she said no? I said, "You know Rachel needs a man in her life, and I'd like to be him."

Joelle laughed. "Don't tell me that you want me to deed Rachel over to you."

"No, of course not." But then I knew I couldn't go on any further.

Joelle put her arms around me and said, "We both need time. It's nice that you have money. Let's get three passages on a cruise somewhere, and we'll get to know each other, and we'll find our way, Oliver."

"I'd like that a lot. They say the South Seas are nice. Have you ever been there?"

"No."

"Neither have I. Call up and get the tickets."

I took her in my arms then and kissed her. When I lifted my head, I said, "I've got one errand and then it's ship ahoy."

"You'd better go now. You promised to take Rachel out and tell her about our new adventure."

As I called for Rachel, I knew that things were going to be different. I didn't know how, but I knew that we were going to find ourselves.

EPILOGUE

I pulled the Land Rover to a stop, and as Eli came out of the cabin, I turned and grinned. "That's Eli. You'll like him."

"Will he like me?" Rachel said.

"Who wouldn't like you? Come on."

We all got out of the car, and Eli, who was wearing the same wrinkled clothes he'd worn the last time I saw him, waited until we got close before he said, "Howdy. How are you folks today?"

"We're fine, Eli." I saw that he had not the vaguest idea who I was, and there was a guarded look on his face. I put my hand out. "It's good to see you again."

He took my hand and shook it, still staring at me strangely. "Do I know you?"

"You ought to. You don't save so many lives you forget about the folks you save, do you?"

Something changed in Eli's face, and he cocked his head to one side. "Who are you?" he said.

"You mean after you stitched up my head and nursed me back to health you don't even remember me? I'm disappointed."

I saw recognition come, and he yelled, "Well, I'll be dipped! It's you, Ollie!" He moved forward and threw his arms around me. When he stepped back there was wonder in his eyes. "What happened to you, boy? You sure don't look like you did when you left here."

"Lots of things have happened, but before I tell you about them I'd like for you to meet two people who are very important in my life."

I introduced Joelle and Rachel, then said, "This fine lady is going to agree to marry me one day, and this young lady is going to agree to let me be her dad."

Eli greeted Joelle and Rachel. "You come on the right day," he said. "I got dinner almost fixed. You like pig ears?" he asked Rachel.

"Pig ears? You mean to eat?"

"Sure, to eat."

"I don't think so. Aren't they hairy?"

"I can see you don't like my fixin's, but me and this feller will go out and shoot somethin'. Maybe we'll catch a fish. You ever go fishing?"

"Yes!" Rachel said, her eyes excited. "I can fish, can't I?" She pulled at my sleeve.

"She's a fine fisherman."

"Well, why don't we go down and set on the bank, and you can tell me what all has happened."

∞

It was a great day. Rachel caught a two-pound bass and nearly jumped in the water after it. We caught enough for a good meal and cooked it outside. I told Eli as much as I thought would be good for him to know.

It was late that afternoon before I found a moment alone with Eli. "That's sure a fine woman you got there," he said, "and that little girl, she's a scudder."

"God's been very good to me."

"I'm glad you found the Lord, boy. You needed him bad."

"You're right about that," I said. I reached into my pocket and drew out an envelope. "I've got a present for you, Eli. I can't pay you back for all you did for me, saving my life and putting me together. But I wanted you to have it."

"A present for me? Why, it ain't even Christmas." I think he expected money in the envelope and didn't seem particularly excited. He opened it, pulled out the papers inside, and stared at it. He didn't move for a moment, and I saw his eyes going over the writing. He looked up at me and couldn't speak. "Why, boy," he said, "this is a deed for two hundred acres right here!"

"It's all yours now, Eli. You don't have to worry about anybody disturbing Jeff's grave."

"But this must have cost a heap of money."

"Not so much. And I like to think about you here on your own place."

Eli was reading the deed again. He couldn't really believe it, but finally he looked up and began to grin. "Well, I'll be dipped. Thank you, boy."

"Come on now. We'll walk around it. You can show me where the corners are. I guess you can read this map."

We walked the land that day, and by the time we got back it was growing dark and Rachel was impatient. "Why didn't you take me with you, Ollie?"

"I'm taking you. Time for us to leave."

"Come on inside, honey," Eli said. "I got a little present for you."

"What is it?"

"I used to fancy myself a wood-carver. I think you'll like my best one—a doe and her little fawn. Come along." The two disappeared inside the house.

Joelle said, "Was he pleased?"

"He sure was."

We had only a moment, but I took her hand and held it tightly. "You know, Joelle, I'm not the man Frank was. I guess I never will be. But I promised him I'd take care of you and Rachel. I want to spend the rest of my life with you and be a dad to her."

It was quiet in the glade. I could hear the doves that came close around the cabin moaning softly in that little fluttering sound they make. Joelle pulled my head down, kissed me, and then as the two came out of the cabin, Rachel chattering loudly, she said, "We'll take care of each other, Ollie."